D.F. JONES

USA TODAY BESTSELLING AUTHOR

THE WITCHES OF HANT HOLLOW 2
GATE KEEPERS

Preface

"The moment you doubt whether you can fly, you cease for ever to be able to do it."
—— **J. M. Barrie, Peter Pan**

Copyright

Formatting by Jones Media

Acknowledgments

I grew up listening to my father spin a story on a dime. He loved spooky tales. I also watched every episode of *Bewitched*. In addition, the inspiration for the books came from my first short story, Antique Mirror, which first appeared in the *Mirror, Mirror, Halloween Anthology 2015*. My writing style has evolved, and it's been an incredible journey. I adore the books and my characters. I trust you will enjoy The Witches of Hant Hollow 2: Gate Keepers.

A special thank you to my incredible critique team for your comments, suggestions, and encouragement during the development of Lavender's story. Thank you, Tessy, Ana, Karen, Barb, and Tia! I respect and value your advice.

To my editor, Alicia, thank you for making my characters shine. I would also like to thank the D.F. Jones team of readers. It is through your word-of-mouth referrals and reviews that help other readers find my titles.

Thank you, Amanda, for taking my vision for the cover and creating a superb design.

Please note that I write alternating points of view with multi-layered plots and sub-plots. I use section breaks to record any point-of-view or scene shifts.

I have placed a **Character Key** in the back of the book for reference. Word of warning, before heading into significant spoiler territory, it is in the reader's best interest to leave the deep dive until you read the books if you do not want to know what happens.

Blurb

Determined to find her mother, Lavender must navigate magic, romance, and time travel across otherworldly realms.

Like many in the Mage Alliance, Lavender Doanhart inherited the gift of magic. Her happy-go-lucky life ends abruptly on Halloween night when a century-old family feud comes to a head, and supernatural forces of light and dark converge on her family's mansion in Hant Hollow.

As a result, the underworld engulfs her sorceress, grandmother and mother, dragging them into the abyss. Call it intuition or just plain magic, but Lavender knows her mother is still alive and is willing to sacrifice her soul to save her.

Commander Brody Whitmore has risen through the Mage Alliance's military ranks, becoming the regent's right hand. Committed and driven to succeed until the day he meets a stubborn and headstrong witch who consumes his heart and soul.

For over a hundred years, Brody and Lavender were inseparable. Then, on the night he decides to propose, the forces of light and dark collide in Hant Hollow, thrusting his magical lady into the battle of her life. The foolish woman thinks she can save him by breaking off their relationship, but he's determined to fight at her side, even if he thinks she's wrong.

Genre: Fantasy Romance, YA Fantasy-Magic, Time Travel Romance

Contents

Prologue

Doanhart Mansion, Hant Hollow

After the Halloween ball, Lavender rushed to her room to change clothes. She had to meet Brody in the hollow. Find out if they had a chance for a real life together.

She entered her closet, unzipped her dress, and kicked off her strappy heels. Pushing past several outfits, she pulled out black leather pants and a jacket and paired them with a white turtleneck.

Lavender quickly slipped on boots and started for the door.

The house shook.

Jerked from side to side, Lavender braced herself in the doorframe as dust fell from the ceiling.

She heard her grandmother, Iris. "Sick? Angry? Hurt? Go ahead and tell me what you really think, Jonathan Rogers."

Oh, God. She closed her eyes and groaned. Grams had kidnapped Jonathan—again.

Lavender pressed her back against the wall.

"I hate you for stealing my life," Jonathan shouted. "For casting me into that cursed mirror for over a hundred years! Want to know what I think? I want to wrap my fingers around your scrawny neck and choke you to death."

Grams laughed loudly. "Your father sealed your fate the day you were born. He left me for your mother. Then Jasmine fell in love with you. I refused to allow history to repeat itself. None of this would've happened if she'd only listened to me."

Lavender peeked out her bedroom door.

Grams and Jonathan struggled on the stairway landing. He went for her throat, but she plastered him against the wall with the full force of her magic. Jonathan was no match for Iris's, er... well, Grams's dark magic. Lavender knew she wasn't either. She had to find Brody. He'd know what to do.

She teleported to the hollow. "Brody! Are you here?"

Someone grabbed her from behind and slipped a hand over her mouth.

"Be quiet. It's me," Brody whispered. "A coup d'etat is underway. The vampires are fighting the werewolves at the river. They're moving swiftly through the hollow to join forces with Iris and her army. My soldiers are surrounding your house as we speak."

Her heart raced. "What about my mother?"

"She's with your grandmother. I'm afraid it may be too late for her."

"No. We have to stop the coup and save my mom. Let go of me."

He held her tight. "I've received word telepathically that Jasmine and Jonathan are prisoners on the third floor." He turned her around. "I need to know where your loyalties lie."

She smacked him hard across the face.

His head didn't move, but he rubbed his jaw. "I didn't mean to offend. Going into battle, I need to know that you are with us."

"You bastard. Yes, I worry about my mom, but I fight for the light. My loyalties have never been questioned. And Jasmine is not just my cousin. She's like a sister to me. We must save her."

"Glad to hear it. Let's fly."

Thunder rolled, and lightning streaked across the sky as Lavender and Brody flew to Doanhart Mansion and entered the third floor. Her heart hammered. Jasmine was in a torture cage.

Grams murmured some spell Lavender couldn't decipher on the other side of the room. Her white gown was torn and billowed in the torrent winds she created. She didn't look a day over twenty-one.

Mom's blond hair stood on end as the energy in the room— electrified. She lifted her hands and joined forces with Grams.

Jasmine's eyes glowed with magic. The metal bars imprisoning her melted away, and she flew at Grams, yelling, "I'm using the same blood magic you used to control others, but this time it's against you. Set Jonathan and the souls in the statues free, or you shall die!"

"Come to play, Jasmine?" Grams taunted. "You've given yourself to the darkness. You are mine."

"Never!" Jasmine raised her hands to the sky and chanted, "Mouijah Stones take Iris and make her pay, take her now, and don't delay."

Chills raced up Lavender's back.

The Doanhart Coven faced each other in a battle of wills—a struggle over good versus evil. Grandmother Iris and her mother, Peony, stood on the side of darkness.

Jasmine, Aunt Isidore, and Lavender fought for the light.

Lavender knew her life would never be the same after tonight.

Aunt Isidore took her place next to Jasmine, allowing their energies to merge.

Representatives from the Mage Alliance rallied. Dreena outstretched her hands and sent a protective shield around her daughter, Victoria, and the mortals in the room while her husband, Raine, threw lightning bolts toward vampires trying to gain entry through the open windows.

Brody pointed at Jonathan and motioned for Lavender to undo his ties. She quickly freed him.

"Open rebellion to the light magnifies the darkness within you, Iris. Submit to the one real power of the light, and the darkness will flee from you," Dreena exclaimed. "Do not, and you will perish tonight."

Blood ran down the walls and dripped from the climbing vines.

Lavender's tummy clenched.

Julius, the vampire who aligned his forces with Grams, appeared in the window. As he crouched to pounce, a werewolf flew behind him and drove a wooden stake through his heart.

Grams screamed. The dark energy emitted a red glimmer around her and Peony. She tilted her head back and cried, "I summon The Lord Darkness. Release your wrath and fulfill my vengeance with your warpath." She drew a knife from thin air and slit it from her elbow to her wrist.

Scraping metal screeched across the hardwood floor as stagnant air choked Lavender. "Behold, The Lord Darkness is here," Lavender's mother, Peony, exclaimed.

A fiery portal opened, and darkness crept inside.

Brody leaned close to Lavender. "I must help my soldiers against the vampires. Stay close to Isidore." He vanished.

"Nooo, Brody," Lavender cried. Suddenly, she couldn't hear anything but a ringing roar. It seemed as if everything around her went into super slow-mo.

"Clasp hands and form a circle of light," Dreena commanded. "Place the mortals within it. Hurry! The Lord Darkness won't leave empty-handed."

The Goddess of Light appeared in answer to Jasmine's summoning of the Mouijah Stones. The ceiling opened to the heavens, and the storm stopped. Her radiance covered the mortals and the followers of the light.

Everyone in the circle braced as the Shadows slithered across the room.

The enemies immediately turned into ash when they crossed The Goddess of Light's threshold.

The other Shadows recoiled from the path and took another deadly turn.

With a hitch in her voice, Peony pleaded, "Help me, Lavender."

Tears rushed down Lavender's cheeks as she watched helplessly. One Shadow took her mother. Her heart squeezed, and a lump rose in her throat. She wanted to save her mother, but The Goddess of Light had immobilized everyone in the circle.

The Lord Darkness entered the room. It was the first time Lavender had ever seen him in person. While he commanded the room, not within the protective shield, his dark eyes seemed kind. How was that possible?

He stared at The Goddess of Light for what seemed like an eternity, then gave her an acknowledging nod and wrapped his arms around Iris. Blood poured from her self-inflicted wound.

She turned to Aunt Isidore. "Release the captured souls encased within my statues." With one last glance, Grams added, "Forgive me, my children."

Grandmother Iris disappeared with The Lord Darkness in a white plume of smoke. It left no smell. It resembled light fog on a fall morning.

The Goddess of Light's radiance released them.

Jasmine clung to Lavender. "Grams and Aunt Peony are gone."

"I couldn't save Mom. I couldn't move," Lavender cried.

Isidore circled her arms around the two of them. "Dark magic has a price, my darlings, and The Lord Darkness always collects the debt."

The Goddess of Light waved her hand, releasing the ransomed souls from the statues. Their light lifted into the heavens. She nodded to Dreena as she placed her hand on Jasmine's head, removing the darkness from her.

Lavender scanned the room. The carnage inside and out made her sick. She dematerialized and transported herself to the riverbank close to the hollow. She collapsed to the ground.

The weeping willows, positioned along the slope, swayed in the night air. They seemed to beckon her. She stared at the rushing water, unable and unwilling to grasp the magnitude of the family feud that rippled into the lives of the other magical beings within the Mage Alliance.

The Lord Darkness and The Goddess of Light had exchanged looks.

No checkmate tonight.

Were her mother and Grams dead?

Or were they pawns in a much larger game to come?

Chapter 1

Lavender's life changed dramatically after the dreadful night her mother disappeared with The Lord Darkness.

Immediately after the incident, the Mage Alliance set an emergency meeting in Jonesboro to alert its members of a power shift. She sat with her family.

Jasmine's husband, the regent, Carlton McGraff, made a plea to anyone still aligned with Lavender's Grandmother Iris to renounce the darkness and join forces with the light. The alliance would revoke membership to those who continued practicing dark magic.

Mage members sitting behind Lavender were spreading rumors about her. *Is Lavender a Princess of the Night? I heard she's just like her mother. No? Yes?*

The gossipmongers cut deep into an open wound of her heart. She wouldn't give them the satisfaction of a rebuttal.

Their distrust set into motion her decision to distance herself from magic and magical beings. From that moment forward, she didn't want to live in the shadow of her mother and grandmother.

The exceptions were Jasmine and her family, who accepted her with no judgments, only love. Aunt Isidore and Uncle Draum had moved into the Doanhart Mansion. The home they built over one hundred years ago.

Lavender had also severed ties with Brody. She didn't want to hurt him, but he was the regent's hand. He had to appear above the fray, and she wouldn't drag him down with her.

She moved out of the Doanhart Mansion and used her inheritance to purchase the historic Red Rose Hotel. Once renowned for its charm and elegance, it had fallen into disrepair over the last twenty years. She spent all her time remodeling the exterior to its former glory, gutting the interior except for the sweeping staircase, marbled columns, and painted skylights.

Max Dupres, a well-known Nashville art dealer, had helped her with the interior design. The renovation took nearly eighteen months.

The first-floor bookstore mimicked an old-world style of ambiance. Recess lighting, pendants, and sconces cast a warm glow on the eighteenth and nineteenth-century furnishings. Custom cabinetry held rare and collectible books. It gave the store a unique feel of a forgotten world but held a promise of romance. By appointment, of course. The store had priceless collections for select clientele and was not open to the public.

The second-floor art gallery showcased Max's clients' and Victoria Frost-Rogers' unique permanent collection. Victoria and Jonathan had married, and they had a beautiful little girl. She worked with Max to host private exhibitions.

Victoria had fallen into the same cursed mirror as Jonathan. The whole fiasco was brought on by Lavender's jealous grandmother, which unleashed Victoria's biological parents, Dreena and Raine. They were superiors in the upper echelon of magic.

Victoria had lived most of her life thinking she was an orphan, only to learn her mother was an immortal of the highest order, a true goddess, and her father, guardian of water and sky. The Elite was top of the food chain for those following the light.

The good news for Lavender—Victoria didn't mesh well with the alliance either, so they became friends.

The third and fourth floors were Lavender's private quarters and alchemist laboratory. Her lab had state-of-the-art equipment where she could grow any herb, root, or plant hydroponically.

Her bedroom suite, living, and kitchen area had fourteen-foot ceilings and two marble fireplaces in an open floor plan. The ceiling skylights had electronic screens to block out the light on days she slept in. Beautifully hand-crafted wood covered the walls and lush, deep red, oriental carpets on the refurbished hardwood floors. The French doors with matching windows on either side led to her outdoor garden sanctuary.

The community of Rockvale had accepted Lavender into their fold. She even attended the local church on Sundays.

Two years later

Lavender woke early and dressed in her signature Boho-style dress. She chose a chunky turquoise and amber necklace. She slipped on bedazzled sandals and went downstairs. She turned on the lights and sat at her bureau plat desk with cut brass inlays. She touched the laptop and activated the screen.

She'd turned the first floor into a rare bookstore to search for any ancient text, scrolls, or books on The Goddess of Light and The Lord Darkness origins.

In the mortal world, the two Gods were myths. This belief gave her the cover she needed to find any path that could save her mother. No one believed her mom had survived. Call it intuition, call it her sixth sense; she knew Peony lived, whether in this realm or another.

Lavender had sensed that good existed in her mother, even though she had deviant sexual practices, which she sought counseling to kick. Driven by sibling jealousy, her mother did anything to gain approval from Grams, which cost her everything.

Her employee, Emily Ellen, a college literary intern, bopped inside the front door. "Hi, Lavender. Sorry, I'm a little late."

"No worries. I just sat down. Would you make me an espresso, please?"

"Sure thing. But, first, I have something to give you." She opened her backpack and pulled out a sealed envelope. "Professor Browning said it might interest you."

Emily Ellen started for the office kitchen. Lavender placed her hand on her forearm. "Make yourself a cup too."

When Emily Ellen left the room, Lavender opened the envelope with trembling fingers. She'd placed an inquiry with the professor weeks ago regarding a manuscript she wanted to acquire.

She withdrew the paper and read a Post-it stuck to the top: *This is from our overseas contact, Browning.*

Professor Browning,

I received the enclosed letter from the monastery at St. Lucian's in the Pyrenees. During its restoration, one monk scholar found several ancient scrolls and relics in an elaborate cavern. Archaeologists date the dwelling to at least fourteen thousand years ago. I think it is the text Ms. Doanhart seeks, and a trip to France may be in order.

Some local scholars discuss the two unknown deities, Yaris and Cetus. I returned to your notes and referenced The Goddess of Light and The Lord Darkness. The two may or may not be the same.

Ms. Doanhart could be the one to unlock the mystery of the strange hieroglyphics not native to the area or the era. She is welcome to inspect the scrolls during St. Lucian's screening process.

I believe it will be in her best interest to see the rare find first-hand. Anyway, the monastery will not allow the scrolls to leave their library. I am available to speak by phone, teleconference, or video chat. Please feel free to share this with Ms. Doanhart.

Sincerely,

Adam Bisset, curator of antiquities

Lavender glanced at the contact information.

Emily Ellen entered the room and handed her an espresso cup.

She took a sip. "Excellent. When does your semester end?"

"Fall break starts next week. I CLEP out of two classes, and the last two are online. What's up?"

"CLEP? You mean the College-Level Examination Program?"

Emily Ellen nodded. "Yes, ma'am."

"Would you be interested in running the store?" Lavender inquired. "I must travel to St. Lucian's once I secure an appointment to view ancient scrolls the monastery found."

Emily Ellen pushed a strand of shoulder-length black hair behind her ear. "Yes, ma'am."

"Will you house sit too?"

"In your suite? You're kidding, right?"

"Provided you water my plants and herbs."

"You can count on me. I'm willing to work on your project too. I'm quite knowledgeable with ancient mythology," Emily Ellen added.

"Thanks, but this is a personal project. I need to see it through myself."

Max burst through the side door with an armful of colorful gladiolus in a Waterford crystal vase. "Hello, my lovelies." He placed the flowers on Lavender's desk.

Lavender's smile went wide.

"Bingo! That's what I was aiming for. I miss you. Let's go play today." He kissed her cheek. "What's this?" He picked up the document before she could stop him.

"Max, that doesn't belong to you."

With a raised brow, he replied, "It rarely does, dumpling." He read swiftly. "Please tell me this isn't what I think it is?" He looked at Emily Ellen. "Be a dear and grab my gallery box out of the car."

She sighed. "My cue to vamoose."

"They *do* teach college kids today." Max snickered as she left through the side door.

"Don't taunt Emily Ellen." Lavender shook her head. "Employees like her are hard to find."

He placed his hand on his hip and tapped his foot on the floor. "Well."

"Deep subject for such a shallow brain."

"Meanie." He shoved her. "Are you going to France? And if you are, I'm going with you."

"It's dangerous, Max."

"Like that's ever stopped me." He pulled a walnut Chippendale chair next to hers and sat down. "So, when are we going? I'll make arrangements with Victoria to watch the gallery."

"I don't know. I just read the letter. Hopefully, next week. Will that work for you?"

"With bells on, honey." He pushed away from the table. "Now, where are the Pyrenees?"

"It's the mountains between France and Spain. My great-grandmother's chateau isn't far. But, Max, no one, especially Jasmine, must know what I'm researching. Are we clear?"

He pretended to lock his lip and throw away the key. "Not a word, my dear. Oh my, I just adore French men. Gotta scoot upstairs. Victoria is on her way."

Emily Ellen returned and handed him the box.

"Thank you, sweetie pie."

Max scaled the massive staircase and disappeared down the hallway.

"I'm going to take a walk to clear my head. I'll start checking flights to France when I return."

"I can do that for you."

"I appreciate it, but you have enough on your to-do lists. Check the vintage editions in the climate-controlled room. Even minor fluctuations in temperature and humidity could create disintegration in the paper or binding."

Emily Ellen nodded. "I got it. Keep the temps between sixty-five and seventy and the humidity levels between thirty-fifty percent."

"How did I get so lucky to find you?"

"How do you know I didn't find you?"

Downtown Rockvale had not changed much since the Doanharts had moved there in the late nineteenth century. As the decades passed, the Doanharts' wealth increased, and they acquired much of the real estate on Main Street.

Her family had kept currency pumped into the community, so the broader Nashville metropolitan area real estate tycoons or foreign investors didn't squash the local businesses.

Only a few mortal descendants remained from when they first arrived in America. They knew about magic and turned a blind eye to anything unusual. The newer families and businesses received glamour to block any memories of supernatural activity.

Lavender breathed in the fresh autumn air as she strolled down the pristine sidewalks. The town was still beautiful, and the Doanharts intended to keep it that way. The Mage Alliance did well to protect its constituents and the mortals that allowed magical beings freedom. She reached in her pocket and hit Great-grandmother Hagatha's number on her cell.

"*Bonjour*, my sweet. I'm so glad you called." Her vocal range could easily reach soprano.

"I'd like to come for a visit and bring a friend, please."

She rattled off in French, "*Oui*. This will always be your home."

"Hagatha, please use English." Her great-grandmother insisted family members call her by her first name. She despised getting old. "I'm coming as an American tourist, but really I'm on a mission to find my mother."

Hagatha didn't reply.

"*Grand-mère?*"

"I heard you, Lavender." Her French accent was gone. "I feel Peony is still alive, but my poor, poor, Iris, I am not so sure," Hagatha cried.

"Yes, I agree with you. I also believe we're running out of time to save her."

"No, my dear. He'll want a trade. There is no other way."

"The Lord Darkness?"

"*Oui.*"

"There must be another way to access the other realm without sacrificing my soul. I'll tell Aunt Isey and Jasmine that I'm visiting you, but please, don't tell them I'm searching for my mother. They'll try and stop me, or worse, get involved."

"I'll keep silent, my precious girl. My home is yours for as long as you like." She paused and said, "Is your friend good-looking?"

"Very. But you're not *his* type, and he isn't *yours*. I'll call you when I have arrangements."

"Not my type? When has any man ever not been *my* type?"

Lavender giggled. "Oh, you will see soon enough."

"Hm. Yes, we shall see about that." Hagatha ended the call.

It would be good to see her again. It'd been a century since Lavender left France for America.

She went through the iron gates of the cemetery next to the church. She waved at Pastor Green, who weeded the fence on the far side of the churchyard. She continued to the oldest section and silently read the names of the dead.

"Missing your old, mortal boyfriends?"

That voice—quickened her pulse.

She turned.

Her heart pounded.

Brody.

He stood around six and a half feet tall, with broad shoulders and a narrow waist. The depth of love reflected in his blue eyes made her tummy flip. His chiseled jaw could rival any Greek God, and his full lips, she inwardly groaned, were delicious.

"Brody. What are you doing here?"

"Checking on you. I came to town with Carlton and Jasmine. They're staying at the mansion for a couple of weeks. I thought maybe we could get together as friends. No pressure." His right brow rose. "I know you don't love me anymore." He waited for her reply.

If only that were true. She did love him. But he'd questioned her loyalty. What would he say if he knew she searched for her mom and The Lord Darkness? "I'm not sure that's such a good idea."

He took her hands into his. "I love you. I know I made a colossal mistake. I should've never questioned your loyalties, but so many lives were on the line."

She withdrew her hands. "Including my mother's."

"Damn it, Lavender."

Pastor Green stepped next to her. "Language, sir. You are on hallowed ground." He turned to Lavender. "Do you know this man?"

She smiled. "Yes, this is Brody Whitmore, a friend of my family."

"I apologize, preacher," he said. "We have much to discuss if you'll excuse us."

The pastor looked at her. "Is that what you wish? Or you may come into the chapel for prayer."

"Prayer?" Brody belted.

"Pastor Green, I apologize for my uncouth friend. I will see you Sunday." She left the cemetery with Brody on her heels.

"You're attending a mortal church? The same church that burned witches?"

She stopped walking. "Would you keep your voice down? These mortals had nothing to do with Silver and Aster. And they do not know I'm a witch. I no longer practice magic, and I have been baptized." She lifted her chin, turned, and resumed her walk.

"Oh, baby, getting dunked in the water by a mortal does not make you baptized. But they preach forgiveness, so you should forgive me." He wrapped his arms around her. "Forgive me, please."

Her resolve weakened.

What she faced—she'd face alone.

She wouldn't risk Brody's life. She shouldn't risk Max's.

If she forgave Brody, she'd lose the will to fight and find her mother. She stopped in front of the Red Rose front steps. "I'll come for dinner this evening. That's all I got for now."

"Then, that's all I need." He pressed a kiss on the delicate skin of her inner wrist.

Oh, she missed him.

Chapter 2

"Max, thanks for going with me to dinner with the fam." Lavender slid inside her 2016 blade silver metallic Corvette Stingray.

He waved her off and got into the car. "I love you and your family. I know it seems I live a perfect life with lots of friends who throw fabulous parties, but the fact is, most of those folks are fair-weather friends. I'm glad Victoria and Jonathan introduced me to your family."

She pulled out onto the street and headed toward Hant Hollow. "My deranged family nearly killed us."

"All families have their troubles, honey," He laughed. "But Iris did scare the bejesus out of me."

The county recently paved the roads of Rockvale, making it easier for her Corvette to hug the curves. Her fingers gripped the steering wheel, feeling its engine's vibrations roar.

"You like the power of this car, don't you?" Max asked.

"I suppose it's a way to substitute my need for power. Nearly three years and counting, I have not uttered one spell or used my abilities in any way. Do I miss it? I miss the exhilaration of mentally crafting magic from scratch and watching it materialize before my eyes just as I imagined it. But magic cost me my mother."

Once out of the city limits, she rolled the windows down and inhaled the crisp air. From the smile on Max's face, he enjoyed it too. Driving down the country roads, she reminisced about the old dirt lanes with only a couple of farms, lots of trees, and sloping hills. The Doanharts lived exceedingly long lives. She was just eighteen when they moved to Hant Hollow at the end of the nineteenth century. Over a hundred years later, several large subdivisions replaced the opened pastures.

But once Lavender turned onto Hant Hollow Road, the present met the past. The Doanharts had purchased several surrounding farms adjacent to their original parcel. Decades passed, and the woods grew thick. Nature's animals and magical beings sought haven within their boundaries. Only the paved road and overhead electrical wires gave way to the twenty-first century. Protection shields kept wandering hunters and hikers off the property.

She pulled into the long driveway leading toward Doanhart Mansion. She visited often, but she never entered the third floor. The Goddess of Light had removed any trace of the dark arts from their home. However, whenever Lavender entered the house, something beckoned her to the top floor. Something dark. She refused to answer the call.

After parking, Lavender and Max exited the vehicle.

She looked at the asymmetrical design with its gambrel roof and arched windows on the black and white façade. Magic kept the home in pristine condition. A decorative fall wreath adorned the red front door. Chrysanthemums in a bevy of colors brightened the sculpted landscaping with several pots on each step.

Peace washed over her, and she breathed a sigh of relief. She loved it here. She loved Jasmine and Isidore, but she'd never live in the house again.

Brody stepped out the front door and walked down the steps to greet her. He glanced at Max and nodded. "Hello." He turned to Lavender and grinned. "I'm glad you came, even with the mortal."

Finis, Jasmine's three-year-old son, rushed out the door. He opened his arms wide and flew to her. "See me, Laven-door, I fly."

She scooped up the child and hugged him. "You're a very bright boy. Did you miss me?"

"Uh-huh." His head burrowed into the crook of her neck.

"What about Uncle Max?"

Finis frowned. "You're not my uncle. You're a mortal."

Brody burst out laughing. "Good one, Finis."

"Touché." Max twirled his finger in the child's curly, dark hair. "I may be mortal, but I bring lollipops."

"I want one." Finis opened and closed his fingers.

"Not until after dinner. Your mother would cook my goose." Max chuckled.

The boy frowned again. "You're not a goose."

"But it could be arranged, Finis." Brody chuckled again.

"Stop teasing Max," Lavender said.

Jasmine opened the storm door and jogged down the steps. "Come here, Superman." She took Finis from Lavender's arms. "Everyone is out back. Mom is showing off her new outdoor kitchen. Carlton is grilling, and Dad is pretending to help." She winked. "I'm going to bathe this young man, and I'll meet you out there in fifteen minutes. Max, would you help me?"

"I'll help pick an outfit for Superman," Max said. "But I do not change poo-poo diapers."

"I not in diapers." Finis wiggled his fingers.

A diaper appeared on Max's head.

Everyone laughed but Max.

Jasmine wrinkled her nose, and the diaper disappeared. "Sorry, Maxie. We're trying to control his magic, but it's challenging."

"Well, that's what I get for hanging with a bunch of witches." He leaned into Finis and wagged his finger. "Naughty boy."

Finis clapped his hands. "Sor-wee."

They went inside and left Lavender with Brody— alone.

Her tummy clenched.

Brody brushed his thumb lightly against the back of her hand. "Walk with me."

Give me strength, Lord. Believing in two faiths seemed better than none.

"Why do I feel as though this is a setup?" She withdrew her hand and followed the curved sidewalk around the house.

"Because it is," he answered. "Just give me a minute or five." He pulled her over to sit in two rustic Adirondack chairs under the large maple tree near the vegetable garden. They had retrieved the last of the tomatoes a week ago.

He took a deep breath and released it. "I've been working on Iris and Peony's case since The Lord Darkness took them. I have recent intel that gives me some hope— your mom is alive." He leaned closer to her. "I also keep tabs on you. Your recent acquisitions of rare books, grimoires, and other collections of magic are illegal. I should arrest you, but love does crazy things to a person."

"You've been keeping tabs on me?" She loved and hated the idea that Brody watched over her.

"The mage council was alerted six months ago that magical beings are disappearing without explanation. My gut tells me you have a target on your head."

"Oh, Brody, it's not like I'm hiding. If The Lord Darkness wants me, he knows where I live."

"This isn't a game. And I know what you're doing, Lavender," Brody said with a raised brow.

Her eyes widened. "What do you mean?"

"Don't play with me. Do you think you can go into the other worlds without alerting the immortals? You wouldn't last one night. And you've not practiced magic in three years."

"I haven't the slightest inkling of what you are referring to." She turned as he grabbed her hand.

"I'm not arguing with you. May I remind you that Iris had enormous power? She practiced dark magic, and it swallowed her whole." He released her and threaded his fingers through his hair. "Do you want to die or worse, have The Lord Darkness take you too?"

"I am not stupid." She knew the risks. Her voice rose. "And you can't tell me what to do. I am not military."

She pushed away from the chair, and before she could say jackrabbit, Brody had her in his arms.

They locked eyes in a battle of wills—waiting for one to give in an inch to the other. She would've allowed him to seduce her in the past, but too much was at stake. If Brody was right and her mom lived, she needed to find her.

He slipped his hand to the nape of her neck and circled his other arm around her waist. He leaned in close—too close. His warm, minty breath kissed her neck. Her pulse thundered; her knees weakened.

She glanced at his eyes, then averted her gaze to those enticing lips. Oh, she wanted to feel Brody's muscular body against hers again.

His mouth hovered over hers.

"Don't kiss me." She shook out of his embrace and shoved him with all her might. "I will not ruin my family's dinner, Brody. You will maintain your distance, or I will break my vow of not practicing magic and turn you into a fat horny toad."

He threw his head back and roared with laughter. "That's the girl I've been waiting on for three years."

"Ugh." She marched away, but not before he caught up with her.

"Lavender, make me a promise." He pulled a bracelet from his pants pocket and held it in his hand. He pointed to the gems. "Black tourmaline to protect you from evil spirits, white quartz paired with the black stones create strong metaphysical powers. Amethyst, to heighten your natural psychic abilities, to call on me in a jam. Jet stone to heal you from injuries, and jasper to drive away any dark energies. Promise me you'll keep it with you. It will not help against The Lord Darkness but deter his minions."

She nodded.

He placed the bracelet on her wrist, and she smiled.

Lavender knew the meaning of each gemstone, but the gesture spoke volumes of his affection.

"Thanks for not pressing me. I've been working on a plan to find my mother. I'm cautious and will use my business to gain insight." She cupped his face with her hands. "Mom is alive. I feel it in my bones. I'll call on you if I get in a jam." She released his face and grabbed his hand. "The bracelet is beautiful, but your caring means more than I can put into words."

"You warm my cold heart with one word, one smile. Lavender, you have me—heart and soul. I will die for you."

"And I—you. Let's pray it doesn't come to that."

"Oh, and about praying, how does the church thingy work? So, they really don't know you're a witch?"

The air turned cooler as Brody and Lavender followed the pebble stone pathway to the backyard. Isidore and Draum had built a fantastic outdoor kitchen with plush seating for entertaining. Mums, zinnias, and pumpkins were casually placed around the area. The river visible from his view brought back so many memories—good and bad.

Flames flickered in the stone fireplace as he watched Jasmine point to Finis, then to the blaze.

"H. O. T. Hot."

Finis pointed. "Hot-ta. Hot-ta."

Brody longed to settle down, and he wanted to marry Lavender. *To have and to hold from this day forward.* He was tired of the endless military campaigns. He had watched his best friend, Carlton, and Lavender's first cousin, Jasmine, build a happy life together.

On and off, Brody and Lavender had been a couple for over a hundred years. She was feisty and fun and didn't take crap off anyone.

Everything changed the night her mother disappeared with Iris into one of the other realms. He missed Lavender so much on some days he didn't want to crawl out of bed.

Isidore hugged Lavender and kissed her cheeks. "Oh, I love seeing the two of you together again."

"Um, we're not together again," Lavender replied. A sucker punch to his gut. "We are just friends." She took Isidore's hand and pulled it next to her chest. "This place is far out."

That's great—just friends.

He stepped over to the bar.

Max mixed cocktails. "What's your poison?"

"Is that a joke, smartass?"

"Woah, big fella. I come in peach." He handed him a rather large drink. "Ah, peach margarita." Accenting on the *rita*.

"Sorry, Max." His eyes narrowed. "You know what she's up to, don't you?"

Max pretended to zip his lips, realizing Brody wasn't playing around.

"When I make promises, I keep them," Max said. "If you want to know what Lavender knows, what she's doing, and where she's going, don't ask me—ask her."

"Where is she going?"

Max turned and swiftly joined the women and the child. The little coward.

The Doanharts loved Max, but he was a mortal, and Brody didn't trust mortals.

Kyewicket, the Doanharts family familiar, was a black cat with eye color that changed with his mood. The cat, nobody's fool, hopped onto the barstool next to Brody.

He looked at the women, then eyed Carlton and Draum cooking.

"I know what Lavender is doing. I know where she is going," he purred.

"Is this a riddle or what?" Brody asked.

Kyewicket hissed. "If you want to know, you must promise to take me with you when you go after her."

"Yeah, okay. So, what's up?"

"Promise, with the witches' honor code."

Brody held up a peace sign and placed his forefinger and middle finger on either side of his nose. "Witches honor, I swear, by The Goddess of Light, now tell me where Lavender is going."

Chapter 3

Biarritz, France

As soon as the jet landed, Lavender and Max went to claim their baggage. The airport terminal wasn't too busy. People talked and walked by them in both directions, with an occasional voice announcing the next arrivals and departures over the loudspeaker.

"I booked us rooms for the night in this neo-baroque manor I thought you'd like," Lavender said.

"The Beau Chateau?"

"Uh-huh."

"I adore Edwardian architecture," Max gushed.

"Yes, it has a panache for sure." They walked toward the exit. "After a thirteen-hour flight, I knew I wouldn't have the energy to pick up the rental car and drive an hour or so to Hagatha's."

"I'm glad. My rear-end is still numb."

She laughed. "When we get to the manor, let's change clothes and grab dinner. Then I'm soaking in the tub and sleeping for eight hours. Normally during a transatlantic flight, I'd conjure up a sleeping potion with just the right amount for deep sleep, leaving no after-effects."

"Sleep—boohoo-hoo. We're in France. Let's party. I do so love the French accent. It gives me a twinge in all the right places. Too bad they hate Americans."

"Not all Americans. You have to give as good as you get."

"Oooh, that sounds nasty, and I like it. Well, at least most of them speak English. I flunked French."

"I know enough for the both of us. I lived with Hagatha for eighteen years. It was much different back then."

"Ah...that's why you opted for the nineteenth-century digs. I don't blame you." She pointed. "Our Rolls awaits."

"We're going to have so much fun." Max rubbed his hands together with glee.

Lavender didn't have the heart to remind him that she was there on business.

As the bellman took their luggage to their rooms, Lavender and Max walked through the plush lobby with floor-to-ceiling bookshelves on one side and two rolled arm sofas with a gray, brown, and cream paisley design on the other. A black baby grand in the corner.

With excitement, Max said, "This is splendid. Oh, look at the fabulous bar. Please, one glass of champagne." He pointed to a sign. "They have fifty different ones. Then we'll change clothes for dinner. I bet they can even arrange a reservation."

"You're impossible" She rolled her eyes. "Okay, one."

They made their way through wrought-iron gates on the other side of the lobby and entered the bar. It had high ceilings, dim lighting, masterfully crafted dark wood, a marble countertop, and several cozy table settings.

Max held the stool for Lavender. Then he sat next to her. He perused the list of champagnes. Before ordering, the bartender popped the cork and poured a bubbly concoction into two crystal flutes.

"*Mademoiselle*, and *monsieur*, compliments of the gentleman in the corner."

Simultaneously, Lavender and Max turned to see a handsome, dark-haired man with a mustache and soul patch, impeccably dressed.

He nodded.

"Let the games begin." Max chuckled.

When Brody learned of the latest call Lavender placed to St. Lucian's, he and Carlton agreed to keep his mission under wraps, at least until Brody knew for sure Lavender's intentions. He shifted his appearance several times during the flight.

Kyewicket rode with the cargo. He claimed the cat and teleported to the hotel. The cat snaked between Brody's legs as he secured a room next to Lavender's with a spell.

"You promise to stay out of sight."

"She'll never know that I'm here," Kyewicket purred.

They went to the room for a few minutes. Brody changed several times before the cat approved.

"You must look French, my friend."

"I look ridiculous," Brody said. "I should be scouring the countryside for members practicing the dark arts."

Kyewicket yawned. "Lavender and Max are here."

Brody peered out the window and watched her exit the vehicle. "What if I can't protect Lavender, and she has placed the mortal in danger, too?" A lump formed in his throat. "I remember the first time I was sent to Hant Hollow. The first time I knew I was in love with her. Love makes us vulnerable."

The black cat stretched onto the bed. "I remember it was the turn of the twentieth century."

"I became quite distracted when Lavender caught my eye. She'd sought me out while I set up military perimeters around the Doanhart's property for the upcoming festival. The look in her eyes had the air backing up in my lungs," Brody sighed. "I fell desperately in love with that spirited witch."

Hant Hollow 1915
The Southern Festival of Summer Solstice

Brody arrived a few days before the festival began. As the military commander, it was his duty to ensure the safety of all magical beings and the humans that would attend the weeklong Medieval Renaissance-inspired event hosted by the Doanharts.

Elite members of the alliance set up luxurious tents along Hant Hollow's hill while smaller tents dotted the glen.

He strode through the area, checking for anything out of the ordinary.

Lavender materialized in front of him, giving him a start. His grin went wide. Before moving to America, he'd met her briefly at Hagatha's chateau. He had wanted to kiss her then, and the urge to kiss her remained.

"I heard you were here." She sashayed around him, trailing her fingertips along his shoulders and down his right forearm. Thick lashes framed brilliant blue eyes. He ached to run his fingers through her silky blonde curls that cascaded over her shoulders.

He bowed, took her hand, and pressed a kiss against the tender, soft flesh. "You are a vision. And a delightful distraction to my duties."

"Come with me."

They ran into the thick woods until breaking through to a clearing next to a rushing river.

"We shouldn't be here, alone, unchaperoned. Your debut comes at the end of the week. You'll have many suitors more eligible than I."

Before he could stop her, Lavender went on tiptoes and wrapped her arms around his neck. She pressed her lips against his with such passion that he lost himself. His tongue delved between the sweet seams, then he gently removed her arms and stepped back.

She giggled, the half-woman, half-child. She was of age but innocent.

He took slow breaths to regain some control of the situation. "As much as I'd like to continue kissing you, I don't want to be reprimanded due to impropriety with a new member."

She clasped her hands behind her back and batted her lashes. "I've dreamed about kissing you for the longest time. And I can safely say you'd never make the first advance, so I took the opportunity, and I'm not sorry. Besides, you're not the first man I've kissed."

Anger rose within him so intense the river water bubbled. The thought of her kissing anyone but him nearly unleashed his beast. "Who? You've not been inducted into the alliance, and it is against the rules."

"They weren't in the alliance." She rolled her eyes. "They're mortal."

"What?"

"Are you jealous?" she asked with a raised brow.

"Hell, yes, I'm jealous. Mortals cannot be trusted. They're liars, cheaters, and thieves."

He cupped her face, memorizing every detail. His heart hammered. "I do not want you kissing any mortals. Understood?"

She nodded. "Well, don't steam up, but I'm working the kissing booth this year. Also, I'm getting inducted into the alliance, which means I will raise lots of money for our main library in Waytherlands."

With gritted teeth, he replied, "I'll make sure not to visit your booth."

"Brody." She leaned against his right arm and looked into his eyes. "You're the only one I want to kiss. I love you."

He took her hands. "You're too young to understand the implications of those words. I'll ask you again a hundred years from now."

The Beau Chateau

In disguise, Brody stepped over to the bar. "*Bonsoir.* My name is Henri Paul, and you are the most beautiful woman I've ever seen."

She nervously glanced away. The old Lavender would've been a hopeless flirt.

"Well, what about me, handsome?" Max asked.

"*Un beau gosse*, or handsome boy," Henri replied.

Lavender spit out her drink.

Max narrowed his eyes, then looked back to Henri. "You had me at *Bonsoir.*"

Henri or, well, Brody laughed.

Max was a funny little man.

Brody/Henri handed Lavender his handkerchief. "I couldn't help overhearing that you're hungry. I have dinner reservations at eight at the little Italian restaurant next to the hotel entrance if you two would like to join me. I hate eating alone."

"We would love to," Max exclaimed and squeezed Lavender's knee. "Where is it?"

"It's walking distance, Max." She stood. "We'll see you at dinner, and thank you for the drink. Um, I detect an American accent, Henri." Her lips pressed in a tight line. She was smart.

"*Oui*, born in France but live in America." Not a lie.

Max stood. "We'll get changed and meet you soon."

Brody watched them walk away, then popped into his room to shower quickly. He anticipated spending more time with Lavender, and maybe he could figure out her next steps with a good meal and a bottle of wine.

Chapter 4

Lavender yelled, "I have suspicions about Henri."

"Come out." Max pounded on the bathroom door. "How long are you going to stay in there? We're going to miss him."

She slammed the door open and stepped out with as much theatrics as Lady Gaga on stage. "Henri won't leave."

Max clapped. "Girl, you look like Sabrina. Forgive us, Elizabeth Montgomery. I haven't seen an outfit like that in decades."

She'd changed her hair into a short black shag. She had applied thick black eyeliner and ruby red lipstick. Lavender conjured up a '60s-inspired mini-dress in pink, blue, green, and yellow paisley pastels.

His gaze went to her feet, and he wagged his pointer finger. "Not the flip-flops. Wear the bedazzled sandals." He stopped. "Wait. Are you off the wagon? You used magic?"

"It feels good to flex again." Lavender twirled around. "Do I look okay?"

"Do you want the short or long version? I have to warn you the long version is in Pig Latin." Max imitated the iconic Uncle Arthur laugh.

She playfully pushed him, then snapped her fingers. Her flip-flops turned into sandals. "Look, you need to play along. I'm Lavender's cousin, Clara. Lavender crashed with jet lag. Then, we'll play the rest by ear. And don't gush so much over Henri. He could be The Lord Darkness incarnate."

"Well, if he is, he pulls it off flawlessly."

Twenty minutes later, Lavender and Max entered the Italian eatery with a killer view of the Atlantic Ocean. The sun was sinking low on the horizon.

A music artist belted *C'est si bon* as they walked along the path.

"There's Henri." Max waved. "See him?"

"You need to chill. Have a cocktail, have two. Please, don't blow my cover."

Henri's eyes raked over her body like hot coals, and his intentions seemed crystal clear—he wanted her sexually.

She didn't plan on using magic against Henri—only if it was necessary. Hopefully, she overreacted. However, most of the time, her empathic abilities were spot on.

Henri pushed away from his chair. "You look different."

Lavender leaned in and planted air kisses on Henri's cheeks. "I'm Clara, Lavender's cousin." She used English with perfect French inflection. "I drove here this afternoon to accompany Lavender to Aunt Hagatha's chateau tomorrow. Lavender was so jet-lagged that she fell asleep. Max and I are starving, so boom, we are here."

"Pity, but I welcome your company."

Her hair rose on the back of her neck. Something was off with this man. Was this man a wizard, a spy, or both?

Henri looked at Max. "*Bonjour.*" Then he turned back to Lavender. "I took the liberty of ordering for us. The specialties are excellent, and they're known for their homemade sauces and bread." He waved to a nearby waiter who came quickly with a bottle of red wine, then Henri sat down next to Max, across from Lavender.

Max sipped. "The wine is robust. Hm, firm, full-bodied." He swirled the dark red liquid, then took another drink. "Blackberry with a hint of vanilla and exceptionally aged tannins."

"Excellent read, Maximus," Henri replied with hoarseness.

Max's cheeks reddened.

It took all Lavender's willpower not to laugh at Henri's flirting with Max.

Because when Henri looked at her, he undressed her with his eyes. He made love to her with the silkiness of his voice, and the way his words rolled off his tongue made her wonder what it would feel like to have his tongue in her mouth and a few other choice places.

Henri spoke about his childhood in France. He used his hands while talking about his real estate business which made him wealthy.

One of his gestures gave her pause. Could it be?

They ate.

They drank.

They laughed.

And they drank some more.

Lavender had fun. But it was more than fun. There was an easiness with their conversation like two old friends.

An electric charge rushed through her veins as Henri brushed his fingers across the back of her hand. By the time the main course arrived, Lavender had learned Henri had descended from a Bourgogne family.

Max was drunk when the waiter delivered the dessert. He made yummy sounds with every bite. The Basque cake had two flaky pastries filled with vanilla cream. "Oh my God, this cake is sooo good."

Henri ordered them each a coffee. He ordered hers, no white sugar, only raw cane sugar with extra cream. That did it!

She'd play along with his deceit a bit longer. Turn up the heat a bit.

Max nodded off to sleep.

"We should get back to the manor. I'll bring the rest of the dessert for Lavender," she said, still in complete Clara disguise.

"We'll walk together?" Henri said. "Max may need help."

Max opened one eyelid and gave Henri the thumbs up.

The waiter handed her a fresh slice of cake and water bottles.

Henri draped Max's arm around his shoulders and held him up with his other arm around Max's waist.

Max giggled. "You smell heavenly, Henri."

"Thanks."

Lavender looked at the almost full moon. The stars seemed so close. Tourist traffic had vanished by the time they reached the manor.

Henri scooped Max into his arms and carried him the rest of the way.

Max nudged into Henri's neck. "My hero."

Lavender chuckled. "You better carry him to the room." She walked ahead through the wrought-iron gates down the hallway. She knocked on the door. "Lavender, are you dressed?"

She turned and shrugged, then scanned the key, and opened the door. "Place Max in the bed, please. I'll go to the pool and see if Lavender is there."

He laid Max on the bed and stepped up behind her—his warm breath kissed her neck. "I'll go with you. I don't want you to go alone in the dark."

Her heart fluttered with excitement walking to the patio.

No one was outside—no lights except the moon.

She placed the palm of her hand on the curve of his cheek. She trailed her fingers down the column of his throat.

His head tilted back, and he moaned.

"You like, or don't like? I mean, you and Max seemed cozy together."

"It's not that. I-I ...," he stammered.

She circled his waist. "If you're married, I'll turn you into a fat rat."

"I'm not married, but I am in love with someone." He frowned. "What do you mean, turn me into a rat?"

"Is your love interest dead?" Lavender continued to toy with him.

"She is very much alive."

Lavender licked his throat, slightly salty and spicy. "Tell me her name."

"No," he whispered, "I won't tell you her name."

She ran her hands over his biceps and down his muscular forearms.

He grabbed her wrists. "Don't do that. You are tearing my heart out, Clara."

She tilted her head to one side. "Why am I tearing your heart out, Brody?"

"What?" He sucked in a breath. "How?"

"When you ordered my coffee."

His eyes widened. "You're not Clara. Lavender?"

She smiled at him and nudged him with her shoulder. "Henri wouldn't have known I don't take white sugar in my coffee, only sugar in the raw."

"That was purely by accident. I thought you were Clara."

Lavender shook her head, and her short black shag turned natural blonde. "Well, I knew you were a wizard after drinks in the bar. I sensed magic within you. But I didn't know if you fought on the light or dark side, so I waited. I listened to your stories. Some I'm sure came from your real childhood."

"Not really. I don't like talking about my childhood." He took her into his arms. "That friggin' mini-dress is driving me mad. I want you, Lavender. Now."

"Your room, not mine."

Brody scooped her into his arms. He kissed her—his tongue gliding along the seams of her lips.

His other hand slid under her skirt. "You can't go wrong with thongs." He nipped at her ear.

She kicked her feet. "Not out here, Brody."

Once next to his room, Brody placed her on the ground and rummaged for his key fob.

"Your room is right next to ours?"

"Yeah, I did that on purpose. And know if Henri had been real, I'd have killed him with my bare hands."

"I love it when you're feisty."

Inside his room, Kyewicket jumped straight up in the air.

"Well, kitty kat, you have some explaining to do." Lavender placed both hands on her hips.

"Darling, you are so out of your depth." Kyewicket swiped at her. "You don't know the people at St. Lucian's, and you haven't practiced magic in years. I requested to come along with Brody to protect you."

"I practiced tonight. Why don't you go on the prowl, Kyewicket? Brody and I have some catching up to do."

She opened the door, and the cat ran out. Once they were alone, she turned to Brody. "Come here, you. I can't believe you followed me across an ocean."

"I can't believe you don't believe it." He wiggled his forefinger. "You come here."

Lavender stepped over to him. "Change back. I'm not making love to Henri."

"Are you sure?"

She nodded.

"Give me five minutes." Brody dashed into the bathroom, brushed his teeth, and sniffed his underarms. *Whew.* He quickly washed under his arms, then swiped deodorant. God, he was acting like a lovesick fool. He stepped out of the bathroom.

Lavender had crawled into the bed in her birthday suit. She snored like a freight train.

He took the blanket from the sofa, draped it around her, and then slipped into the bed. He pulled her into his arms. "Are you sleeping?" He kissed the top of her head and caught the sweet scent of green apples and citrus.

"So, I have a confession to make." He looked down at her. It was easier to say what was on his heart when she slept.

Her breathing was steady.

"Don't be mad at Kyewicket," he whispered. "He loves you. I love you too. We both have witnessed how losing your mom has changed you. I enlisted his help at your family's outdoor dinner party. Don't get me wrong; the rest of the Doanharts are concerned too. There's something off about St. Lucian's. I cannot find the monastery on any GPS, including the mage's surveillance system. I will not allow you to go alone. Please don't beat me up."

Lavender started thrashing on the bed.

"Oh, honey, wake up. You're having a nightmare."

He turned her around, and her lips were turning blue. He placed his fingers on either side of his temples and shouted, "Doctor Conway, come right away. Do not delay, Doctor Conway."

A five-foot-five older-looking gentleman with bushy white eyebrows and gold wire-rim glasses popped into the room. "Move you, brute." He shoved Brody to the side. "Can't you see? She can't breathe." Dr. Conway placed his hand on the sole of her foot. "No fever."

The doctor snapped his fingers, and a stethoscope with a large suction device appeared. He placed it on Lavender's stomach. "Ah, I should have known." He put his hands on either side of her face; her mouth gaped. "Binding worm, hear me, come out now, or I will come in, then I'll personally deliver you to The Goddess of Light. Now, up, up, up, you schmuck."

Lavender started coughing.

"Wastebasket, please," Doctor Conway said.

Brody practically threw it at him.

Lavender started puking, and the longest, slimiest, slug-looking monster slid out of her mouth.

Brody heaved twice.

The doctor grabbed the worm by the tail. "Good God, man, it's a bug. Ha! Immobilitis." He blinked twice, and a transparent canister appeared. He shoved the binding worm inside and sealed it. "It will take twenty-four hours to interrogate the beast. She needs to rest. Doesn't Hagatha live close by?"

"Yes. I think so," Brody replied. "It's been a long time since I visited the chateau."

"Thirsty," Lavender croaked.

Doctor Conway whipped his right forefinger. "What's your favorite milkshake?"

"Chocolate."

He placed the drink on the side table. "Good, then it tastes like chocolate. Drink it up, and it should kill any larvae."

Lavender puked into the basket again. She swiped her mouth with the back of her hand, then wrapped a blanket around her and came to a sitting position. "Please tell me that thing didn't leave babies in my belly."

Doctor Conway handed her the milkshake, then pulled a humongous magnifier from his long white coat pocket and placed it over her stomach. He leaned in and shook his head. "All gone. We caught the beast before it did its worst. Those nasty worms are dreadful once they take root in the intestines."

Brody asked, "What is it?"

The doctor pursed his lips. "I don't have time to explain, not that you'd understand." He looked at Lavender. "Go to Hagatha's, and don't leave the house until I have the results."

"Why?" Brody and Lavender said in unison.

"That was a killer binding worm. Thank goodness I was only in India. I will call on you at Hagatha's in the morning." He turned to Brody. "Do not leave Lavender's side. If she gets sick again, call me right away." Dr. Conway disappeared in a cloud of white mist.

Brody pushed the hair away from her forehead. "I'm calling Max. He'll pack for you. I have a vehicle. We'll drive to Hagatha's without delay. Someone wants you dead, and I don't have time to look at the hotel footage."

"Do I have time for a shower? I feel icky. I will be sick again if I think about that slug in my belly. At least the milkshake helped."

"Good, get in the shower. I'm calling one of my guys. He is excellent at surveillance."

Lavender crawled out of bed on shaking legs. "I'm good." She threw one hand up. "Just a little dizzy. A shower will help." She went into the bathroom and shut the door.

"Christian Birch, calling Christian Birch. I need an in-depth search."

A loud knock at the door. "Henri, Henri, are you awake? It's Max."

Brody turned back into Henri and opened the door. "Come in, Max."

"Who's in your shower?" Max's voice rose. His hands went into fists. "Where is my friend?"

"It's not what you think. Max, just calm down. I'll explain it."

"You French frog, you, pond-scum." He tackled Henri to the bed.

Brody materialized. "Max, it's me."

Max's eyes widened as he straddled Brody.

Christian Birch appeared. "I do not judge, boss."

"Oh, good grief. Max, this is Birch."

"Do you want to tell me what the hell is going on?" Max rolled off the bed.

"No time. I'll catch you up on our way to Hagatha's. Please pack for Lavender, and we'll meet you outside in twenty minutes." Brody waved his fingers, and his suitcase opened and packed itself. "Birch, go with Max. And heads up, someone just tried to kill Lavender."

Max gasped, throwing his hand over his mouth.

"If I were a betting man," Brody said, "I'd say it has something to do with St. Lucian's."

Chapter 5

Lavender clutched her midsection and glanced at the full moon rising in the sky. "Do you think someone hexed me at the restaurant?" She turned to Brody. Kyewicket curled at her feet.

His hands gripped the steering wheel while he sped down the country roads, putting miles between them and the manor. "Binding worms require a certain level of expertise. It's not a spell that's transatlantic. My immediate thought is someone here does not want you to go to St. Lucian's. Tell me why you're going. What book are you trying to acquire?"

"I've gathered a substantial amount of information regarding our ancestry. It's more than I was ever taught in school or by Grams. Based on what I've found, I'm not sure what happened to my mother was an accident. I thought the war between Jonathan and Grandmother Iris was all about Jasmine," Lavender said. "Maybe part of the conflict was over Jonathan's father, but I came across two ancient books alluding to a universal rebellion in the otherworld. Iris was involved somehow. Maybe Jonathan was supposed to have been a blood sacrifice."

"We know Iris used blood magic, but why Jonathan?"

Lavender glanced at Birch. "Are you trustworthy?"

"Ask your lover." Birch crossed his arms over his chest.

"He's trustworthy, Lavender. We're all on the same side, so let's keep things civil," Brody replied.

"I don't want to place you in any more danger than I have to, Max. Forgive me." She snapped her fingers, and Max fell asleep instantly. "There are degrees of blood magic. Iris was in love with Jonathan's father, Thomas. She had a child with him that died. Her wrath would've increased her power exponentially using Jonathan's blood, but he was not a wizard or a warlock."

Brody nodded. "What's the tie-in? Why are you here?"

"I'm not one hundred percent sure, but I think it has to do with The Goddess of Light being a Pleiadean and The Lord Darkness an Orionnite. So, I think my family directly results from that otherworld war."

"In outer space? Seriously? And you're what? An alien witch, is that it?" Birch asked.

"Maybe. Why is that so far-fetched?" Lavender scowled. "I've read many rare scrolls and collections alluding to ancient civilizations coming to Earth long before humanity existed. Maybe, they taught our ancestors magic. Do you think we're the only ones in the cosmos? Look, Brody has vouched for you. The information I know can place you in danger, too. Don't act smug. If you don't believe me, then I do not need your help."

"Birch, zip it." Brody glanced at Lavender, then back to the road.

"We travel to another realm when we visit Waytherlands. Humans do not travel into parallel or multiverses, but we could." Lavender exhaled a deep sigh. "I have my notes in the cloud. You are welcome to read them once we arrive at Hagatha's."

"I won't lie. You've lost me a little too," Brody added. "Why do I feel you're leaving out something important?"

Brody clenched his jaw. "If what you say is true, you are in way over your head. You're asserting that alien species and the deities governing our race are the same, and they're at war. That's more than the mage military can handle, not counting the mortals on the planet."

"Don't you think I know that?" Lavender wrung her hands. "The text I'm to view should confirm my suspicions. If I'm correct, then we'll need to convene the council. It will change everything they taught us to believe."

"And that's exactly why someone tried to kill you. You're getting too close to information that could change our world and possibly human existence. I'm going with you to St. Lucian's, and don't give me any arguments," Brody said. "I wonder. Could hybrids live on the planet? Do they possess the same potential for magic?"

"Jonathan and Victoria's child is a hybrid. We can talk to them when we return. Brody, I'm glad you followed me. I want answers too. No arguments from me. Witches honor." Lavender smiled and made the code of honor sign. "I need to sleep. I can't go to the monastery half-ass."

"True, we all need sleep, but first thing in the morning, Birch will retrace the steps of the waiters, housekeepers, cooking staff, and bartenders during our dinner. Everyone is a suspect. We'll find the responsible parties who poisoned you."

Birch interjected, "Once we get to Hagatha's, we'll go off the grid and only use our most trusted sources in France. Hopefully, Doctor Conway will have the name of the monster's creator."

She pointed at the upcoming street. "Take the next right."

Brody followed her directions. The bright moon made the leaves shimmer silver across the valleys and revealed the snow-covered mountainside. He glanced to his right. He thought he saw someone flying in the air, but no one appeared when he looked again. Nervous, raw energy made him second guess himself. He wouldn't tell the others until he was sure.

"I haven't visited Hagatha's in a long time," Brody said. "I haven't seen the Doanhart matriarch in over one hundred years."

"Heads-up, Hagatha doesn't like to be reminded of her age." Lavender rolled down her window and stretched her arm outside, allowing the chilly wind to cup her hand. "We've entered the veil of protection. Just look at those stars. Smell that sweet air. I'm home."

"Brr, that's cold," Kyewicket purred. "Roll the window up or increase the heat."

She closed the window, scooped the cat into her arms and covered him with her jacket. "I'll keep you warm."

The shield peeled away the layers of protection, and in seconds, they entered the Doanhart property. "Would you look at that, Birch?" Brody said.

"Beautiful. It's like stepping back in time, except for the asphalt," Birch replied.

"The moon shines like the sun." Brody slowed the speed.

The village vanished from sight, leaving an abundance of nature unspoiled by humanity. The road straddled a natural rock ridge as Hagatha's chateau came into view.

"It hasn't changed much since the 1500s. The Doanharts have protected the mages against persecution since we built the chateau." Lavender reached back and nudged Max. "Wake up. You're missing the fairy tale view."

"Wha-what?" Max stretched, then his eyes widened. "*Magnifique!* Is this Hagatha's?"

"Yup," she replied.

"You grew up here?" Max asked.

"For the most part. I went to school in a nearby village." Lavender smiled.

"It's mind-boggling that a place like this still exists." Brody slowed the car as he pulled through the wrought-iron gate.

Lavender turned in the seat to face Max. "The medieval architecture, with its thick walls, made it a virtually impenetrable fortress. I can't wait for you to see the gardens. Even when it snows, they're gorgeous. The staterooms are rich in history."

"I've died and gone to heaven," Max said. "Pinch me."

Birch complied.

"Ouchy." Max punched Birch in the arm. "Haven't you heard catchphrases before, you big oaf?"

Birch threw his head back and laughed. "Where did you find this adorable human?"

Max frowned. "At the Five and Dime, where else?"

"I like you." Birch playfully shoved Max.

Brody came to a stop in the circular drive.

Hagatha came down the front entrance steps. "Lavender, I sensed you were on the property. Oh, sweet girl, it is good to see you."

Lavender exited the vehicle, then embraced the woman. "You haven't changed one bit."

Brody slid out and waited for Max and Birch to exit the vehicle before approaching the reuniting women.

Hagatha kissed each of Lavender's cheeks. "Who are these handsome warlocks?" She paused and looked at Max. "You must be the human my American family loves so much."

"Guilty." Max turned several shades of red.

"This is Max, and next to him are Brody and Birch."

"My, my, you have handsome friends. Oh, have you eaten?" Hagatha asked.

"Yes, ma'am," Max said. "And thank you for speaking English."

"No need to thank me. You are an American, after all. Well, let's get you inside and settled into your rooms. I'm sure you need rest."

As they entered the chateau, Stealths immediately gathered the luggage and disappeared.

Lavender brushed the hair away from her face. "Remember the Stealths hired at home?"

Max nodded. "Yes, they're tall, thin, and invisible from a sideways glance." He winked. "And known for their discretion."

Hagatha giggled. "I have a full staff, a head housekeeper and housemaids, my chauffeur, and a stable groomer. They've lived with me for centuries, so they're family to me. Cook takes care of the kitchen. If you need anything, snap your fingers twice, or use the bell pull in each room. Our exceptional Stealths work in silence and prefer communicating telepathically, but they will make an exception for our human guest."

The interior of the chateau hadn't changed either, Lavender thought, with its French Renaissance style. Checkered tiles, crystal chandeliers, corbeled walkways, massive mirrors in ornate Italian frames, and vaulted exposed beam ceilings. An original Da Vinci painting hung over an elaborate stone fireplace, and seventeenth-century tapestries covered the walls.

"Close your mouth, Max." Lavender chuckled.

"Hagatha, will you adopt me?" he replied.

"But of course. Andre will show you to your rooms. Please make yourself at home, and I will see you all in the morning." Hagatha vanished out of the room.

Andre, the Stealth, extended his arm toward the hallway. "If you'll follow me."

A flood of childhood memories came over Lavender as she walked up the imperial marble staircase. She and Jasmine on silver trays, sliding down the steps like sledding down snow-covered hills. Or the time they had learned to fly, and Lavender flipped over the top tier banister, free falling. Jasmine had swooped beside her and yelled, "Fly, my darling, soar to the heights." The squeals of their laughter had often echoed in the enormous halls.

In those days, the Doanhart family had been so close-knit. She never imagined the horrific division of ideologies in a million years.

Today, their little troop seemed weary and worn as they climbed the stairs.

Hagatha had updated the stone and brick hallway with whitewash. It created a warmer, airier touch.

As a child, the gray, drab stone scared her. Ghosts and goblins had occasionally appeared in the knight's armor or mirrors. But her mother had assured her it was only her brilliant imagination. Mom made everything seem brighter before Hant Hollow before Dale Rogers and Iris had twisted her soul.

Andre stopped at the first guest room. "*Monsieur Dupres*, your room, sir. The private bath is on the right. Please feel free to use the tapestry bell pull next to your bed if you need service."

Max seemed stunned and at a loss for words, which was rare. "I'll see you in the morning, sweetie." He yawned and kissed her cheek.

The next room was for Birch. He went in without comment.

Brody took her hand. "Will you stay with me?"

"Not tonight. I'm exhausted and afraid I wouldn't get any sleep in your room." She reached up on tiptoe and kissed him lightly on the mouth. "I'll take a rain check."

Brody drew her up and leaned in close. His eyes searched hers, then gazed at her lips. He looked back into her eyes. "I intend to collect in full."

She smiled, and he kissed her again before entering his room and closing the door.

"Andre, do I get my old room?"

"*Oui.*"

Lavender ran the rest of the way and threw open the door.

Everything looked the same. The door closed, and Andre vanished.

She kicked off her shoes and jumped into the plush canopy bed with a mile-high mattress that enveloped her like an old friend. She snapped her fingers, and she wore a lilac silk nightgown.

Lavender slid in between the sheets and, seconds later, drifted into a deep sleep.

Chapter 6

Lavender woke to birds chirping a cheery tune outside her bedroom windows. Streams of brilliant sunlight pooled on the floor of her room. Giddy, as a schoolgirl, she relived the warm sensation of being in Brody's arms last night.

Oh, she wished she hadn't gotten sick.

He had never let her down. She felt terrible that she had pushed him away.

No more.

She intended to embrace their relationship again.

She threw her legs over the side of the bed, her feet not quite touching the floor. The lavender scent in the room made her smile. Hagatha hadn't changed her room one bit.

She sighed, then got up and opened the closet door. It was much bigger than she remembered and full of new, expensive-looking clothes.

"Bless your heart, Hagatha." Lavender's fingers caressed each color-coded outfit. "Hmm." She fumbled in her small bag and pulled out her phone. "Temperature in the Pyrenees."

"Sunny and twenty-two degrees with snow showers late morning."

"Yikes." The coast and the mountain temps differed significantly. With the phone in hand, she said, "Convert to Celsius."

"Minus five point five Celsius."

She'd forgotten how cold it could get in the mountains, but the array of autumn colors was nothing short of spectacular.

After a hot shower, Lavender opted for an oversized cashmere sweater with high-waisted jeans and paired it with brown shearling boots.

She grabbed a winter scarf and the black fur-lined parka from the back of the closet.

Max would want her to coordinate.

Lavender giggled, wiggled her nose, and changed the black coat to a warm tan.

Stepping into the hallway, loud laughter echoed downstairs as she hurried to the kitchen. It held much warmth and many fond memories.

The cozy room reminded her of the fun times at Hant Hollow before Grams' jealousy destroyed her family.

She shook her head. She would not think about that today. She was in France with the man she loved.

The smell of bacon frying made her mouth water.

Brody, Max, and Birch sat on the bench opposite an open fireplace. The logs crackled with flames.

Lavender noticed Hagatha and raced to her, and they embraced. Lavender couldn't help it. She cried like a baby.

"My dear girl, it's going to be alright." Hagatha took Lavender's hands. "You are so beautiful, so like your mother."

Lavender sniffled as Hagatha whirled her finger and offered a handkerchief.

"You must eat. Cook made all your favorites."

Cook nodded, then busied himself at the stove and pulled out a tray of warm croissants from the oven.

"I am starving. That smells wonderful." Lavender hiccuped.

Max's hands cupped a large coffee mug. "Sleep well? I slept marvelously." He blew the steam, then sipped.

"Yes, I slept great." Lavender went to the cupboard, pulled out a cup, and filled it to the brim with the piping hot brew. She added raw sugar and thick cream, then glanced at the liquid and mentally stirred the concoction with a spell.

Cook placed an assortment of breakfast meats, baked French eggs drizzled with butter, warm croissants with melting chocolate on the worn oak table, and pitchers of orange juice.

Hagatha clapped her hands, and placed settings with linen napkins materialized along with the silver and crystal glasses. "You should see our home in the summer." She looked at Max and winked. "We throw great parties."

Everyone filled their plates and ate in silence for about a minute.

"Well, honey, everyone who knows me— knows I love to parr-tee." Max grabbed a sausage link with his fingers and bit it in half. Then he exaggerated the *guttural R.*

Hagatha popped to the other side of the table and caressed his bald head. "Would you like to have sex with me?"

Max choked.

"Are you okay, Max?" Lavender burst out laughing. "I don't think I've ever seen you so flustered."

"Oh, hush up." He turned to Hagatha and placed his hand on her forearm. "Thank you kindly for the offer, but I'm gay."

"I can be a man for you, my sweet." She twirled her hand, and she was a super-hot man.

Max's mouth gaped. "Um. Um. You'll have to let me think about that for a bit."

"*Mon coeur,* it is not a proposal. It's only sex." Hagatha switched back to herself.

The whole kitchen erupted in laughter.

"Oh, oh, Lavender, I almost forgot." Hagatha snapped her fingers and materialized in the rocking chair next to the fire. "The curator working with the monastery left you a message. They're expecting you this afternoon at two."

"Two? Has Doctor Conway called?"

"No word from the doctor. Darling, are you sick?"

Lavender didn't want to worry her. "No, just a bug." She took a bite out of the chocolate croissant. "Cook, you have excelled in your culinary skills."

He grinned. "Thank you."

"Someone hexed Lavender with a killer binding worm last evening." Brody pushed away from the table, picked up his plate, and took it to the sink. "We need time to vet what happened to you yesterday before you go to St. Lucian's." He leaned against the counter and then crossed his arms over his chest.

"That's my cue." Birch stood. "I have work to do. I'll return when I get any deets." He reached for Hagatha's hand and kissed it. "I'll take you up on the sex offer, that is, if Max gets cold feet." He chuckled. "Cook, *c'était absolument délicieux!*" He glanced over his shoulder. "Max, that means it's real good," he said, elongating his syllables to inflect a Southern United States accent.

Lavender popped over to Max and draped her arm around his shoulders. "Don't tease Max. He's my dearest friend. And I love him."

Birch shrugged and vanished.

Max waved her off. "I'm a big boy, Mommy, and please stop the magical chairs. I'm getting dizzy. Hagatha just caught me off guard. They don't talk like that at the Rockvale Church." His smile widened. "You know, where you were baptized."

"Baptized? What is this, *mon cher*?" Hagatha asked.

"Long story for another time. Did Mr. Bisset leave his contact information?"

"*Oui*, in the library on my desk." Hagatha turned to Cook. "Is it okay if we leave you with the mess?"

Cook's cheeks dimpled. "No worries. I'll clean the kitchen. Formal dinner tonight, *n'est-ce pas?*"

"That's right. Formal. Say eight o'clock, everyone?"

Max and Brody nodded approval.

"Formal? Have you guests coming to dinner?" Lavender took her dishes to the sink. She leaned against Brody's arm.

"But, of course, my dear. My great-granddaughter has returned home."

"Please, may we move the dinner party to another day? I have lots of work. And, it's going to take me a little time to adjust to your French palate," Lavender said. "Most of the time, I eat salads or drink protein shakes."

"No wonder you are so skinny," Cook said. "A couple of weeks with me, and you'll be right as rain."

"Come, my darlings," Hagatha interjected. "Let's go to the library so we may discuss Lavender's itinerary."

The library had twenty-foot-high cathedral ceilings. The seventeenth-century French desk and chair overlooked acres of elaborate gardens with the Pyrenees as a backdrop.

Books filled the sage-color-washed shelves, trimmed in leather to protect the bindings. The shelves held rare collections and manuscripts never seen by mortals on two levels.

"I designed the new library. The dark wood needed a facelift." Hagatha walked over to the fireplace, clapped twice, and flames appeared. "Did you know I had an affair with the artist?" she asked, nodding to a painting above the mantel.

"You had an affair with Delacroix?" Lavender inquired.

"*Oui,* I broke his heart." Hagatha's age was a mystery— centuries, possibly a thousand years old. She never revealed her actual age. She still loved playing the coquette. "It is why he never married."

"This palatial room has effortless interior design," Max said. "I'm envious of your skills."

"I could teach you everything I know." Hagatha sidled next to him.

"That's what I'm afraid of." Max laughed. "The art collection alone is worth millions."

"You are an art dealer, no?" She eased down on the ivory sheepskin settee. "You see the monetary worth of art. But this art speaks to my soul. I would never sell it."

"Enough already with the artsy-smartsy shit," Brody interrupted. "Where's the curator's contact information?"

Hagatha frowned. "In the drawer."

Brody took out a piece of stationery, and Lavender snatched it from his hands.

She read the address. "11475 Abellio. The name doesn't ring any bells."

"It's off the D19. The road is treacherous and hidden if memory serves." Hagatha went to the shelves closest to the fireplace and withdrew a book. "Hm. I'm not sure I remember a monastery close to the location. However, ancient ruins abound in the mountains. The Pyrenees are full of magic and myth." She held it in front of her. "Book, show me Abellio Road."

A hologram appeared out of the pages into the room. "It looks like the forest to me." Lavender stepped closer. "Ah-ha! There, it's barely visible in the thicket, but I see it. May I take the book with me?"

Hagatha nodded. "I agree with Brody. Call the monastery. See if they'll reschedule for tomorrow."

"I will call, but if they can only see me today. I'm going." Lavender picked up the book when the doorbell chimed.

Andre ushered Dr. Conway into the library, then backed out and closed the door.

"Dr. Conway, won't you sit?" Hagatha pointed to the settee.

"No time for that, Hagatha." He nodded to Brody and Max, then turned to Lavender. He took out a folded piece of paper and adjusted his glasses. He cleared his throat. "My dear girl, you are a victim of a deadly binding worm. It's good that Brody called me immediately, or things could've turned out much worse." He handed her the paper. "The Princess of the Dark Night is responsible for your bug."

"Which one? That sect of witches disappeared." Lavender was stunned. "They escaped when Iris took down Urslina after the Southern Festival of Summer Solstice in 1915. Are they practicing in France?"

"It seems so." The doctor pushed his glasses up on the bridge of his nose. "The worm exploded before I could extract any further evidence."

Brody took out his mobile and swiped the screen. "Birch, the Doc is here. Urslina's hags placed the binding worm spell." He nodded, saying nothing, and his face stayed emotionless for a few more minutes. He put the phone back in his pant pocket. "Birch has found our contact. He said a group of radical witches formed a new coven. He's unsure of the deity helping them. He's confirming the sources now." He stepped over to Lavender and held her hands. "Call the curator. Tell him you have food poisoning and see if he'll move your arrival time."

"Urslina's witches declared long ago that they'd get revenge on Iris and our family." Lavender appreciated his touch. "Maybe, they intend to take a pound of flesh from me. I wonder if they're connected to St. Lucian's."

"There's only one way to find out," Brody said. "Call the curator."

Lavender nodded and snapped her fingers. Her phone appeared in her hand. "I'll be back." She left the room, strode across the foyer, sat next to the double staircase, and then placed the call.

"*Bonjour*, Adam Bisset speaking."

"Hello, Monsieur Bisset, this is Lavender Doanhart. I've been a bit under the weather since my arrival and wanted to see if it's possible to reschedule our meeting until tomorrow?"

Silence.

"Monsieur Bisset?"

"I'm afraid that's out of the question. Two o'clock today is my only availability, as I'm leaving for a tour in Egypt. I cannot say when I'll return. The monks will seal the scrolls for a later viewing if you cannot make it."

She stood. "No, no, don't do that. My associate and I will arrive at two."

"Your associate?" he asked. "I was unaware of an associate."

"Since the scrolls are ancient, I brought my colleague, Mr. Whitmore, for a consult. He's an expert in antiquities." Lavender didn't wait for a reply. "See you at two." She hung up and paced the floor before heading back into the library. "We have to go today. He's going on tour and doesn't know when he'll return."

"I'm going with you," Brody said.

"I told him I was bringing my consultant, Mr. Whitmore, as a specialist in all things old." She sat next to Brody and looked at the doctor. "Are there any residual effects from the binding worm?"

"There's a slight chance your spell casting may go awry. For example, you want to turn the little American into a cat, and instead, he turns into a chimpanzee." Dr. Conway looked over the rim of his glasses. "But the odds are slim. Call me if you need me. I'm due in Provence." He whirled his hand and disappeared.

Kyewicket stalked into the library. "I'm going with you, Lavender, in case you get into trouble."

"That's what she has me for." Brody picked up the cat and rubbed his ears. "But if you insist, you may come under the cloak of invisibility.

"What do you want me to do?" asked Max.

"Hagatha can take you on a road tour. The villages are charming with stone houses and bridges. You'll love the Romanesque architecture and art museums. Dress warmly. Snow is expected."

"Be still, my heart." Max fluttered his hand over his heart. "Do the art galleries take credit cards?"

"Your money is no good here, my pet." Hagatha added an 'R' with the rolling of her tongue. She laughed as she lashed out with a claw-like gesture going in for the kill.

Lavender said, "Hagatha, behave."

"I will need alcohol and lots of it." Max wiped his brow.

Chapter 7

Brody opened the Toyota 4Runner passenger's door for Lavender, and Kyewicket jumped in and settled into the back seat. Hagatha's vehicle would make navigating the snow on the mountain's upper elevations easier.

"I'm glad you're with me." Lavender cupped his face with her hands. "When I booked the trip, I wasn't scared of anything, but now I'm not so sure. Anything from Birch?"

"Nothing." He kissed her lightly on the mouth. "I will protect you, my love. Get in, and we'll talk on the way."

She slid into her seat and strapped on her seatbelt.

He reached the driver's seat, then pushed the engine button. The vehicle roared to life. "Tell me how you found Adam Bisset."

"My intern, Emily, referred me to Professor Browning. He teaches at Silver Meadows University. He's the dean of Philology and specializes in studying oral and written histories. His emphasis is on classical languages. He also deals in rare collections. I met him when I first opened for business. He put me in contact with many dealers, including Adam Bisset."

"How did you find Emily?" Brody listened intently but stayed focused on the hairpin turns along the winding roads. The scenery was amazing. The farther into their route, the more he relaxed because the vehicle handled well.

THE WITCHES OF HANT HOLLOW 2: GATE KEEPERS

"I bought an ad with the campus placement center. Emily was the best applicant by far, and she's irreplaceable." She leaned on the console. "What's going on in that brain of yours?"

"Emily might everything you say, but she sounds too good to be true. If I were doing an investigation, she'd be top on my list of suspects."

"Emily? Oh, no, seriously?"

"Seriously. Someone tried to kill you last night. I've already initiated a search on Emily, the good professor, and Adam Bisset. Birch is incredibly good at his job. If they check out, we move on to Hagatha to find out who she told about you coming to France."

"Oh, what if Emily finds out? I'd be apt to suspect Hagatha's friends. It seems more logical," Lavender said.

"Perhaps. I will leave no stone unturned. If there's nothing amiss, Emily will never know, and Hagatha will want to help. Birch is fast and reliable. The information he uncovers just might save your life."

They drove deeper into the forest, climbing elevation with every mile, er, every meter. Snow soon fell in sheets, making driving a bit more challenging. "Check your phone navigation. I'm not picking up Abellio Road on the SUV's GPS."

"The road is about a mile up ahead on the left." Lavender turned up the heater.

"What are you hoping to find at St. Lucian's?" he asked.

Lavender scratched her cheek. "I'm looking for the Gate Keepers. They may have access to Mom's location. What did you find out about her?"

He avoided disclosing information about her mom for now. "Legends state the Gate Keepers are Gods. They're incredibly discerning regarding who enters the parallel realms and other worlds."

"We're close."

Brody slowed the car to a snail's pace. "I don't see anything but forest."

"Do you see that cross?"

"Yeah. I see it." He came to a complete stop. "That's an ancient pagan cross. It has strange markings, probably Celtic, with the intertwining dragons. Did you know the knot used to hold weapons?"

"Really? It could also be a remnant of the Cathars too."

"The Cathar Christians who broke away from the Roman church and were massacred?" He pulled forward to examine it more fully, and the forest opened to reveal another road with stone pavers.

"Uh-huh. I read a few articles on them. They were pacifists. And the Romans tried to wipe them all out. No telling what scrolls they found. The Vatican probably stashed them."

His GPS pinged. "Looks like we've arrived."

He turned onto the road and scaled a narrow upward climb. The forest wall closed behind them, obscuring the former path. "No doubt about it. Magic abounds in these hills."

The snow stopped suddenly.

The sun burst through the clouds with a brilliant blue sky. "Beautiful, gorgeous." Lavender fidgeted in the seat. "I can't believe I've never seen this place before. The village is in the distance, and the rolling snow-covered hills look like a Christmas card or fairy tale."

"May I remind you that fairy tales are often based on horrific origins with real beings."

"Don't be a Debbie Downer." She rubbed his upper arm. "Let's just revel in the magic until we arrive at our destination."

Brody kept his thoughts to himself as a malevolent air seemed to envelop the vehicle.

He glanced at Lavender. She was breathtaking, positively glowing with radiance. His instincts screamed for him to turn around, to escape while they still could.

Orbs of light swarmed the SUV.

Lavender turned to Brody. Her eyes glazed with wonder. "Do you see the faeries? Aren't they spectacular?"

"No. As soon as I find a place to turn around, we're heading back to Hagatha's for reinforcements. Depending on the species, fae can turn into evil monsters."

"Oh no, Brody. You're wrong. They are full of light."

Trying to break her spell was no use, so he chanted the song of protection under his breath. "Oh Goddess of light, hear my plight, take these faeries from our sight." The burdened, snow-lined branches seemed to open like fingers on a hand. The orbs floated back into the woods and disappeared. He sighed with relief.

He parked, then placed his hand on her knee. "You, okay?"

Lavender blinked several times. "What happened?"

"I believe the fae mesmerized you." He caressed her face with one hand.

"The multi-colored orbs were fae." More of a statement than a question. "How extraordinarily frightening."

"They're something else. Baby, do you feel the negative energy?"

Before she could answer, she noticed the monastery.

"Ancient Romanesque or Byzantine structures. Brody, that castle is from the eighth century or earlier. I count fifteen crenellations, maybe more." She opened the door as if in a trance.

"Wait, Lavender," he said.

Too late. She'd slammed the door.

He turned off the engine and exited the vehicle.

Kyewicket jumped into his arms, and he quickly tucked the cat into his coat.

They rushed to join Lavender before she reached the front entrance. "Stay close to me. There's something about this place I don't like." He reached inside his pocket, pulled out his phone, sent Birch and Hagatha the location coordinates, and added *send in the troops if we aren't back by nightfall.*

A tall man with jet black hair, dark features, and brown eyes approached them. "Lavender Doanhart, I'm glad you made it." He looked at Brody and said, "Welcome, friend. I'm Adam Bisset, curator for The Temple of Entia."

History radiated from the stone walls. Lavender knew the telluric currents often ran underground or through the sea, and some say they created spiritual hallucinations or otherworldly communications between individuals sensitive to ley lines.

Witches and warlocks were extremely sensitive beings.

Ley lines tie specific landmarks to historic structures. America's founding fathers used them to design Washington, D.C.

The hair rose on her arms and the back of her neck.

"I'm amazed I've never seen or heard of St. Lucian's." Lavender tried to engage Adam to read his emotions. "I grew up in France, not too far from here, and I thought I knew everything about this place. The castle is incredible, and my God, the view is heady."

"Some of the people in the nearby village are descendants of the original residents of this great castle. They're wary of strangers." With a gesture of his hand, Adam pointed to the entrance. "After you."

Lavender hesitated. She noticed the look of concern in Brody's eyes and his stance's rigidness. He wanted her to turn and leave, but she had come too far to stop now.

"The dank earthen scent lends itself to the age of the structure." Adam approached a monk and whispered something she couldn't hear. He turned to Lavender and Brody. "Devon will take you to change into sterile clothing. We cannot risk contamination of the scrolls."

Lavender and Brody held hands as the monk led them down a long, dark hallway. The sconces on the walls illuminated their path with a dim glow.

She leaned over to Brody. "Guess they don't believe in electricity."

The monk turned and placed a finger over his lips for her silence. He ushered them into a room with electricity—tapestries on the wall dated by her guestimate the 1200s. Devon pointed to the closet without a word and backed out of the room.

"Lavender, something is very wrong about this place and the people living here."

"Yes, I feel it too. I shouldn't have brought you here. You shouldn't risk your neck for my mother." She opened the closet and took out the sterile garments, first putting on white gloves, then slipping on the coveralls over her clothes and coverings for her boots.

Brody's fingers were too big for his gloves, so he magicked a pair. "I'm not here for your mother. I'm here for you." He pulled on coveralls and the mesh slippers over his boots. "If we need to split quick, grab my hand, and think of Hagatha's."

"Will do." She leaned close and whispered, "Someone is watching us."

"Yeah, ever since we turned onto Abellio Road."

Devon waited for Lavender and Brody in the hallway. He motioned for them to follow him. Minutes later, they entered a state-of-the-art climate-controlled viewing room.

"There are thousands of manuscripts and scrolls secured in this room and many more in the castle's library," Adam said. "Many of the documents contain universal knowledge, dated before the 1500s. The ancient scroll you're about to view predates the earliest known writings, and some consider it transcribed by the Sumerian descendants. Modern-day archeology is more akin to forensic science, you dig?"

Neither Lavender nor Brody laughed at Adam's joke.

"The specialists that have observed the scrolls could not reveal any new findings. However, I trust, as does the museum within the monastery, that Lavender may shed some light on the meaning of the scrolls."

Lavender glanced at Brody. "Take notes." She sat at the examining table, itching to get her fingers onto the ancient text. Carefully, she adjusted the light attached to the reading magnifier and examined the document's material. The words hit her hard in the chest. How did she understand their meaning so quickly?

Her heart raced. The spit in her mouth dried.

She read to herself:

Seven sisters of light with seven wizards of the night—a truce between the two royal families no more to fight. Each sister must wed a wizard. All is well until the eighth sister seizes the heart of a certain mister, destroying ties through royal lies.

Lavender calmed her racing pulse. "Is this the only scroll?" She inhaled and exhaled evenly.

"What does it say?" Adam's voice rose with irritation.

Brody stepped between Adam and her. "Back up, Hoss." Electricity fired to his fingertips.

"It's okay." Lavender touched his forearm. "Adam is only curious. I'm sure he means well."

Adam cleared his throat. "I apologize for my curtness. I'm curious about what the document says."

"I'm only guessing, and my thoughts may not reflect the text." She would not reveal the truth but would give the curator a nugget to see if he had anything else to offer. "Two warring tribes made a peace treaty, and broken rules led to strained relations." She asked, "Was anything else found with the scroll?"

The curator stepped over to a rather large oil painting and opened the back to reveal a safe. He carefully punched the security code, and the door sprang open. He picked up an object, brought it to the examining table, then lifted the protective sleeve to reveal a sculpture resembling a fertility Goddess. "They found this near the scroll."

"That's an Omphalos Stone," she said. "It creates telepathic connections like a two-way radio. May I inspect it without my gloves?"

Adam seemed to think over her request, but he reluctantly agreed. "Please be careful."

Lavender took off her gloves, then sent a telepathic message for Brody to do the same. She waited for a couple of minutes to see if perhaps Adam or someone watching them would stop her. She stood, then held the stone.

Lavender read the text on the sculpture aloud. "The troubled one calls me to the heavens." The vibrations released a shrill tone she thought would split her eardrums.

Adam went to his knees, screaming.

White rays of light shot forth from the stone.

"Set the artifact on the table." Brody touched her shoulder. "Then move away from the light."

It was too late.

Wind and electrical currents swirled about the room.

Kyewicket stuck his head out of Brody's garment.

Lavender clutched the cat and Brody as the illumination engulfed them.

The Pleiades Realm

Darkness and pain—Lavender trembled. Her knees went weak. "Aw, man, I hurt." She blinked several times, and her vision returned. "What the heck happened?"

Nothing looked familiar.

White walls, white bedding, white rugs, and she was in a white dress too. She still wore Brody's bracelet.

Her heart pounded, pumping adrenaline through her body. She glanced at the reflection in the gilded mirror—and gasped. The Goddess of Light looked back at her.

Not the Goddess—her. She placed her hand on the full-length looking glass, then looked at her hands, and touched her face.

No shimmer, no glamour. No obvious portal.

"How am I the Goddess of Light?"

"You're not. You've possessed her body." Kyewicket materialized at her feet. "Shush. We're not alone."

A slender young woman entered the room. "What are you waiting on? And where did you get that scrawny beast? Shoo, be gone with you."

Lavender scooped Kyewicket into her arms. "Please don't yell at my cat. Why are you yelling? My head hurts. Who are you? And where am I?"

"Funny, Yaris. Really? You're playing that old trick again. Let's see. I am the seventh sister of the seventh son. My name is Cora. I'm older than you. You are the eighth sister. And if we don't make it to the garden party, our royal parents will flog me because you are my responsibility." She grabbed Lavender's hand. "Let go of the cat. I won't tell Mother."

"My name is Yaris."

"Yeah. Keep telling yourself." Cora chuckled.

Lavender whispered to Kyewicket, "Please be careful and stay here until I return."

"I must look for Brody and a way home." Kyewicket purred. "I promise to be careful. I can shift."

The cat disappeared.

Good, his magic worked.

Did hers?

"Neat trick, cat, and who is Brody?" Cora asked.

"I cannot say. The feline must belong to Brody."

Cora tugged at her sleeve. "Come on, Yaris. Father is announcing my betrothal to Cetus, one of the seven wizards from Orion. Be thankful. You're number eight." She rolled her eyes. "At least you're not for sale."

"You are the seventh sister. Are you marrying the seventh brother? Oh, I mean, wizard?" Lavender followed Cora down a white corridor. Everything in every direction was white, including their long white empire waist gowns. "What's the significance of you marrying Cetus? And why is everything white?"

"Sister, you are losing your mind. The significance of me marrying the last wizard seals the peace scrolls, silly. And what is white?"

Didn't Cora know the color white?

Lavender and Cora rounded the corner, descended a white winding staircase, and ran out the front double doors. Cora released her and strolled to a group of women chatting near a spectacular gold water fountain with what appeared to be champagne.

Lavender wanted alcohol but was afraid to eat or drink anything until she knew it wouldn't kill her or make her sick. She marveled at the gardens surrounding the veranda. Trees with magnificent pink, coral, and lavender blooms held a heavy scent of vanilla, and their branches had a variety of fruits from the same tree.

What wouldn't I give to test the foliage and its medicinal properties?

The grass was greener than anything she'd ever seen before. Flower arrangements in oversized porcelain jars, with the same hieroglyphs as the scrolls, were placed near each corner of a walking path.

Where was Brody? Was he alive?

Music played, but Lavender saw no instruments or artists.

Loud cymbals clanged.

Cora pulled Lavender to join the group of women.

She mentally counted seven and eight, including her. They must be the seven sisters. She was number eight.

Lavender remembered the text on the ancient scroll: *Seven sisters of light dance with seven wizards of the night—a truce between the two royal families no more to fight. Each sister must wed a wizard. All is well until the eighth sister seizes the heart of a certain mister, destroying ties through royal lies.*

Lavender, or well temporarily, resided within Yaris's physical shell, the eighth sister. Something must happen to the Goddess of Light.

"The wizards are entering the gardens." Cora stood on tiptoes. "See them?"

The men wore gold-threaded, black tunics and silk pants with various jewels around their necks.

Lavender spotted Brody, and she nearly shouted his name.

Cora frowned. "Do you know the last wizard?"

"He seems familiar. Should I know him?" Lavender wrung her hands.

"Cetus is my husband-to-be. If you've embarrassed me, so help me, Zeus, I will tell Mother." Cora stepped away from Lavender in a fit of fury and disappeared into a white tent.

An auburn-haired beauty, reminding Lavender of Iris, approached. "Don't be too upset with Cora. She doesn't want to marry anyone. None of us wished for husbands. Are you okay, Yaris? You look unwell."

"I'm having memory issues today. I fell and hit my head. What's your name?" Her head did hurt.

"My name? Um, Raella, sister number six." She playfully shoved Lavender. "Are you serious?"

"Yes. I must've blacked out. I have no memory of this place or you. Please don't tell anyone." Lavender strolled along the path with sister number six.

"Yaris, the Black Flame Faeries devour dreams." Raella leaned in and lowered her voice. "They may very well eat memories too."

"It's probably from the fall. I'm sure I'll recover soon, but until then, please name the sisters and the wizards."

Raella pursed in lips and tilted her head to the side. "If you're not better by tomorrow, promise to see Moria, sister five. She stands next to Cora, and she's our best healer." Raella said, "The others left to right are Nona, sister one; Ravvyn, sister two; Dreena, sister three; and Thagna, sister four."

It was Dreena. Why? No, how was she here? Lavender would question her sanity if she hadn't seen Kyewicket and Brody.

Where was she?

Would Dreena remember her?

Dreena looked at her, then turned toward Ravvyn.

The wizards mingled with the crowd.

Brody made his way to her.

Please, Goddess of Light, let him remember me. Please, let Brody remember me. What am I saying? I am the Goddess of Light. If I'm her, then where is the real Yaris?

"What are the wizards' names, and to whom are they betrothed?" Lavender leaned against a rock wall with shimmering colors. If Brody remembered her, they'd dash inside the hedge labyrinth to speak privately.

Raella blushed. "We are to marry at the same time. Cetus and Cora's engagement is the reason for the celebration. Are you sure you don't need Mother?"

"No. I will be well soon enough. Please continue."

"Once we drink from the fountain of life, the weddings will occur on the same day in the Great Hall of Ahmen."

"Where is that?"

Raella touched her forearm. "I'm going to get Moria." She left and disappeared into the crowd.

Brody stepped over to her. "Do you remember me?"

"What is your name, sir?" She popped her hand on her hip.

"I asked first." He winked.

Lavender punched his arm. "I'm serious, Brody. We're in deep trouble." She grabbed his hand without waiting for a reply and raced through the maze until she felt sure they were alone. She searched his eyes. "Brody?"

He swept her into his arms, rubbing his freshly shaved face next to hers. She forgot her troubles in an instant. His masculine scent of heather and spice had her heart beating double time. "Lavender, my love, I thought I lost you. I thought I'd never see you again." He held her tightly.

Tears glistened in the deep pools of his blue eyes. She knew at that moment she would never again ask him to wait for her or question her motives about marriage and forget commitment issues—she wanted to have Brody's babies and live life large.

Lavender swallowed hard. "I feel the same way. But we don't have long to talk. Have you seen yourself in a mirror? I'm assuming you see me, and I see you, but everyone I've encountered thinks I'm Yaris, the Mage Alliance's Goddess of Light." She snapped her fingers, and a mirror appeared. "Magic, thank goodness."

He took the mirror and looked from side to side. "I'm The Lord Darkness? Are you kidding me? I knew I wasn't myself. Where's Kyewicket?"

"At least my magic works. Kyewicket is looking for you and a way back to our time." Lavender glanced into the looking glass before it vanished. "What do they call you?"

"Cetus."

"Great. I think we're the ones that instigate the ancient scroll's prophecy. Brody, I think we may be the Gate Keepers." She glanced over her shoulder, then back at him. "I learned Cetus and Yaris's sister, Cora, are betrothed and must drink from the fountain, which initiates a mass marriage ceremony to seal the peace I read about in The Temple of Entia's scroll." Tears rolled down her cheeks. "Brody, you can't marry anyone except me."

His grin warmed several degrees. "I never thought I'd hear those words from you. Are you saying you want to marry me?"

"You bet your boots, Mister!" She threw her arms around his neck. The moment her lips touched his, the stars aligned. Her clairvoyant skills were working.

His mint-flavored mouth brushed softly against the seams of her lips—his kiss, the conduit for a much larger scene to unfold.

She would die before she allowed Cora to marry Cetus.

Yaris, are you here? Can you hear me, oh Goddess of Light?

Lavender didn't wait for an answer. She broke from the kiss. "We must flee."

"I've not had the time to get the lay of the land. Kyewicket, come hither?"

The cat appeared, licking its paw. "No time to explain the dynamics of our predicament. Cora's mother, the queen, looks for Yaris and Cetus. Cora suspected something between them and sought help from the galaxy's matriarch. We must move fast, away from the royal grounds and the castle. Follow me through the maze." He bolted.

Lavender and Brody raced after Kyewicket through twisting turns and abrupt stops. It was as if they were trapped mice. The parallel with her own life wasn't missed. She had lived in a self-made labyrinth since her mother disappeared and was frustrated with her family's attempts to intervene in her self-imposed isolation.

What an idiot. Brody loves me, my cousin and aunt love me, and Max loves me. Am I going to lose everything for my bone-headed determination to find Mom?

Chapter 8

The Village

Max peered across the library at Hagatha. *How old is she?*

"I'm as old as the wind yet young as a newborn fawn. I also read minds, Max. How about we take a trip to the village? It could be hours before Lavender and Brody return."

With a wave of his hand, Max said, "I didn't bring winter clothing."

She narrowed her eyes and then made a circular motion with her forefinger, magically changing his attire. "I think that'll do. Do you want to take the car or just pop over?"

"Let's go by car. I want to see the mountains in the daylight. And great choices on the threads. I'm a huge fan of double-breasted pea coats and adore chunky scarves. I'll stay warm and look incredibly stylish. I've often wondered how witches guess sizes."

"Trade secret." Hagatha chuckled. "Let's take the Jeep. It's supposed to snow most of the afternoon."

Minutes later, Max sat in the passenger seat while Hagatha drove along the icy road. They entered the village with awe-inspiring brightly colored buildings, snow-covered rooftops, and a canal winding its way through the center of the charming town. "It's like a fairy tale."

"'Cinderella' and 'Sleeping Beauty' originated in France. You should see the village at night. We have a light show that goes year-round." She pointed to a stone pedestrian bridge. "We have a legend that states if you kiss your lover on the walkway, your fates are sealed forever."

He laughed nervously. "Let's not try that, okay?"

"Max, you are too cute. If I wanted to seal you to me, there's nothing you could do to stop it." She parked, grabbed her small purse, and tucked it into her long silver fox coat.

"I don't know whether to fear or adore you."

"Both."

They exited the vehicle.

"My friends own a vineyard not far from my property and have a wine bar in town. Care to taste a rare French vintage?"

"Oh, goodie, I love French spirits." He rubbed his hands together, ignoring her previous remark about love potions. "I want to see everything."

"We shall. There're quaint cafes, art galleries, and novelty shops to explore."

The snow fell lightly around them. The dwellings blocked most of the wind as they entered Crush, the wine bar. "*Bonjour*, Stephan."

Stephan's chubby face lit with a smile. "Hagatha, what brings you to our little hamlet on such a frigid day?" He kissed each of her cheeks, then took her hands into his. "You are radiant, my dear."

Hagatha demurely glanced to the floor, then looked at Max. "This is my American friend, Max Dupres. He's an art dealer visiting for a few days. I thought you could treat him to your secret vintage." Her right eyebrow rose.

"Do you think he's ready to try such a rare treat?" Stephan smiled at Max.

"I do," Hagatha replied, then turned to Max. "The white grapes here love the cooler temps. It makes a superb Chardonnay. Stephan and Mel's vineyard was once an ancient seabed. The terroir creates a Champagne with a hint of saltiness that's purely magical if you're game."

Max pursed his lips. His gut instinct told him not to try it, but his adventurous spirit won out. "I am in your hands, Hagatha."

Stephan left them. No one else was in the establishment.

"I drank way too much yesterday, so I'll only have one glass. I'm anxious to see the rest of the delightful village." He took off his pea coat and gloves but left on the scarf.

Hagatha opened her winter fur and leaned back in the chair. "I was teasing earlier. Don't fear me. I would never hurt you. I sense you love a good time, and that's all I'm offering you for the day."

"I've been around a few witches and warlocks over the last several years—some super nice, some not." He sighed with relief. "I feel you're more powerful than any witch I've met. So, I won't lie. I'm a tad bit apprehensive. I appreciate your honesty, and I love having fun."

"Good." Her grin went wide. "How are Jasmine and Isidore? I've only seen videos and images of Finis. He's such a beautiful boy."

"They're wonderful. Each one of the Doanharts has a genuinely kind heart, and little Finis is a spitfire."

"I think I'll make a trip to America soon. I should've visited before, but Iris and I were constantly at odds. I love her very much, but she blamed me for sending her to America. I never dreamed the locals would harm Silver and Aster. I do hold myself accountable for their demise. I suppose my guilt has kept me away long enough."

Max placed his hands atop hers. "It was a long time ago."

She inhaled and exhaled deeply. "I should have seen it coming—all of it. But the expanse of the Atlantic made it harder to interpret what was going on. Now, Lavender is placing herself in danger. I feel it."

Stephan returned with a bottle and two glasses. He poured one for Hagatha. "This special wine has aged for ten years. It is crisp and has a secret ingredient."

She swirled the liquid and took a sip. "Excellent."

Stephan poured Max a glass. "I'll pop into the kitchen and grab a small plate of goat cheese, fresh bread, and homemade jams to sample."

"I don't understand how the French stay so slender. I gain ten pounds just looking at a piece of cheese." He took a drink of the wine. He closed his eyes and allowed the wine to sit in his mouth long enough to taste its power. "Wonderful. I'd love to buy a bottle and ship it home." He sipped again.

"That particular bottle is not for sale. I'm sure Stephan can find a suitable replacement."

Stephan placed the edibles on the table. "Mel will be sorry she missed you. She's in Paris for the week visiting her mother."

"Please make sure you send her my love. Also, would you find a comparable bottle to ship to Max's address in America?" Hagatha inquired.

"*Oui*, Mademoiselle."

Max withdrew his business card and handed it to Stephan. "Thank you."

"My gift to you, Max," she said.

Hagatha's face seemed illuminated with a halo over her head. He squinted, then blinked several times. The bar came alive. The stools started dancing and twirling, and the walls breathed in and out. "What's happening to me?" His voice on slow-mo. The lavender field swayed in the oil painting next to them, and Max could've sworn he caught the scent.

He laughed. He couldn't stop. "Did the wine have acid?"

Hagatha giggled. "Only a few patrons can taste the first fruits of Stephan and Mel's vineyard. It is a mild form of LSD. I assure you the effects are not long-lasting."

"I did acid once in college, but it wasn't this nice. May I touch your face?" Max asked.

Hagatha nodded.

He caressed her cheek. "So soft, like velvet. You're so beautiful. Your green eyes are the most spectacular color."

"Eat some bread and cheese." She removed his hand.

Max looked at the plate. The cheese smiled, and the bread winked. "Um, I don't want to eat them. They're sweet looking." He scooped a spoon of jam and ate it. Moaned, "Oh my God, this is fantastic. It tingles in my mouth."

Stephan came to the table. "I'm glad you're enjoying it."

"Send a package to the house, Stephan. I'm sure Max will want to try the bread and cheese later." Hagatha handed Stephan a wad of cash without counting it.

Max tried to form words but kept chuckling at the effort. He reached into his wallet and pulled out his credit card, and his billfold vanished in thin air.

Hagatha grabbed his hand. "Let's go to the art gallery next door."

He drained the rest of the glass, then gave her a thumbs up.

Snow fell as they walked along the pathway. Max opened his mouth and allowed the flakes to land on his mouth. "Vanilla milkshake. Oh, I thank goodness I can talk again." He slipped his arm around Hagatha's shoulders and sniffed. "You smell like honeysuckle on a hot summer day. I could eat you up."

Hagatha looked at him. "Maxie, you are too sweet."

"Aw. Jasmine and Lavender call me Maxie." He snickered. "I hear smells and smell sounds." He roared with laughter. "I haven't had this much fun in decades."

They toured several art galleries. He selected three pieces to ship home.

Max held Hagatha's hand as they left one establishment, huddling together to keep warm. "Ooh, it's like we're on a movie set. The village sparkles. Where to next?"

"Do you like candy?"

"Is the pope catholic?" He laughed. "The winged creatures on the spires are moving again."

"They are friendly and good luck to those who witness them."

Hagatha ducked inside a confection shop, and Max followed.

"Bonjour, Maurice, this is my friend from America, Max. What are your specials today?"

Maurice brought over a mirrored plate full of treats. "We have different colored marshmallows, swirls of chocolate-covered cherries, and butterscotch. Try one of each," he replied in English with a thick French accent.

Max popped a marshmallow in his mouth. "Mm. So good." The chocolate jumped onto his hand. He blinked several times. "Marvelous." He chewed slowly, savoring the silkiness of the chocolate not found in a box. "Butterscotch to go."

Maurice packaged the treats and handed Hagatha a golden bag with blue trim. "I put a few of your favorites too, Miss Doanhart."

"You are too good to me," she said. "Don't tell Cook. He gets mighty jealous."

On the way back to the Jeep, Hagatha said, "One last stop." She pointed. "This church has several Renaissance murals. You must see them."

His footsteps echoed, entering the sanctuary.

Max could've sworn he heard a choir singing, but they were alone. He stopped before a series of three frescos of divine beings with allegorical writings in French. "The medieval murals are stunning, but the angels are sad." He sniffled. "Why are they so unhappy?" He looked at Hagatha.

"I don't think they're sad. But if they make you feel bad, we'll leave." She slipped her hand into the crook of his elbow and leaned on his shoulder. "Let's go home."

He nodded. "They are brilliant."

They raced to the vehicle like two teenagers, laughing along the way.

Once inside, Hagatha started the engine. On the short drive to her estate, she cranked the radio with salsa music. She had him doubled over with laughter. Driving onto her property, she pulled around back and clicked the garage remote.

Max had fallen asleep.

She nudged him gently. "Do you feel okay?"

"I feel superb. But I may lie down for a few minutes."

She walked him to his room and tucked him into bed. "Sweet dreams, my new friend."

He fell fast asleep.

A couple of hours later, Hagatha went into Max's room to rouse him for dinner. She watched him sleep for a few minutes. "Wake up, sleeping beauty."

He blinked several times, yawned, and gave her a warm smile. "Are you sure I can't get a bottle of Stephan's magical wine?"

"No, my pet." She shook her head. "Are you angry with me?"

"Why would I be angry? I had a blast and slept great." He sat upright.

"Dinner will be ready soon if you'd like to take a shower and get dressed."

He stood, leaned over, and kissed her forehead. "Thank you, Hagatha, for an illuminating day I'll always remember. I think I will shower. I didn't bring formal attire for dinner."

"The dinner is not formal. I canceled my guests. Please wear whatever is comfortable. I'll be downstairs." She paused at the door and turned to him. "Oh, I have replenished your wardrobe."

"Oh, you are too kind." He bowed with his hands in prayer mode.

Hagatha dressed for the evening, selecting a dark blue velvet jumpsuit with matching shoes, her hair sleek at her nape, secured with a diamond comb. She descended the stairs and went to the library for a cocktail before dinner.

Birch paced in front of the fireplace.

"What's happened?" Hagatha asked.

Birch stopped short. "Did you receive a text? Any word from Brody or Lavender?" He ran his hands through his thick, dark hair. His eyes were full of concern.

She reached into her pocket and pulled out her phone. "Brody left coordinates to their location. Are they missing?"

"He texted to send the troops if they weren't home by dark. It's dark. What have you been doing?" Birch asked.

"None of your business."

"Great, you had sex with Max. Perfect. A sensational end to a terrible day."

She rolled her eyes but didn't reply to his crude comment.

"I called in a few recruits who wait in the kitchen." Birch frowned. "Do you want to come with me to St. Lucian's or stay here with the American?"

Max entered the room.

"I'll go with you," Hagatha replied. "Max will stay here." She turned to Max. "I added my contact info to your phone. Please call me if Lavender and Brody return."

Max nodded.

Birch stalked out of the room.

"What's going on?" Max's brow furrowed.

"Lavender and Brody are missing. They should've returned by dark." She turned to Max. His face turned ashen. "Do not blame yourself. Lavender knew the risks." She whirled her forefinger and changed into military attire. "Come with me into the kitchen. Cook will make you a plate."

Tears welled in Max's eyes. "I should've gone with her. I came here to protect her."

She caressed his face. "Darling, you cannot protect a witch. You're her emotional support. You must remain calm. Come now, Cook has prepared a feast for a king. It would be a shame to waste it."

Birch gritted his teeth as Hagatha entered the kitchen with Max.

What did she see in the human?

He shook his head. He couldn't think about his desire for the witch until they found Brody and Lavender.

"Irick and Adel, meet Hagatha, Lavender's great-grandmother," Birch smirked. He could practically see the steam escape her ears as he introduced the warriors.

Lavender said, not to mention Hagatha's age. He didn't.

She shook each warrior's hands. "We must hurry. Every second they're missing is a chance they may not return. Birch, you have an SUV?"

He nodded.

"Max, I'll let you know anything we find out. Text me if they return. Reception in the mountains is sometimes sketchy." She squeezed Cook's hand. "You may contact me telepathically. Take care of our guest, please."

"*Oui.*" Cook straightened his broad shoulders.

Outside, Irick and Adel got in the back while Hagatha slid into the front passenger seat of the black SUV.

Her face looked like stone. No emotion.

Birch followed the GPS directions until they reached 11475 Abellio. He turned onto the road. "Are you familiar with St. Lucian's?"

"No. It's a Christian monastery, not pagan. I didn't know it existed until Lavender told me, and I did some research. There's something odd about that place."

The afternoon snowfall made the roads more treacherous. The SUV started sliding toward a steep ravine. He used magic to bring the vehicle to a safe stop. His pulse raced like crazy. "Are you okay?"

"I'm fine. We're close. I see the lights." She pointed through the trees.

He closed his eyes and used magic to wrap chains on the tires. He wasn't taking chances. Magic could only go so far, and that ravine could've caused them serious harm. He inched forward until the chains made traction, then drove slowly to the abbey and parked.

Hagatha didn't wait. She jumped out of the SUV and raced to the entrance.

He rushed to her side with Irick and Adel behind him.

"Hagatha, what are you doing? We have no idea what or who is inside."

The roar of the wind made it hard to hear Hagatha, but the determined look in her eyes spoke volumes. He stepped in front of her and beat on the door several times before a monk opened it.

"May I help you?"

Hagatha shouted, "I am here for Adam Bissett."

The monk's eyes widened as he allowed them to enter the foyer. "Mr. Bissett is indisposed."

Hagatha extended her hand toward the monk. Fire flew from her fingertips, barely missing the priest's face. "I suggest you take me to him immediately, or I will bring the abbey down."

The monk's voice quivered. "Follow me." He led them through dim corridors and two flights of steps. He knocked on the door, and another clergyman opened it. "These people are here to see Monsieur Bissett."

The other monk straightened his shoulders. "Mr. Bissett has had a terrible shock. He cannot speak."

"There's going to be a lot he can't do unless you get out of my way." Hagatha brushed by him.

In a small room, on a twin bed, lay Adam Bissett. His hair was white as the sheets that covered him. He stared at nothing, unblinking.

She looked at the monk who was tending Bissett. "What happened to Lavender and her companion?"

The monk stayed silent.

Her hands fisted. "Tell me or so help me. You will need more than a bed to recover."

The monk relayed the arrival of Lavender and Brody. He told them about the climate-controlled room and the ancient scrolls they'd examined. "From what I can gather, Monsieur Bisset handed them an ancient sculpture, and...."

"And what?" Birch shouted.

"They, they disappeared. I found Monsieur on the floor, screaming."

"What?" Hagatha shrieked.

The monk wrung his hands. "They vanished within white light that accompanied a sonic boom. When I found Monsieur Bissett, he muttered the light took them."

"Took them where?" Hagatha stepped next to Adam's bedside. She took his hand. "Show me the sculpture, show me the light, show me what caused you such a fright." Her face paled. Panic rose in her chest, making it hard to breathe. Suddenly, she turned to the monk. "Take me to the room. I want to see the scrolls and sculpture."

The monk shivered. "The ancient scrolls are still on the table, but the sculpture is not—it became the light."

Chapter 9

The Black Flame Forest

Lavender ran as fast as her feet could carry her. A sharp pain bit into her side. Darkness approached as Brody and Kyewicket followed her into the dense forest.

Kyewicket stopped. "The Black Flame Fae live in the woods. They've promised to help us."

"Do you trust them?" Brody asked.

Lavender turned to him. "Do we have a choice?"

An orb of light bounced around them before materializing into the most beautiful, luminous, winged creature with dark features and brilliant pale blue eyes. The being bowed before Lavender and then straightened. "You are here to save Yaris?"

"Do you see Yaris standing here?" Lavender was on the verge of hysterics.

"I see you, Daughter of Doanhart, your friend, and your familiar. We do not have time to speak. The royal guard is in pursuit. Do you and your companions fly?"

Brody stepped forward. "We do, but where are you taking us?"

"To safety. Follow me. The forest is dark and dangerous."

"What is your name?" Lavender asked.

"My name is Crystal. Stay close to my light."

Lavender lifted off the ground and soared through the dark and perilous forest with only the light of Crystal's orb as a guide. Branches scratched her arms and face and nearly made her crash more than once. Her magic was slightly shaky, and she had no clue where the faery was taking them.

Crystal shouted at the trees, and their branches moved, opening a straighter path.

Her instinct told her Crystal was good, but they were in a different realm. Maybe the rules didn't apply the same way. She concentrated on the glowing light before her. She didn't dare turn to see if Brody and Kyewicket followed for fear of getting lost.

Strange sounds screeched through the woods. Would the darkness swallow them whole? Her throat constricted.

Is Yaris safe?

"Yes," came as a whisper on the wind.

Lavender sighed in relief.

They flew faster. The midnight moon rode on their backs. The wind whipped Lavender's face as she spiraled downward, deeper into the darkness.

Was this a test, trial, or punishment?

Her fierce determination to find her mother gave her courage.

Will Crystal help us? She asked the wind.

Yes.

She thought of the fairy tales she had read about forests. *Yikes, bad things happen in the woods.* Brody had told her earlier that some fairy tales had true elements. Which ones?

Stop it, Lavender. Some good things happen too. The prince saves Snow White, and the big, bad wolf eats stones and dies, Brody answered her telepathically.

Not practicing magic hindered her. Weary and wary, she continued to fly. She would not give up or give in. Too much was at stake. Not only her mother, but Brody, Kyewicket, and most importantly, she thought, the Goddess of Light. Deep within her bone-tired body, she must continue and persevere to save Yaris, or the Goddess of Light would disappear and possibly, endanger magic itself.

Despite whatever beasts lived in the depths of this dark place, she intended to overcome her misgivings, buck up to her frights, and steady her nerves to what was coming.

The wooded kingdom of the Black Flame Fae came alive with thousands of lights within a circle of trees. Crystal landed in an open meadow full of bustling activity, and they landed beside her.

Fae, trolls, elves, and other beings went silent and bowed before her.

Brody's arm circled her waist, and Kyewicket slipped between her trembling legs.

"Are you okay?" Brody asked.

"A bit nervous, but I'm fine."

Crystal released a tune, and other fae rose and joined her with a most harmonious yet relaxing arrangement. "She is here. She is here. No more shall we fear because she is here."

Lavender looked up at Brody.

His eyes seemed filled with wonder at the spectacular light and melodic sound.

She glanced at Kyewicket, curled at her feet, asleep.

A throne of vine and branches rose out of the ground with a massive male that towered over most of his subjects. He stared at Lavender with kind eyes. He had long white hair and wore a white gown. Majestic came to mind, yet something about him gave her pause.

Light beams shot from his crown. A hush fell over the crowd.

Crystal stepped forward and knelt before him. "Oh, giver of the flame, King of the Fire Throne, the Daughter of Doanhart is here as you predicted. She is here to save us."

"You have done well, my child." He motioned to Lavender. "Come, Daughter of Doanhart, that I may see you more clearly."

Brody stepped in front of Lavender. "Forgive me, King of the Fire Throne, but I am her protector. May I have your assurance that you mean no harm?"

The king chuckled, then belted out laughter. "Brave, Brody Whitmore. I have seen you too in my visions."

"You see our true form?" Lavender inquired.

"I do. However, my subjects only see Yaris and Cetus. Come forth with Lavender and Kyewicket too."

"There is something about the king that reminds me of someone," Lavender whispered.

Kyewicket purred, "The Wizard of Oz."

The king inhaled and exhaled as they approached the forest throne room. Trees opened their gold-dipped branches to reveal a royal walkway with sparkling jewels that casts shimmering shadows of light.

Lavender swallowed hard as he approached her. His ginormous hand cupped her cheek.

"You possess Yaris in our realm, as does Brody with Cetus. Young love should be celebrated, not sold. The royal families have forgotten love. They will want your heads for defying them."

The king walked around them. "How did you get here? What form of travel?"

Lavender and Brody exchanged nervous looks.

"Do not fear, my children. I protect the woods. The royal guard will not find you. I will parlay with the King and Queen of Pleiades on your behalf. He is my brother." He whispered, "Except for a chosen few, my subjects only see Yaris and Cetus. You will use those names during your stay with us. Is that understood?"

Brody answered, "Understood if you explain how you know our real names."

"I don't understand how we arrived here." Lavender searched the king's eyes. "I don't understand how we can save you."

"Tsk, tsk." The king raised a bushy brow. "We will speak on the subject later. For now, you require rest. I will have Crystal take you to your rooms. Eat and sleep. We will speak again in the morning. We have much to celebrate." He waved to his subjects, then retreated underground.

A flurry of excitement buzzed within the arena of the fae.

Crystal gestured toward a huge tree. "I have the royal rooms ready for you."

The royal rooms?

Lavender scooped Kyewicket into her arms with Brody at her side and followed Crystal. They didn't speak.

Lavender was amazed by their surroundings. Multicolored strands of lights flickered in the city, carved out of wood and stone. An assortment of jewels adorned the arches and walkways. "Brody, it's a community of magic."

"We've fallen through the rabbit hole." Brody chuckled. "It is magnificent, but we need to stay on alert. I have so many questions. And as you know, magic can be good or evil, and some practitioners use both."

Crystal looked over her shoulder. "The king will answer your questions. He's a visionary. He sees the future. He knew you would come here. I assure you while you're in our care, you are safe."

"Crystal, do you know what will happen to us?" Lavender asked.

"It's not for me to say. I am only a servant as we all are to The Royals of Pleiades."

"Okay, I understand, but you are taking us to royal rooms. Does that mean we're royals?"

"He said you were slippery." Crystal frowned.

Brody inquired, "Who? The king?"

"You will be treated as royals during your stay. Yaris and Cetus are royals. Most of the fae recognize that."

Crystal took a path over a wooden pedestrian bridge to a home carved from within a redwood tree. She opened the door. "Your rooms are inside. I am at your service day or night. I am also your guard, stationed here to protect you." She closed the door and took her post.

"Why do I feel like we're captives?"

"Maybe we are, maybe not." Brody gazed out a floor-to-ceiling window. "This is what I call a treehouse. It's unreal. The living area is bigger than my old apartment in the Boro."

The interior furnishings bathed in swaths of golds, greens, browns, silks, satins, and velvets created a warm ambiance—one floor with dividing screens to separate the quarters.

Kyewicket jumped on the king-sized bed. "It's not the Ritz, but it'll do." He curled into a crescent and tucked his head to his chest. Within minutes, he was snoring.

"I'm going to take a bath in the soaking tub." She yawned. "I need to unwind before sleep, but first, let's check out the food."

The kitchen area was a bit smaller, but platters of food were on silver trays, and jugs of ale waited for them to sample. "Do you think we can eat their food? We're in a different realm. Our bodies could have serious allergens with side effects."

Brody grabbed a pastry with what appeared to be meat and took a bite. "Oh, man, I don't know what I'm eating, but it's delicious."

"Really?"

He nodded and poured himself a tankard of brew.

She chose a puffed pastry. "Yum. Sweet cream cheese."

They sampled a variety of foods. Some mouthwatering, some okay, and one had the consistency of snot that nearly made her puke. A large mug of ale washed it down.

"I think I may pass out and take a bath in the morning."

"The best idea I've heard today," Brody replied.

She snapped her fingers, and she wore silky PJs.

Brody took off his clothes and slid between the covers, naked.

She got in and cuddled next to him. "Brody, are you scared?"

His big, strong arms surrounded her. "Scared is not the word I'd use. Outnumbered, probably. I'm worried about finding a portal that'll take us home. But if I must live anywhere else in the galaxy, it's with you."

She nudged her face into the crook of his neck, her arms entwined with his. "Ditto. Brody?"

"Uh-huh?"

"I love you," she whispered.

"I love you too, kid."

The Pleiadian Court

Cora, along with her sisters, walked solemnly to court. Their shoes echoed in the corridor.

The royal guard posted sentries at each entrance and near the tall glass windows. Sunlight beams streaked the floors with green, red, and purple hexagon orbs.

The court requested the Black Flame Fae liaison to appear during the inquest.

Whatever happened today was not her fault.

Why had Yaris fled with Cetus?

Surely, they knew the king and queen would banish them or put their heads on a pike. The only word counted in their realm, although the Orionnites would undoubtedly voice concern regarding Cetus's disappearance.

The Pleiades had been divided long ago between the royals and the fae. However, her uncle, King of the Fire Throne and ruler of the Black Flame Fae, would use the opportunity against her father for his gain.

She took a deep breath and exhaled.

Ravvyn squeezed her hand. "Yaris is fine. Father loves her very much. He is just but also wise."

Cora appreciated the sentiment, but she had seen the king's fury. Ravvyn had not.

Cora and Cetus's marriage would have completed the prophecy and sealed the peace between the royal families, but that chain of events no longer existed.

Her parents, King Valdoor and Queen Octavia, sat on blue velvet tufted thrones inside the royal courtroom. Regal, chins lifted, and shoulders back.

Cora did the same.

Forest murals on the walls were trimmed in delicate earth tones, while decorative rugs covered the white marble floors. Heavily armored knights stood close to them. Their duties protected the royal family and their guests.

Courtiers stood on either side of the room. They thrived on gossip and drama.

A hush overcame the crowd as she and the sisters went before the throne. They lined up by order of their birth.

The tall, thin advocate for the Orionnite wore a long black coat. He slammed his fist on the ornately carved wooden podium. "Where is Cetus? What have you done with my lord?"

The Orionnites stomped their feet and clapped their hands.

The advocate shouted, "This has been a trick to destroy our royal lineage and cause discord in our land."

King Valdoor remained calm. His voice steady, he said, "I have word that Cetus, and my daughter, Yaris, are in the Black Flame Forest with my brother, King of the Fire Throne." He pointed. "His representative, Emir, will offer an official report."

Cora watched Emir approach the other podium, directly in line with the advocate. He was the most breathtaking fae. He wore a gold headband with diamonds and rubies, complimenting his luxurious wavy dark brown hair that matched his kind, expressive eyes surrounded by thick dark lashes. He had a firm jawline and full lips. The sleek purple garment set off his broad shoulders.

Where are his wings? They were not visible, and she blushed, thinking about his physique under the clothing.

"I come on behalf of Odar, King of the Fire Throne and ruler of the Black Flame Fae. Yaris and Cetus are comfortable and protected by his good graces. He is willing to parlay for their safe return."

The advocate screeched, "Parlay. Did I hear you correctly, faery? We demand you return Cetus to the Orionnites, or this planet will suffer the full force of our military." Again, the Orionnites stomped and shouted in agreement.

King Valdoor waved his hand. "Silence. What does my brother want?"

"He wishes that you lift all restrictions from the Black Flame Fae, and they be given full citizenship within the realm, with the ability to travel freely within the galaxy without fear of imprisonment. King Odar also requests you restore him and his queen to court." Emir stood with his back straight, his shoulders squared, and his chin lifted. He seemed fearless, but what he requested would create chaos among the elite.

King Valdoor leaned back on his throne. One hand rested over the queen's hand, and the other gripped the armrest. "Bring me proof that my child and the seventh son of Orion are safe, and I will consider King Odar's proposal." His jaw clenched. The fire in his eyes expressed his fury. "Do not, and I will invade the forest. Not even a twig will remain."

Cora understood all too well that her father was buying time for the royal guard to rescue Yaris.

"The marriage contract between Cetus and Cora is null and void," the advocate exclaimed. "If Cetus returns unharmed, we will keep the peace, but if he is injured in any way, all contracts will cease, and our great army will bring war to your shores."

Father stood.

In two strides, the king towered over the advocate. "The marriage contract between Cora and Cetus may be void, but he will marry Yaris, or the magic we'll unleash in the galaxy will cause catastrophic harm to all of your people. Are we clear?"

The advocate showed no apparent signs of fear. "Agreed."

Cora sighed in relief. No marriage for her, thank the stars.

Yaris and Cetus would wed; after that, she could not fathom how the king would punish them.

Father looked at his daughters and smiled. He went to Queen Octavia, offered her his hand, then escorted her from the great hall. Once they were out of sight, the noise in the hall exploded with chatter.

Cora made her way to Emir. "You are very brave or very foolish to confront the king in such a manner."

Emir chuckled. "Your father doesn't scare me." He turned and walked toward the doors that led into the courtyard gardens.

"You're not afraid of King Valdoor?" She caught up with him.

"No. Are you?" Emir asked with a raised brow.

She thought for a second. "Sometimes. I worry about my little sister. I'm afraid he will banish her when she returns or worse. Are you leaving for the forest?"

"My duty is not complete. I must prove your sister and her companions are safe." He searched her eyes, and her stomach dipped.

Without thinking, she replied, "I will accompany you to the forest. I will prove Yaris is alive and well."

He crossed his arms over his massive, muscular chest. "You are either very brave or very foolish."

"Touché." Cora laughed. "I'm probably both. Will you allow me to change clothes for the journey?"

"You must leave word with your parents." He breathed deeply. "I will not risk my people's lives on the whim of a royal."

"I'll speak to the king." She wanted to ensure Yaris was safe, but Emir intrigued her, and she hadn't seen her uncle in eons.

"I'll wait until dusk. I'll carry on without you if you don't return to the gardens."

Cora gave him a quick curtsy, then materialized to her bedchamber.

Chapter 10

Brody watched Lavender sleep. She breathed steadily, but her brow furrowed. He wanted to wake her, kiss her, and tell her everything would be alright, but would it?

Instead, he patiently waited for her to open her eyes.

Kyewicket left earlier. The cat wanted to get a feel of the terrain in case they needed to flee. He was a cool cat in every sense of the word.

Lavender snuggled closer to him. Her arm draped over his bare chest. She mumbled, "What time is it?"

"I'm not sure they keep time here. No clocks." He brushed a strand of hair off her face.

They locked eyes, searching for the right words to say, but there weren't any.

"Do you think we'll ever return home?"

He wanted to lie but didn't. "I sensed yesterday that the Fae King is up to something. What— remains to be seen."

Lavender set her hands on his chest and rested her chin on top of them. "Were you able to sleep at all?"

"Eh, not much, but enough. I'm a warrior. I don't need much sleep to function." He threaded his fingers through her hair. "What about you?"

She didn't reply at first. She gave him an intense, smoldering look, and when she wet her lips—it was his undoing. "Make love to me, Brody. I need you. I—I want you so much. I'm so sorry I kept you away. I'm sorry I wasted time we could have spent...."

He placed his forefinger over her lips. "Don't. We can't change the past. We don't know the future. We only have here and now."

Lavender was on him fast, kissing him hard, her hands roaming over his body.

He flipped her onto her back and took charge. He'd waited for years to make love to the only woman he'd ever loved, the only woman he would ever love. "You're mine. Say it."

She nodded. "I'm yours, and you're mine, always."

Heat fused their bodies, each losing control, their hearts beating as one. Having Lavender back in his arms again was like going home. Making love to her was like renewing his soul.

It was intoxicating.

He'd thought she didn't love him. He'd been wrong.

He would die for her—kill for her too.

His mouth ground against hers as the undulating motion of her hips brought him to the brink of orgasm. He paused, looked into Lavender's loving eyes, and kissed her gently. He caressed her cheek with the palm of his hand, then trailed kisses down her slender throat to her firm, round breasts and back up to her luscious lips. Her skin flamed hot, inside and out— *pure bliss.*

"I have thought about you every day and night since you left," he said, his voice hoarse.

"Oh, Brody, I've missed us." She gasped, "I've missed this too, not gonna lie."

He groaned as he nuzzled her throat. "You and I are meant to be."

Her face rubbed his, her breasts crushed against his chest as she moved out from underneath him and climbed on top. She rode him fast and hard. It was brutal but also exquisite. She held onto him as if her life depended on it.

It was more than he could take. He released.

She collapsed on him, then slid beside him, her arm resting against her forehead.

The silence stretched into minutes.

"I'll wash your hair like the old days," he said.

She propped on her elbow. "I'd like that."

Kyewicket popped into the room. "Rah-ow!"

Lavender and Brody were in the tub.

"Hate to interrupt, but please get dressed," the cat purred. "I have some interesting news. I'll wait in the other room." He was glad Lavender was back with Brody, but he didn't want to see them do their thing. *Yuck.*

Kyewicket paced. There was no time for relaxing or lounging. No time for lovemaking. He had way too much information to relay.

A few minutes later, Lavender and Brody joined him in the sitting area close to the paned windows. "On my search and find mission this morning. I met Sprite, a mini-fae. She took me on a tour of the community." He licked his left paw.

"And?" Lavender pressed.

"Well, it seems Queen Goldengrace, the former matriarch of the Black Flame Fae, was forced into marrying King Odar to keep the peace and save the beings that call the woods their home. He and his knights commanded the forest after his exile, or he would've otherwise burned it to the ground. Sprite approached me. The queen has requested your presence."

Brody's eyes shut tight. He shook his head. "No. It's a trap." He looked at Lavender. "I will go. It's too dangerous for you."

"Brody, I love your concern. But I'm meeting with the queen. We are all meeting her. We don't need to separate again, including you, Kyewicket."

Kyewicket stretched, then strolled to the door. "Crystal is guarding the door. Sprite stated the fae is an assassin for King Odar. He has no intention of releasing us."

"I knew it," Brody shouted. "My gut instinct about the 'Gandalf' lookalike is true." He snapped his fingers and covered himself and Lavender in sleek body armor that looked like tiny dragon scales. "The gear will help protect us. Cat? May I?"

"No. I shift quickly. You both are the bargaining chips for the king's plan back to court."

Lavender stepped over to the door and extended her fingers toward the Black Flame Fae guard. "Sleep Crystal, sleep deep, and allow us to pass, or I'll throw you out on your scrawny ass."

"Good one," Kyewicket hissed. "Sprite's waiting for us at the end of the pedestrian bridge."

Lavender reached for the door, and Brody stopped her.

"Wait. The king may have other spies. I suggest using the protection of invisibility to travel." He swirled his forefinger, and magic dust whirled around them. "Let us walk unseen among the fae. Protect us while on our journey today. Only allow us, Sprite, and Queen Goldengrace clear vision as our main safety provision." The trio shimmered. Their disguise kept them unseen.

Kyewicket led Brody and Lavender out the door, down the treehouse steps, and along a crushed-stone pathway. Dwarves worked skillfully hammering metals, and Duendes tilled land with different types of vegetables. Kyewicket noticed the change of command as the king's guards lorded over the forest's magical beings. He growled, then took a secondary path curving around a tree line that seemed to disappear but revealed a luscious garden and another wooden bridge.

Sprite's wings fluttered.

Kyewicket raced to her. "We travel under the cloak of invisibility."

The little faery's eyes widened. With a whisper, Sprite said, "On the other side of the bridge is a secret garden where my queen awaits you." She motioned for Kyewicket, Brody, and Lavender to follow.

Lavender's stomach churned. Her chest tightened with every step.

What if the queen meant them harm?

She was hyperaware of every sound, of every being they passed along the route to the bridge. Defying the king, and placing his assassin under a sleep spell, could potentially imprison them or, worse, get them killed.

She'd love to explore the woods if she weren't so scared. The trails in Rockvale and Hant Hollow gave her solace. The woods here were unpredictable. She would be brave. Brody and Kyewicket didn't deserve to see her fall apart as sheer terror quaked her insides.

A turquoise stream bubbled and gurgled under the wooden bridge.

Sprite took out a wand and recited undecipherable words. A vine-covered door opened into an oasis that could rival Eden. The enchantment seemed surreal.

Lavender was awestruck. The stone path turned into a soft grass walkway, and on either side, one garden morphed into a different one. She spotted irises, sweet William, wild daisies, feather reed grass, marigolds, purple vinca, silver lavender, variegated hostas, red canons, and so many more. The symmetry of the ever-changing design resembled a flock of birds creating patterns. It took her breath away.

A white gazebo sat amid the garden's beauty and within its shelter, the queen.

Queen Goldengrace's ethereal qualities mimicked a medieval version of a fairy God-mother. She sat regally on a stone bench. Her long yellow hair shimmered like cornsilk and flowed over porcelain-like shoulders. Perfect ruby lips, a small nose, and even her pointy ears were delicate. She wore a long sky-blue gown. Her pale hands rested in her lap. She straightened when she noticed them.

The sadness in her pale blue eyes made Lavender want to hug her. "Thank you for meeting me." She assumed she spoke fae, but the queen's English was spot on.

Sprite came forward; her tiny frame knelt before the queen.

Lavender and Brody did the same.

Kyewicket hopped on the bench and purred.

The queen took him in her arms and stroked his ears. The cat had excellent empathy skills.

"Well done, Sprite." The queen motioned to the bench next to hers. "Please sit, Lavender and Brody. Our time is brief. The king will soon notice my absence."

Lavender and Brody still didn't speak but followed the queen's orders.

"King Odar has visions. He also uses me to keep my subjects safe. I am fae, but I'm a witch too. I can assist you with safe passage home. Within the underground castle walls is a secret room with a looking glass well. It is a portal."

"I'm in," Lavender blurted. "Oh, I'm sorry for interrupting you, Queen Goldengrace."

The queen waved a dismissive hand. "My husband uses Yaris and Cetus to escape exile. He wants back at court and requests freedom for all living beings in the forest as a ruse. He will hand over Yaris and Cetus to his brother, King Valdoor, who will punish them rather severely, then Valdoor will take vengeance on the forest and those dwelling within. As you may have suspected, Yaris and Cetus are The Goddess of Light and The Lord Darkness in your realm. What you may not know, Lavender..." The queen turned her head.

Lavender's chin dipped toward her throat. "What?"

"Please continue, Your Highness." Brody squeezed Lavender's hand.

The queen's head tilted to the side. "I must hurry. The king is searching for me. After the festival, Sprite will bring you here. Then I will take you into the palace's under-ground." The queen vanished.

Sprite's wings fluttered as she took to the air. "I must check for spies. The king will not approve of Queen Goldengrace's plan. Please do not mention this meeting." The tiny fae flew away.

Lavender sat speechless for several minutes. She turned to Brody. "The night of my mother's disappearance, I noticed the deities exchanged glances. How they looked at each other reminded me of how I look at you, Brody. If they are in a relationship here, maybe they are in our realm too. Maybe, my mother and Iris are safe with The Lord Darkness. Do you think?"

"You're jumping to wild conclusions." Brody dragged his hand over his face. "Damn fine pickle—we're in." He stood, pacing back and forth in front of Lavender. "What was the queen going to tell you? We must do everything in our power to save Yaris and Cetus. Saving them may very well be our only salvation. The woods aren't the only thing at risk. The Goddess of Light and The Lord Darkness balance our realm's existence. The entire Mage Alliance is at risk if something happens to them. Everything happening to us seems intertwined."

"Yaris is royalty. So maybe you are too in our realm. That's got to be it." Kyewicket jumped into Lavender's lap. "We're in royal rooms. You are Yaris, and Brody appears as Cetus. I think it's our destiny to be here."

"Oh, my head hurts." Lavender stroked Kyewicket's back. "Brody?"

He turned to her. "Yes, baby?"

"The Mouijah Stones. Iris controlled them first, then Jasmine. It brought them directly to The Goddess of Light's home. Maybe it took Jasmine here. Do you think we're related?"

Kyewicket purred, "Finally paying attention, eh?"

"What do you mean, Kyewicket?" Brody asked.

"I'm not sure, but the Doanharts seem intricately tied with the deities who oversee us."

"But the Mage Alliance includes all supernatural beings, not just witches and wizards. The implications are dizzying, and Hagatha, oh my God." Lavender frowned. "She must be worried sick." She needed to concentrate. "I can't connect with Hagatha from this realm, but maybe I can communicate with the Goddess of Light."

She closed her eyes and mentally pictured the Doanhart Mansion, the library, and the Book of Spells. Iris had made her memorize each spell, curse, potion, and charm. Somewhere inside the book was an incantation to speak with the Goddess without the Mouijah Stones. She must know the truth.

She blinked several times. Was Jasmine in the library?

Too much information too fast made Lavender nauseous.

"Open your eyes, Lavender. You're weaving," Brody said. "Are you okay?"

She had it—the spell to speak with the Goddess.

A wave of darkness encompassed the room.

Lavender couldn't keep her eyelids open. Her lashes were too heavy.

She tried to speak and couldn't open her mouth.

What's happening to me?

Chapter 11

Hagatha's Chateau

Max stared at the plate of food Cook placed before him on the table. "I appreciate it, but I don't think I can eat a bite. I'm worried about Lavender."

"Lavender is a strong witch." Cook took the bench opposite Max. "She's capable of taking care of herself. I remember her as a child. She was precocious." He laughed. "I watched her and Jasmine blossom with beauty, brains, and magical abilities."

"What if Hagatha and Birch disappear too? Who will I call? What will I do?"

Cook pushed away from the table and went to the cabinet. He pulled out a bottle of whiskey and grabbed two glasses. He poured a shot for Max and one for himself, then sat next to Max. "Take a drink. Once your nerves settle, I suggest you call Jasmine and Isidore."

"Brilliant. Let's see, seven hours difference to Hant Hollow, so Finis should be getting ready for a nap." Max sipped the whiskey. He stood then placed his hand on Cook's shoulder. "What's your real name?"

"Call me Cook. Everyone else does."

"Are you a warlock?"

"I prefer wizard."

Max's brows lifted. "Alrighty. Excuse me while I call Jasmine, then I'd like another shot of 1792, please. It's been a while since I drank Kentucky Bourbon, and you can tell me how a wizard and a warlock differ."

Max left the kitchen and went into the library. He withdrew his phone and looked at the bars—only three.

He prayed and hit Jasmine's contact number. It rang four times before she answered.

"Max? Is everything okay?" she asked.

His lips trembled as he forced himself not to cry. "No. It's not. Lavender, Brody, and Kyewicket are missing." He rattled off the information about Adam's letter regarding the ancient scrolls. "Lavender swore me to secrecy, but she's been gathering information about her mom. Hagatha and Birch left hours ago to search the monastery, the place where Brody last texted. She's looking for Peony."

"Slow down. What monastery?" Jasmine inquired. "She's what?" Her tone showed she wasn't thrilled about the news.

"Don't shoot the messenger. Brody is with her. He and Carlton have been keeping tabs on her." Dang, his slip of the tongue would put her poor husband in hot water.

"What?" she yelled. "Carlton knew about this and didn't tell me?"

He listened to her rip a litany of foul language.

"That's not important. Can you—you know, call on the stones? Ask the Goddess what the hell is going on. I'm a nervous wreck. I don't know what I'll do if Hagatha can't find them, or worse, she disappears too." He paced in front of the large window. The France trip he had planned was supposed to be fun. "Jasmine, are you still there?"

He could hear her breathing.

"I'm still here. I'm trying to rein in my anger. I'll deal with Carlton when he returns to Hant Hollow. I'm sure we can figure out something between Mom, Dad, and me. Max, are you at Hagatha's?"

"Uh-huh." He sniffled.

"Don't cry. You stay there. I'm not mad at Carlton, I promise. I'll summon the Mouijah Stones. With any luck, the Goddess of Light will find Lavender and send her home safely. I'll call when I receive any news, and you do the same." She paused, then added, "I love you, Maxie."

"Promise witches honor. And I love you too."

"I promise, Max. Witches honor."

The call ended.

He swiped the tears from his face and slowly walked back into the kitchen.

Cook stoked the fire to a crackling blaze.

Max scanned his broad shoulders and narrow waist. *How did Cook stay so fit?*

He shook his head, stepped to the sink, and peered out the windows. The moon on the snow lightened the darkness. The wind howled, and he shivered, not from cold but sheer terror. He was in over his head and didn't know how to help his friends.

Cook stepped behind him. His warm cinnamon breath hot on Max's neck.

Max wanted to cry like a big baby in Cook's arms. His heart raced.

Cook spun him around. There was a hunger in the wizard's eyes as he gazed at Max's mouth, then back to his eyes. "I got you." His strong jawline softened when he smiled, and his cheeks dimpled.

Well, he didn't see that coming. "I'm glad somebody does." Max's knees weakened.

"Let's have a drink by the fire." Cook led them to the rocking chairs next to the fireplace. "Sit, please. I'll tell you how I met Hagatha."

Cook was silent for a few minutes. He placed his hand on the mantel and stared at the flames. "We met around seven hundred years ago, after Hagatha and her coven moved to France. I was a young lad when Rome's military invaded our village not far from here. They butchered my family. Hagatha and several other witches rushed to our aid, but they arrived too late. Hagatha welcomed me into her home. She became my surrogate mother."

Cook glanced at Max. "She taught me the ancient secrets of magic, and through time, I excelled. Hagatha urged me to branch out on my own, but I wouldn't leave her. I will never leave her. She protected me during a time when pious fools burned folks like me at the stakes." He stared into Max's eyes. "There's so much I'd like to tell you, Max, but I'm forbidden."

"I knew witches lived long lives. I had no idea how long, though. Seven hundred years, you say? Well, you age superbly." Max chuckled. "You don't have to break any confidences or rules on my account. I have dealt with my share of idiots during my lifetime."

Cook cupped Max's face. "I'm glad."

"Me too."

All fear and anxiety melted away. Looking into Cook's eyes, Max knew he had found his soul mate. He'd searched his entire life and never thought he'd find love, but love had found him.

Hant Hollow

Jasmine fumed. She closed her eyes and took several breaths.

How had she not seen Lavender's pain?

They were like sisters instead of first cousins.

She'd only seen what she wanted to see, and now Lavender was missing.

She glanced at her time-bending watch. Her father, Draum, worked in Waytherlands at the Library of Magic, but her mother, Isidore, would arrive home soon with Finis for his afternoon nap.

Jasmine must call on the stones. She raced into the library.

Intricately carved mahogany bookshelves lined the walls. A beveled-edge mirror hung over the Italian marble fireplace's mantel, and an oversized white sofa was in the middle of the room. Vintage Aubusson rugs covered most of the wood plank floors.

She had spent countless hours in the library reading her favorite books or brushing up on magical skills over the last century, and she knew every inch of the room by heart. She hurried past the Doanhart Book of Spells displayed on the large podium next to the eight-foot paned window with dark green velvet drapes trimmed in gold fringe.

She flew to the second level, where rare hand-written books were kept. She passed the rolled scrolls and ancient leather-bound texts, then stopped.

She hadn't called on the Goddess of Light since Iris and Peony disappeared.

She trembled and extended her fingers. "Mouijah Stones of truth and light, I need help, I need insight." The divine box with inlaid pearls appeared on the shelf. She opened the lid and looked at the two sun discs with embedded rubies and ancient magic words. She grabbed one sphere, and incandescent light filled the room.

One minute Jasmine stood in the library.

The next, she was in the presence of the Goddess.

Streams of light burst forth with brilliance. "Hello, Jasmine. It's been some time since we spoke. How may I assist you?" Her stunning appearance took Jasmine's breath, but it did not compare to the deity's strength and compassion.

"Lavender, Brody, and Kyewicket are missing. Do you know what happened to them?"

She stepped next to Jasmine and pointed to a white bench under a red maple. Doves circled above them. "Please join me."

Jasmine glanced around. The only time she'd materialized into the divine location, she hadn't noticed any trees or life. Yet, this time it surrounded her—a colorful archway of alternating white and purple wisteria trees swaying with a warm, gentle breeze.

Animals in the woods tended to be shy, but here, they reminded her of *Snow White's* friends. The birds sang sweet melodies. Small bunnies hopped near the celestial, and she smiled. The little creature gazed at her with pure adoration.

Jasmine sat with the Goddess for a minute or so, neither speaking.

The longer she waited, the more anxious she became.

The Goddess took Jasmine's hand. The vibrational energy exchanged between them made the hair on her arms rise. "I am aware of their disappearance. While I want to give you information, I'm forbidden."

Jasmine thought her brain would explode. "Why are you forbidden? You're divine. How is that possible? And if you can't tell me what happened, with all respect, may you at least tell me if they're safe?"

"They are safe." The immortal's kind eyes expressed love.

"Will they return home?" Her stomach churned.

The calm displayed by the divine being was unnerving.

"Do I take it that Lavender isn't returning?" Jasmine thought she might pass out or puke.

"Do you know what self-fulfilling prophecy means?"

Jasmine released a breath. "Yes. If I expect something and believe in it hard enough, it will happen."

"Life-altering events unfold as we speak. Should I utter one sentence regarding Lavender, I could very well change the outcome. I won't risk it. Do you trust me?"

She searched the Goddess's pale blue eyes. "Yes. But I don't understand."

"I'm sorry for causing you pain and confusion." She kissed Jasmine's forehead. "I will always watch out for you and your family. I promise one day you will understand."

White mist engulfed Jasmine. She materialized on the second-floor landing of the library.

The front door opened, and she heard Finis running down the hall. "Mommy, Mommy, Mommy. I home. Where are you?"

Jasmine popped in front of her son, went on bended knee, wrapped her arms around his little body and cried.

"What's wrong, Mommy?" Finis asked with concern. The child's brows knitted together.

Isidore placed her hand on Jasmine's shoulder. "Lavender is missing." Not a question, but a statement. It was uncanny how her mother could read a situation so clearly—one of her magical gifts.

"Yes, Mom. And I can't help her."

"Let me put Finis down for a nap. You put on the tea kettle." Isidore took Finis in her arms.

"Mommy needs me." He rubbed his eyes.

"Mommy will be okay, my darling boy. Take a good nap. Daddy should be home when you wake," Isidore added.

Jasmine went into the kitchen and put the tea kettle on. She scratched her brow while contemplating her conversation with the Goddess of Light. "She knows."

"Knows what?" Carlton came in the back door. He took off his winter coat and hung it on the rack in the mudroom.

She pointed her finger at Carlton. "I have a bone to pick with you."

"Tea first, then you may scold me." Carlton took her in his arms. "Oh, you're serious. What's up?"

"Are you aware Lavender has been looking for her mother?" Jasmine raised a brow. "She, Brody, and my cat are missing."

He kissed her cheek. "I plead the fifth."

"That doesn't fly, Regent. My dearest cousin, your right hand, and my cat are missing. What do you know about the monastery?"

"Lavender's been looking for your Aunt Peony since she disappeared. I kept tabs on her with Brody to keep her out of trouble. I don't have to remind you how your cousin sometimes acts." He took her hands, and she withdrew as the kettle whistled. "She's impetuous."

"That's putting it mildly."

Jasmine opened the chamomile box and measured tea for three. She took the service with honey to the kitchen table. "You should have told me."

"You're right." He sat at the table. "I didn't want to worry you. Based on Lavender's computer, the monastery has an incredible library full of lost secrets. I believe there is a text at the abbey that may have information about your Aunt Peony and the origins of our magic."

"You hacked her computer?" She handed Carlton his tea as Isidore came into the room. "I had to."

"So, you allowed Lavender to pursue her adventure, knowing it was dangerous." Jasmine tapped her foot on the floor.

He sipped his tea. "You and I both know once Lavender gets something in her mind, she's relentless."

"I called on the stones and met with the Goddess." She pursed her lips.

"Does she have information on Lavender?" Isidore entered the kitchen, took her cup, and joined them at the kitchen table.

"She knows something, Mom, but she's not sharing the details with me. Something to do with a self-fulfilling prophecy." Jasmine sipped the hot beverage. "Something major is happening, and we have to sit and wait. It's agony."

"Not necessarily. Is Hagatha home?" Isidore inquired.

"She's at the monastery."

"Hagatha has a shew stone. It can see beyond realms." Isidore looked at Jasmine and Carlton. "I have a sense Lavender is no longer within ours. The only way to know for sure is to ask the black glass. Hagatha has one that's said to be as old as time itself."

"Don't worry, Jasmine. The mage military is on call. Brody enlisted Birch along with two of my best warriors. They will find them." He leaned back in his chair. "Know that Brody loves Lavender, and she loves him. They are together. And Kyewicket is an asset too. He's one smart kitty."

"Mom, will you call Hagatha?"

Isidore smiled. "Of course, I will use the phone in the library."

Jasmine had never seen a shew stone.

She barely remembered Hagatha.

It's funny. Jasmine hadn't thought of her great-grandmother since she left France.

* * *

St. Lucian's

Hagatha adjusted the extension light to help magnify the ancient text in the abbey's climate-controlled room. Adam Bissett had the scrolls carbon-dated, but she knew magic was why the text remained in mint condition instead of looking like tree bark.

The ancient royal families' language had been preserved. The papyrus held two opposing philosophical views on magic plus information on physics, music, and the secret of the magi's longevity over death. Some of those same sentiments rang true today in the Mage Alliance, including the tug of war between light and dark magic.

The monk scholars in the room watched her every move.

The revelation within the story would've shaken their faith.

And even with infrared imaging, high scanning resolution, or a particle accelerator, humans would never interpret its contents correctly, or they'd misread the intent.

She eased away from the table. "May I ask where you found this scroll?"

The head monk, or priest, took one step toward her. "We were repairing part of the cave system under the castle. Several rocks unearthed a ceramic jar with the text and the sculpture that sent your friends into the light."

"May I see the jar?" Hagatha asked politely.

The priest nodded. "I will retrieve it from the vault if you kindly reveal what's in the text."

Hagatha glanced at Birch then back to the priest. "Get the jar, and I will illuminate you, but I also wish to see where you found the items in the cave."

The priest tented his hands in prayer mode, bowed, and retreated from the room.

Only one monk remained with them. Hagatha walked over to him, and his back pressed against the glass wall enclosure. She wiggled her finger. "Sleep."

Hagatha looked at Birch. "I'm going to make a replica of this document. Do you have room in your coat to hide the scroll?"

"Yes. What is in the text?"

"I'll explain later." She turned to the text, wiggled her fingers, and said, "I see two scrolls overlapping."

Birch went to the table.

Hagatha handed him the scroll. "Hide it. I will wake the monk, and you ask for the loo, then hide the relic in your vehicle. They can have the fake. They'll never know it's a forgery. Make sure your warriors guard it with their lives. And be quick." She snapped her finger, and the friar woke.

Birch said, "Where are the restrooms?"

The monk looked between them. "Take that door and turn right in the corridor. You will see the sign."

Birch ducked out the door.

Hagatha sat at the table and continued to read.

She was elated. The scroll rightfully belonged to the Mage Alliance. She would personally deliver it to the Library of Magic in Waytherlands.

Her cell rang. It was Isidore. "Isey, I can't talk. I'll call you when I get home."

Isidore asked, "Do you still have the shew stone?"

"Yes."

"Lavender is not in this realm. Find out where she is, please?"

"It's not *where* she is that's our problem. She's time traveled with her friends. I am sure of it. I must go." Hagatha didn't say goodbye. She ended the call as Birch returned to the room, followed by the priest.

"This jar held the ancient text. There wasn't a blemish, not a scratch or crack. It is magic, no?" The priest was astute.

"Magic or divine intervention." She swallowed.

"Yes, I believe so." He nodded. "Would you like to see the grotto?"

"Birch and I would love to see the underground cavern."

Hagatha knew one more item was missing. She sought the dagger that changed her life— forever.

Chapter 12

The Black Flame Forest

Cora changed out of her formal clothing and donned a royal military uniform. She strapped on boots and grabbed her satchel, including a restorative draught, a magic potion, and a dagger with encrusted rubies, the Dagger of Destiny. She may need them since her wizardly skills far exceeded anyone in court except her mother.

She nearly skipped down the stairs and out through the back gardens. She planned on embracing her sister once she found her. Yaris had saved her from a loveless marriage.

Did Yaris love Cetus?

There was no time to think about that now. She was on her way to meet and somehow disarm her father's number one rival, her uncle, King Odar. She would travel alone through an enchanted forest with Emir. *Alone with the delicious fae. Hm.*

Her breathing labored at the thought of Emir undressed, perhaps water glistening on his torso. Her cheeks heated at the idea of running her fingers through his dark wavy mane.

He had better not have left without her. The thought sped her pace until she spotted him waiting for her at the edge of the manicured grounds. She exhaled deeply and halted before him.

Emir bowed. "We must hurry. The night is upon us." He turned his back to her and ran through the maze.

She raced to keep up with him.

Cora had a taste for adventure and never thought of the woods as dangerous for one instant. She had not been alone in the forest since her father banished King Odar from court. Her uncle had taken one-third of the royal guard with him.

She looked at the magnificent trees. A strong wind rustled their leafy branches. The trees were talking to each other. "I understand the trees."

Emir grabbed her hand. "You only think you understand them. They see you as the enemy. Stay close to me, and do not veer from the path."

Her heart fluttered while holding Emir's hand. And she agreed. The trees didn't like her at all. "It's not my fault. My father makes me angry too," she shouted to the woods.

"You're not like the other court members." Emir chuckled.

"I am unlike anyone except maybe Yaris. Do you think she's safe?"

"They are safe. My mother watches over them."

The wind died as darkness surrounded them—replaced by strange noises and screeching birds.

She bumped into Emir. "Oh, I'm sorry. It's so dark. I can't see."

Emir turned and squeezed her hand. "I will protect you. The forest and I are on good terms if you don't venture from the trail. We'll set up camp near the river, and we should make it to King Odar by morning."

"You have a noble heart."

"There is nothing noble about me, milady."

"Are there wild beasts in the woods?" she asked while stepping over brush and stones.

"We are all wild in the woods, milady. Do you trust your father's word if we return Yaris and Cetus unharmed?" He offered his hand to help her step over a downed log.

"He'll stand by his word to King Odar. However, he will punish Yaris severely. He may even banish her from court or, worse, kill her. But I have a plan to save Yaris and Cetus." The rush of the river met them at the next turn. It gurgled and babbled over moss-covered stones winding its way through the forest. "The path ends."

"For the night. It will return when the new sun breaks at dawn." He reached in his bag, pulled out a quilt, and placed it on thick, plush grass. Then he pulled out a loaf of bread and a hunk of cheese. He offered her the food, but she wasn't hungry.

"I'm too excited to eat. I've never been away from the palace at night." She sat on the covering and drew her knees to her chest.

"So your father agreed to you accompanying me?"

She pursed her lips. "Um. I left him a note. My father wouldn't allow me to go with you unchaperoned. He's drinking Dragon Ale tonight, so he won't read it until morning."

"Fig-fatten. You've placed my people and me at risk." He shook with anger. His jaw clenched.

Her gaze went to the ground. No one other than her parents had ever raised their voices at her. "Do you want me to go back to the palace?"

"It's too late for that." He jerked off his sleek purple garment.

She gasped. Emir was the most beautiful creature she'd ever seen. His wings jutted and lit with intricate designs. She wanted to touch them but decided against it.

He shouted words she didn't understand, and when he glared at her, she saw nothing but contempt.

Tears brimmed on her lashes. She couldn't stand being in his presence, so she ran. Twigs jerked her hair, and wiry branches bit her face and arms. She didn't stop until she heard a monstrous cry.

Cora stopped in her tracks.

She looked behind her, to the left and the right.

It was too dark. She couldn't see a thing.

Emir had told her to stick to the path, not to deter from the trail. She'd left her satchel on the quilt, so she didn't even have the dagger for protection.

Her shoulders tightened. Her heartbeat was nearly bursting.

A glimmer of light appeared, moving closer to her as she crouched behind a tree.

"Don't be afraid. I won't harm you. Cora?" Emir landed without a sound. He stepped next to the tree. "Come out, Princess. You are hiding in an angry troll's tree."

She bolted and crashed into him.

They rolled together down a steep incline. The scent of the dampened ground and leaves filled her senses as they came to a halt.

Emir enveloped her in his arms. "Are you hurt?" He was trembling.

"Nothing but my feelings." She panted.

"What are feelings? Do you require attention to those feelings?" He was quite sincere.

"Feelings are emotions like you were angry at me, shouting words that I didn't understand, but the intent was clear. I ran because you hurt my pride. You hurt my feelings." She placed her hand over her heart.

His face softened. "Please do not run away from me again. King Odar would have my head."

"He'd cut off your head?"

"Worse. He'd cut off my wings. Come, let's go back to camp." He held Cora's hand through the darkness, his wings lighting her path.

"King Odar needs to be held accountable for atrocities toward friend or foe." Cora fumed.

"He is our ruler. Losing his niece or hurting his niece would warrant my wings."

She timidly reached out to touch his wings, and they disappeared. "Where did they go?"

"Only my wife may touch my wings."

The sting of his words hit her hard. "You're married?"

At the campsite, he busied himself, making a small fire. "I'm not married, but the Black Flame Fae take relationships most seriously."

"My father takes relationships seriously too. I'm glad Yaris ran away with Cetus. I'm not a fan of arranged marriages."

"The Black Flame Fae may fall in love by choice. We choose our mates. Well, most of the time." He joined her on the blanket. "Every soul is free. Your soul is free to choose whether you're exiled or in court."

"My soul is free to choose— if only that were true."

Emir stretched out on the quilt with his hands behind his head. "Look at the stars above our heads. They stretch across the vast Universe. The same is with souls. Souls are as numerous as the stars and just as vast. One person cannot own your soul, even if enslaved. Your father does not own your soul. That is the one thing which is yours. Never forget that."

She eased down to lie beside him. Her body barely touched his, yet it ignited a passion within her heart. "You are incredibly wise and kind. I'm sorry I ran away. I have a confession to make."

He propped on his elbow and searched her eyes. "What would you like to confess, Goddess?"

Hearing the endearment in the timbre of his voice resonated with her resolve to admit the truth. "You won't get angry?"

"I will control my temper."

She released a breath. "While I want to help my sister and Cetus, I came on this journey to be near you."

"Me?" He frowned.

"You struck me to my core at court. You are brave and beautiful. I have learned, on our journey, that you speak truth and wisdom, but when your arms wrapped around me, in that free-falling moment, the only thing I wanted was to feel your lips next to mine." She blushed and looked away.

Emir gently turned her to him. "You are a stunning Goddess. I am merely fae. We are star-crossed, Cora. If I kiss you, and that kiss leads us to love, what will happen next? Do you think your father will welcome me to court as an equal?"

She sat crossed-legged. "I do not need court. I have never needed the pomp and circumstance either."

He placed his hand on top of her knee. "You are not merely a Goddess, Cora. You are the seventh sister of the Pleiades."

"That may be true. But shouldn't that give me the right to forge my destiny? To choose the one whom I'll spend in eternity."

He kept his eyes on her. "You should have the right to choose. All beings should have the inalienable right to pursue their life course. Rulers should not force anyone into a life that's not of one's making. Rulers should not force unjust laws on their people. All beings should have the right to pursue happiness without constraints. And you will live forever...I will not."

Her voice quivered. "But I forbid you to die."

The flickering flames cast shadows on Emir. "And that is something a Goddess would say. Although it won't make it real unless I seek the secret of longevity from the sorceress who holds the mysteries."

"There is a witch who offers immortality? Does she live in the woods?" She bit down on her bottom lip as she waited for his reply.

"Cora, would you like me to kiss you?"

Her eyes widened, and she nodded. "I would like that very much."

He patted the quilt. "Lie beside me."

Her tummy fluttered, but she complied.

He turned onto his side, and his hand slid through her hair. He cradled her head in his hand.

Cora wanted to close her eyes but didn't want to miss one minute of her first kiss.

By the light of the two silvery moons, Emir crushed her lips with his, it wasn't gentle, but by the Gods, it was perfect. She had led an exemplary life until this evening. She would never let him go, even if it meant she would be banished.

In the still quiet woods by the babbling brook, Cora fell in love with a fae.

Emir woke before the sun.

Cora lay in his arms.

She had the face of an angel. He had never touched such soft skin. Her amber-colored eyes changed hues while he kissed her. He had wanted much more, but a relationship between a deity and a fae was impossible and forbidden.

What had he been thinking?

He would remember Cora's kiss for the rest of his life. He would search for his mother's sister if she meant what she said. Serena was the sorceress that held the secrets of life over death. He shook his head.

Cora would come to her senses as soon as she met King Odar. And when she finally married, his heart would break into pieces.

Emir cringed. King Odar would not cut off his wings for kissing his brother's daughter. He would celebrate it as a victory. The King of the Fire Throne would never know true love. He stripped Emir of his title and made his mother his queen by force. Queen Goldengrace was the absolute ruler of the woods; one day, she would be again, even if it killed him.

Cora stirred in his arms and blinked. "Mm, Emir, you're as good as you look. Kiss me again."

His grin went wide. "Didn't you have enough kissing last night? We must travel. King Odar waits for my return. You never told me how you could save Yaris and Cetus."

"My father stated at court that Cetus and Yaris would marry. He has no intention of fulfilling his boast. He will kill Yaris for betraying him and the kingdom. The only way to save her is for King Odar to marry them before we return to court."

"Out of the question. Royal marriages are a public spectacle. They must seal the prophecy." He trailed his fingertips along the curve of her face. "King Odar marrying them would incite a war between the two royal kingdoms."

"No. It won't. If Cetus marries Yaris, she can take my place. I will relinquish my right as the seventh sister of Pleiades. Yaris will seal the prophecy, and peace will endure in the Universe."

"Don't get your hopes too high," he replied. "King Odar will want to know what he gets out of the union. Anyone who thwarts his plan pays for it dearly."

"I will think about it while we continue on our journey." She asked, "How long before we arrive?"

"The path over the river is open. We should arrive within the hour."

He stood and offered her a hand, then she threw her arms around his neck and kissed him on the mouth. He quickly withdrew from her embrace. "The woods are watching. We must be careful in the light of day."

Cora reached for her satchel and pulled out a dagger with encrusted rubies. "I will kill King Odar and my father if it frees the woods, the fae, and my sisters."

Emir placed his hand over her mouth and whispered, "Shush. That's treason."

Lavender, Brody, and Kyewicket left Queen Goldengrace's secret garden and followed Sprite back to the common area. Lights of many colors dotted the landscape and the forest.

The Black Flame Fae community buzzed with laughter and chatter. Streams of gold and silver ribbons fluttered from the tree branches. Faeries, elves, dwarves, goblins, and trolls worked effortlessly together, organizing a fantastical celebration. Musicians and dancers practiced on the royal blue and gold trimmed carpet before the king and queen's table. Food and beverage booths were on both sides of the arena.

The crowd swell gave them adequate cover.

Lavender grabbed Brody's forearm. "Cora's here." She pointed next to the Dragon Ale sign. "I wonder who the tall fae is standing next to her?"

Sprite hovered next to Lavender. "That's Prince Emir. He's Queen Goldengrace's only son."

Brody crossed his arms. "He looks like his mother and nothing like King Odar."

"Prince Emir is elfin nobility. His father, Winterwood, was killed by King Odar and his guards when they invaded the forest. We're no longer permitted to call him a prince. Emir works as an emissary to King Odar. He does the king's bidding."

"To whom are they speaking?" Lavender asked.

"The queen's sister, Serena, that's odd because the king banned her from the community. Powerful women who possess magic threaten him."

Brody rubbed the back of his neck. "Why?"

"Long story." Sprite fluttered above Kyewicket.

The cat jumped onto a low-lying branch, eye level with the fae. "We must find out if Cora is on our side or the royals."

"I'll inquire about Cora. But you must dress for the celebration. It's in honor of Yaris and Cetus. Shall I escort you back to your rooms?"

Brody shook his head. "No. But I want a mug of ale. Is that permitted?"

"I'll send ale to your rooms."

Lavender turned to Sprite. "I think the party is a trap. Something feels off."

"The queen has more loyal subjects than King Odar knows. One day we will rise against his tyranny. The queen will protect you." Sprite vanished.

Lavender glanced at Cora, and they locked eyes.

Cora weaved through the crowd. "Yaris." She kissed Lavender's cheek and ignored Brody entirely. "May we speak in private?"

"Our rooms are close. We may talk there while I dress for the celebration."

They wound around the path and went up the walkway.

Crystal, the fae sent to guard Lavender, was still under her sleeping spell.

Brody opened the door for Cora. "After you."

"Shouldn't you wake that faery?" Cora frowned.

"I will speak to her. Cetus will show you inside, and I'll join you in a minute."

Lavender looked around before leaning in close and whispering in the guard's ear. "Open your eyes. No longer do you work as King Odar's spy."

Crystal tilted her head. "How long have you been standing there?"

Lavender placed her hands on her hips. "Long enough to know that you sleep on the job."

The fae bristled. "My apologies. I'm not sure what happened."

"Our little secret," she said. "I stepped out to see if you would get Dragon Ale for Cetus. The celebration starts soon."

The fae bowed. "I will return." She vanished, leaving a trail of golden glitter.

Prince Emir approached Lavender. "Is your sister inside?"

Lavender narrowed her eyes. "Are you a friend of Cora, or do you work for King Odar?"

"I am both." His eyes brightened.

"I met your mother, Queen Goldengrace. I must know where your loyalties lie." Lavender wanted to trust Emir.

He straightened his shoulders and lifted his chin. "It's better we talk inside your suite."

"I agree." She ushered him inside. She wanted to tell Cora and Emir the truth about Brody and her. If they had a chance of escaping to the queen's mirrored room, they'd need help.

Lavender inhaled sharply.

No matter how frightened, she would not cry. She needed to think clearly.

The foursome stood looking at each other.

The silence lengthened, then Lavender stepped forward. "We don't have time to dawdle. Can we trust you?" She looked between Cora and Emir. Each nodded.

"My real name is Lavender Doanhart. I come from the twenty-first century and the planet Earth." Lavender summarized the drama that brought Brody, Kyewicket, and herself to the Pleiades and its forest. She remained silent for a moment to allow her words to sink in. "You look skeptical." She went to the mirror on the wall. "Cora, look in the mirror and tell me what you see."

The seventh sister peered into the mirror. She mumbled to herself. "It's not possible." Cora turned to Emir. "Do you see what I see?"

He moved to stand next to Cora. He looked at the mirror, then looked at Lavender. The reflection in the mirror was Lavender, not Yaris, while the flesh and bone took on Yaris's appearance. "Are you a witch?"

Brody moved in quickly and circled his arm around Lavender's waist. "She is a witch. I'm a warlock." He pointed to the cat. "And so is Kyewicket. Emir, we did not appear here in your realm voluntarily, but your mother said she would help us return home."

"Did my mother tell you that she and her sister Serena are also witches? I don't think your presence here is a coincidence."

"We do not want to possess Yaris and Cetus," Lavender said. "We need our bodies back to travel through the looking glass well in the palace."

Cora shook her head. "No. No. No. Don't you see? Lavender and Brody are the ones in love, not Yaris and Cetus. They must marry. They must." She brushed the tears from her eyes.

"I will not allow you to marry anyone but me." Emir took Cora into his arms.

Should she tell them about the Goddess of Light and The Lord Darkness, who reigns over magic on Earth?

"Something happens to Yaris and Cetus." Lavender swallowed hard. "Um. They no longer live within the Pleiades or Orion. They're still divine and immortal and govern magical beings like Brody and me."

"I agree with Lavender." Brody shook his head. "Something happens here, maybe at the celebration that sets Yaris and Cetus's future into motion." He turned to Emir. "If your mother and aunt are witches, is it possible Yaris and Cetus are bestowed with the same gifts and abilities?"

Cora interjected. "All deities have varying degrees of abilities you call magic. What differentiates my family from the fae is intent."

Emir frowned. "Explain."

"My father and uncle use their influence to enhance their dominion. They crave power and control and don't care how they obtain it or who it hurts. They don't care about their subjects or family and often use half-truths to meet their needs." Cora paced the length of the room. "Magic used by the fae is solely for the benefit of their colonies and people. How do Yaris and Cetus govern you on your planet? And is Earth within our galaxy?"

Kyewicket purred. "Yaris is the Goddess of Light. She controls good witches. And Cetus is The Lord Darkness. He has power over the evil ones or misguided ones."

"I think our magic originates here. I don't think it's a consequence. Earth and the Pleiades are in the Milky Way Galaxy." Brody picked up Kyewicket and scratched his ears. "My friend may be oversimplifying their duties, but he is somewhat correct."

"An ancient sculpture acted as the conduit to bring us here. Do Queen Goldengrace or Serena use sculptures when casting spells?" Lavender asked.

"The Goddess sculpture?"

"It looked like a fertility relic but did not arrive with me."

"No, it wouldn't." Emir sat on a sofa and placed his face in his hands. He looked up and said, "I'll find Serena and bring her here. She's the only one who can answer your questions."

Lavender prayed that Serena could shed light on their predicament. "We'll get dressed for the festival and wait for you."

"I'll go with Emir." Cora squeezed Lavender's hand. "We'll find a way to help you to return home and get Yaris back too." They left through the front door.

Crystal entered with a pitcher of ale. "I hope this pleases you, milord. I'll be outside if you need me. Mugs are in the cupboard."

"Thank you." Brody saw her to the door, then turned to Lavender. "What are we supposed to wear to this shindig?"

Lavender strolled into the bedroom and opened the ornately designed armoire. She retrieved a white velvet dress trimmed in gold and laid it on the bed. "Super lush fabric, and dig the handcrafted gold belt with pearls. But I am not wearing those undergarments. What if I have to pee?"

Brody fingered a kirtle. "But this one has rubies and sapphires."

"The only jewels you need to be concerned with are the ones hanging between your legs." She belly-laughed, and he did too.

Lavender snapped her fingers, and the dress appeared on her. "I feel like Guinevere in King Arthur's court. Will you be my Lancelot?"

"The Arthurian tale is tragic. I will be your knight. I will not reprise the role of Lancelot."

She snapped her fingers again.

Brody wore a rich black velvet tunic with a lace-up neck. The slashed sleeves revealed a gold satin inner sleeve, and he paired it with black brocade paneled pants and high boots. He opened his arms. "I lived through the Renaissance. Get me a mug of ale, wench." He winked.

"Let's both drink a mug. I need something to settle my nerves." Lavender moved into the sitting area.

Brody handed one mug to Lavender and gulped ale, then belched. "Pardon."

Kyewicket stalked around them. "Can you run in that dress? Can you fly?"

"Does a duck quack?" She arched a brow. "Yes. I might not have lived during the middle ages, but I've worn my share of long dresses. Thank God for Marlene Dietrich ushering in a new era of fashion."

"I dated her," Brody chimed in.

Lavender punched him in the arm. "You did not."

"I like it when you're jealous." He drew her up and kissed her. "Remember, whatever happens after dark, stay close to the cat and me."

"Meow, I have a name."

"Yes, you do." Lavender crouched down and kissed Kyewicket's nose. "You be safe too. Jasmine would kill me if something happened to you."

He hissed, "I can take care of myself."

A knock at the door echoed in the room.

Brody waved Lavender behind him and opened the door.

Emir allowed Cora and his Aunt Serena to enter, then followed them inside. "This is Lavender, Brody, and Kyewicket. They have questions."

Serena wasn't as beautiful as the queen, but her energy of love set Lavender at ease almost immediately—until she spoke. "I am a witch." She withdrew a wooden carving that resembled the relic at St. Lucian's. "I brought you here."

Lavender's eyes widened. "What? Why? Why did you do it?"

"My sister and I are the first witches. You and Brody are inhabiting Yaris and Cetus's bodies." She stepped over to Lavender and placed her hand on Lavender's abdomen. "You are with child."

"I'm what?"

Brody stammered, "We're what?"

Serena looked at Brody, then Lavender. "You have your minds, but your bodies belong to Yaris and Cetus."

"Yaris is carrying Cetus's child. Lavender, you cannot return home until the child is born." Serena walked around them. "Attempting to travel through the looking glass well would kill the infant and you."

Brody labored to breathe. "That child is ours, not theirs."

"The child may be yours in spirit, conceived in love, but it is biologically divine and connected to Yaris and Cetus." Serena grabbed a mug of ale and guzzled it.

Lavender placed her hand over her belly. "I'm pregnant?"

"Yaris is pregnant." Serena placed the empty mug on a wooden side table. "You must take care of her and her unborn child."

Chapter 13

Celebrating the Doanharts

Brody offered Lavender his hand as they exited their rooms. Kyewicket followed closely behind, intent on finding Sprite to relay the good news. Yaris was going to have a baby.

Lavender didn't feel pregnant. "I have so many questions. I mean, do I carry to full term? Possessing Yaris's body is weird enough without carrying her baby. Oh, Brody, how will we ever survive to go home?" She squeezed Brody's hand.

"Do not worry. I'll protect you and the baby." Brody's jaw clenched. "I don't care what that old crone said. That child is yours and mine."

"She does have a point, though. This isn't my physical body, and that's not yours." Her thoughts raced. "We've been on and off together for over a hundred years. God knows we've had tons of sex. Yet, never once did I get pregnant."

"We can't overthink that now. We must act as if nothing has happened before King Odar, so we can flee to Serena's home in the woods when the time presents itself."

Dusk turned into darkness. Multicolored lights and torches filled the festival. Music had the partygoers dancing in the street along the route to King Odar's table. The community members wore elaborate costumes in bold colors of violet, canary yellow, cyan, red, and emerald with impressive headdresses and unique feathered masks that complemented their attire. One fae walked on stilts, swaying with the beat while blowing golden-like glitter into the air.

The jubilance of the crowd stunned her. They cheered for Brody and Lavender as they entered the banquet area.

Brody leaned in and whispered, "They think we're rock stars."

Lavender wanted to laugh and cry at the same time. She nodded.

Crystal ushered them to velvet chairs beside the king and queen.

Cora, Emir, and Serena were not seated at the royal table. Lavender didn't see them at all.

King Odar wore a jewel-embellished tunic in full regalia. He rose, took Lavender's hand, and kissed it. "Please join the queen and me." He slapped Brody on the back.

Queen Goldengrace dressed in a royal blue gown made of silk with puffy sleeves and fur trimmings. Her hair was swept up and secured with pearl-embedded combs.

Servers brought dishes in staggered intervals. Dragon Ale flowed like water among the citizens. The king ate heartily, but the queen only nibbled.

Lavender leaned over to the king. "Thank you for the marvelous feast."

"The party has just begun, my dear. Eat. Drink. Dance." He leaned in and said, "We celebrate the Doanharts this evening."

She looked at Brody.

The thought hit her like a ton of bricks.

Celebrate the Doanharts.

Yaris and Cetus were with child.

Was Hagatha the baby in her womb?

The food looked incredible, but Lavender couldn't eat one bite. She was in shock.

Brody ate a small meal but matched the king's drinking ale mug by mug.

The king wiped his mouth with a cloth napkin and threw it on his plate. A server swiftly removed the food from the table and vanished.

A hush fell over the crowd when the king stood.

"Welcome to the celebration uniting the Black Flame Fae community and the royal families. This evening we take the opportunity to offer our hospitality to Yaris and Cetus. Dance, my friends. Celebrate with me!"

Brody leaned into Lavender. "Dance with me."

Lavender followed him onto the makeshift floor covered with a crimson paisley rug. It had been decades since they waltzed. Brody took her right hand and placed his left hand on the small of her back. With the rise and the fall of the melodic tune, they danced.

Others joined them on the floor.

His face pressed next to hers. "Do not look alarmed. The royal guards have swarmed the meadow. Something is afoot." He glanced around. "Do not leave my side for any reason. We may need to teleport into the forest if altercations unleash."

King Odar stood and clapped his hands. The music stopped.

Lavender watched as Cora and Emir approached the king's table. Her pulse raced.

"It looks as if I'm honored with not only one niece but two." The king stepped away from the table and onto the banquet floor. He bowed to Cora then said, "Seventh sister of Pleiades, why have you come?"

Cora's hands remained behind her back. She looked the king straight in the eye. "Uncle, you sent Emir to negotiate for the safe return of Yaris and Cetus. I felt it my duty to accompany him to assure my father that his daughter is safe. I am grateful you have bestowed your kindness on my younger sister."

The king dragged his hand over his white beard. "How do I know you aren't here to hurt your sister?" He turned to Lavender, then looked back at Cora. "It seems you were to marry Cetus, and he ran away with your sister. Sibling jealousy is a vicious rivalry."

Emir stepped beside Cora. "King Odar, she vowed to King Valdoor the safe return of Yaris and Cetus. However, your grace, the Goddess Cora, has concerns King Valdoor will banish them for disrupting the peace treaty between the Orionnites and the Pleiadeans. She may have a plan."

Cora relayed her scheme for Yaris and Cetus to wed.

The king listened, then his face turned red. His fists clenched. "Who are you to interfere with my plans? Quite frankly, once you've returned home, it is no concern to me what your father does to his wayward daughters. I desire to return to court and for all community members to have free mobility to move about the Pleiadean domain." He took a menacing step toward Cora. His eyes bulged. "You have jeopardized everything I have labored to achieve."

Lavender and Brody moved next to Cora and Emir.

Brody said, "We agree with Cora. Marriage would solve all issues with the alliance."

Queen Goldengrace stood. Her hand went to her throat. Her eyes scanned the forest.

"Cora, did your father approve of you traveling alone with a fae at night?" The king narrowed his eyes on Cora.

"No. I came of my own accord."

"You have ruined my plans!" King Odar shouted, "Guards, arrest them at once until I decide what to do."

Suddenly Cora brandished a dagger and lunged at King Odar's throat. "Die, you pig!"

The king dodged the thrust of the knife, but it sliced his right shoulder. The royal guard advanced on the crowd.

The king reared his fist against Cora when Serena appeared in a cloud of black smoke. Her cackle was loud and clear. "Do not threaten my people, you coward." She held a carved staff with a crystal ball on the hilt in her right hand. She slammed it into the dirt. "Stand still." The entire population froze.

Serena stepped over to Queen Goldengrace and tapped her shoulder, releasing her from the spell.

"What's happening, sister?" Goldengrace asked.

"The prophecy is true. Yaris and Cetus are with child. I must take them deeper into the forest. She must bear Yaris's child before we send Lavender and Brody through the looking glass well."

"Please take Emir with you. King Odar will want to make an example out of him."

"We'll not fight today, but judgment is coming soon for the likes of him. Magic him to the dungeon. I'll turn his guards into goats. Allow the Black Flame Fae to take back the woods."

"I will do as you wish but know that the royal families will come to fight. Our people are in grave danger."

"Tell King Valdoor the truth. Tell him that his daughters are safe after fleeing King Odar's wrath. Inform him I will send the Goddesses home once we are certain our community is safe, and he must vow the Goddesses will not suffer at his hand. King Valdoor must give freedom to all beings that live within the forest and return the sovereignty of the land to Emir. He is the rightful heir to the throne. Make him swear an oath on his kingdom."

"I swear it."

Serena turned King Odar's guards into goats as Queen Goldengrace called on her army to imprison King Odar, still immobile. "I won't undo the spell cast on Odar until I know King Valdoor will accept the truce."

Serena took her staff and swirled gold dust around Lavender, Brody, Kyewicket, Emir, and Cora. "Come with me, children, follow me home to the glen. You'll receive food and comfort in my den. The infant brings change, and magic will reign once again."

They appeared in front of Serena's home. She slammed the staff into the ground and sent a protective shield that shimmered outward around her property so no one besides her sister could enter without consequence.

Lavender held onto Brody with one arm and Kyewicket with the other.

Cora and Emir stared at them, then they all looked at Serena.

"My home is yours until the babe is born. My sister and I will arrange for your return to your time and planet." Serena strolled along the stepping stones to the front door of her rustic yet whimsical cabin. Her home's A-framed thatched roof seemed to extend to three stories.

The weary group followed the witch through a rounded doorway. The spiral staircase looked a bit rickety. The stone fireplace went from the ground floor to the roof's peak. She let Kyewicket down, and he yawned, curled on a rug next to the hearth and promptly fell asleep.

Lavender wanted to cry.

She wanted to go home.

She missed the streets of Rockvale, the Red Rose, and the Hant Hollow's property.

She missed her family.

She reminisced of the skinny-dipping days, lazily floating on the river and making mad passionate love to Brody under the willows. "I'm going to have a baby, Brody. She is going to take my child."

Serena turned to Lavender. "The child is not yours," she answered gruffly. "The physical body you inhabit does not belong to you. Please understand that the prophecy will bring magic to your world."

"Why did you bring us here?" Lavender asked.

"All in good time." Serena plopped onto a plush sitting chair.

Brody lifted Lavender's chin with his forefinger. "Remember, we are together, no matter what."

Serena waved her hand, and her formal attire switched to a long tunic with a brass belt. "I have rooms on three floors. Close your eyes and imagine the perfect space that will ease your anxiety. I am on the ground floor. Lavender, Brody, and Kyewicket are on the second floor, and Cora and Emir will reside on the third floor.

Cora's face flushed. "I cannot share a room with Emir."

Serena rolled her eyes. "Yes, Goddess, you and Emir have already shared a bed under the stars. There are no judgments here. I suggest you get acclimated to your rooms. I've added clothing and personal grooming items for your stay. The bathhouse is outside. I must rest to renew the energy that magic spent, and we'll talk more later." Serena fell asleep in an overstuffed chair. Her legs stretched out on a matching hassock.

Lavender and Brody went upstairs with Cora and Emir.

On the stairway landing to the second floor, Cora reached over and kissed Lavender on the cheek. "You may not be my blood sister, but you are in my heart. Everything will work out for the best."

"How can you be so certain?" Lavender clipped.

"Faith," Cora replied.

Brody asked, "In what?"

There was an awkward silence before Emir answered for Cora. "Our realm is full of magic and mystery. There are celestial beings who watch out for us. I cannot explain how I know we are in the presence of angels. It's just a feeling."

"I believe in angels." Lavender sighed.

Brody grunted. "I'm super glad you have faith in angels. I'm a skeptic. I believe in the here and now. I do not believe in destiny or fate."

"Never say such things." Cora gasped. "That's how calamity takes place in our lives."

"Never mind, Brody." Lavender squeezed Cora's hand. "He believes in Yaris and Cetus. They are the deities that guide magic in our world."

"It is all so confusing." Cora glanced at Emir and smiled. "I suppose we'll go to our rooms and see you downstairs in the morning."

Lavender nodded without speaking.

She and Brody entered the bedroom with a mixture of dark and light wood covering the walls and floors. A plump feather mattress with several quilts and blankets looked inviting. The stone fireplace crackled with flames.

A single window looked out into the forest. Lavender sensed something or someone watching them from within its depths but did not alert Brody. He was already on pins and needles, judging from the tightness in his face and across his shoulders.

"I'm not frightened, not really." Lavender leaned against his shoulder. "I feel safe here."

"I'm glad you do. I'm going to change out of this ridiculous costume, and then I'm checking Serena's shield for any weakness."

"Brody, don't go yet. Let's rest for a few minutes. Please wrap your arms around me. When I fall asleep, you can check the grounds."

He scooped her into his arms and brought her to bed. He slid in next to her and drew her close. He kissed her forehead and the tip of her nose. "Rest, my love. I won't leave you until you're snoring."

She giggled. "I do not snore."

"Oh, yeah, baby, you snore big time." He chuckled. His fingertips traced her face. "I don't mind it. It's sort of cute, like when you sneeze."

"How do I sneeze?"

"Ah-chew-wee," his voice squeaked.

"Well, you sneeze, big shoe." Lavender laughed. "It's the little things that mean a lot."

His fingers went through her hair like a comb. "Sleep. Rest. Snore."

Once Lavender fell asleep, he rummaged through the massive wardrobe with the same ornate designs he had seen on the sculpture at St. Lucian's. The hieroglyphics seemed to be a part of the Pleiadean written language.

Brody inhaled and exhaled. He didn't care for the clothes Serena had chosen for him. Instead, he looked at the dressing mirror and snapped his fingers. He wore his military uniform and boots, then magicked a long black trench coat with various weapons, including a stopwatch.

The folks in this realm may not observe minutes and hours but keeping time helped Brody put into perspective day and night. His ability to summon was getting stronger by the minute.

He stepped to Lavender's bedside and weaved a protection spell over her until he returned. He took two long strides, opened the well-oiled hinged door, then silently closed it again. Cora and Emir's muted voices drifted away as he descended the stairs.

Kyewicket's head popped up when he reached the first floor.

Serena's head was bent over a leather-bound book. She looked at him. "I think you will find my protection shield intact, but if you insist on checking for yourself, take this charm. Beings that live in the forest do not exist in your world."

"I thought you were sleeping." He placed the necklace around his neck. "You need to come clean and explain why you sent for us. You've placed the woman I love in harm's way, not to mention a questionable pregnancy. How risky is it to give birth to a deity?"

"It pleases me how much you love Lavender. She needs someone upon whom she can depend. As far as why I called you here, that dear boy is a conundrum. I cannot risk the child by explaining the details, but once the infant arrives, I will explain all."

"And how long does pregnancy in your world last?"

"When the moons are full."

"I need a little help here. I see no calendar or clocks or moons. How am I to know when that happens?"

Serena moved away from the table and walked to the window. "Come and see for yourself."

He joined her. Two half-moons were visible.

"The cycles of our moons are similar to your lunar course." Serena looked at his stopwatch and smiled.

"Are you saying Lavender will give birth in less than fifteen days?" Brody frowned.

Serena nodded.

"So help me, if anything happens to my girl, I will hold you responsible, and I am not one to be trifled with." He cursed under his breath and stormed out of the house. Kyewicket raced to keep up with him. Brody stomped around the side of the home and followed the path to the woods in the back.

"Lavender is strong," Kyewicket said. "She will survive."

He stopped abruptly. Tears welled in his eyes. He hadn't cried since losing his family a long, long time ago.

"It's okay to cry, Brody." Kyewicket threaded his legs. "It's not a show of weakness."

Brody swallowed hard, trying to push the emotions away, but the thought of losing Lavender was more than he could bear. The tears flowed. His shoulders shook as he sunk to the ground. "She is the only reason I wake in the morning. She's everything to me."

Kyewicket jumped into Brody's lap. "She loves you too. She has since the first moment she met you. I know Lavender can be a handful, but her bravado and flirtatious ways hid her fears and insecurities."

"I would never reject Lavender." He scratched the cat's ears. "Never. Not in a million years."

"I know, and so does she. Remain strong. Ready yourself for battle. King Valdoor will come for his daughters."

"How do you know?"

"I pay attention." Kyewicket jumped off his lap. "The rumblings at the party stated the king and his army are on their way to the Black Flame Forest. The king will want to save face in court and with his Orionnite visitors."

Brody came to his feet. "Then let's get to it. We'll check the protective shields. King Valdoor's magical abilities will be stronger than ours. We'll trap him in the forest."

Chapter 14

Lavender woke disoriented and looked at her rapidly growing belly—what the...? *How could it have gotten so big, so fast?*

The mere sight sent chills up her spine.

A foreboding took her breath away. Heart pounding, she tried to stand on her trembling legs. *Impossible.*

She opened her mouth to scream for Brody and found her vocal cords weren't cooperating either. The enormity of her predicament had rendered her speechless.

Serena entered the room in a flash. She took Lavender's hands into hers.

"Look at me and follow my breathing. Inhale slowly, then exhale. In one, two, three, four, out one, two, three, four." She demonstrated.

Lavender focused on Serena and followed her instructions. Tears streamed down her face, and her ragged breathing brought on hiccups. It took some time for Lavender to regain her composure. "Where is Brody?"

"He's checking my protective shield. That warlock loves you very much."

"Yes, he does. Serena, the baby is growing too fast. I'm terrified." On the brink of hysteria, Lavender had been running on instinct ever since they had arrived in this world. She'd relied on Brody's strength and his rationality. "You must tell me. Is the child I'm carrying Hagatha?"

Serena said, "There is a danger to you and the child if I reveal too much information."

"Why I'm here? Where do I fit in this insane scenario?"

"I know it must be difficult for you to understand. You are carrying a full-blooded God in your womb. The gestation for a divine being is around fourteen or fifteen days. Your body will change rapidly. But rest assured, I have seen you deliver the child safely."

"I cannot go any further without knowing something about my circumstance carrying this child. It is your game plan."

Serena glanced to the floor before she redirected the conversation. "Do you think you are up to going downstairs?"

Lavender nodded.

Serena helped her stand. "Steady."

"Did Hagatha know about you? Did she know this would happen to me?"

Serena's fingers brushed over Lavender's face, causing a sense of peace to descend on her. She breathed a sigh of relief. Lavender didn't want to alarm Brody, so she vowed to be brave.

"Come downstairs. Cora and Emir couldn't sleep either, and they're cooking soup. Brody and the cat should be back soon."

Lavender looked at her tightening clothing. "I'll need bigger clothes."

Serena whirled her finger, and Lavender appeared in a beautiful long blue empire dress with a gray sleeveless tunic and comfortable slippers.

"Thank you." Lavender placed her hand over her stomach and rubbed. "I am really pregnant. It's surreal. I mean, Yaris is pregnant. If I'm here, then where is Yaris?"

"We'll talk downstairs."

Lavender followed Serena down the winding staircase to the small kitchen. Something smelled delicious, and she was ravenous.

Cora's eyes widened. "Oh my, you are with child."

Emir stood and offered Lavender his wooden chair, which she accepted gratefully.

Brody opened the front door, and his eyes went straight to Lavender's stomach. He rushed to her side. "Baby, are you alright?"

"Kinda weird, huh?" She gave him a half-hearted smile.

Kyewicket circled and curled next to Lavender's feet.

Cora brought her a wooden bowl with no spoon. "It's tomato soup."

Lavender turned the bowl up and sipped. "It's wonderful." Bread and hunks of cheese were on the table with a pitcher of milk, water, ale, and pewter mugs.

Everyone made polite conversation during their modest meal. Once the table was cleared and the dishes washed, Serena brought out a large leather-bound book and a crystal.

"Please close your eyes and clear your mind," Serena said while giving each a few minutes to meditate. "Yaris and Lavender, Cetus and Brody are inextricably intertwined until after the child is born. It is the love shared by Lavender and Brody which encourages the love between Yaris and Cetus. I will attempt to show you a glimpse of the future using my crystal. You may open your eyes."

Lavender and the rest of the party gazed into the shew stone.

Swirling white clouds turned stormy gray. Yaris and Cetus held their infant child before the Pleiadean royal council. Men in tall black hats and long black robes shouted accusingly at the young family.

King Valdoor slammed his hand on the armrest of his throne. "Yaris, you deliberately sabotaged our treaty with the Orionnites. They've banned Cetus from ever returning to Orion's Belt. You have given me no choice. I forthwith strip you of your title. I order death for you, Cetus, and the infant at first light. You have embarrassed the kingdom. Get out of my sight."

The clouds churned again, turning blood red.

Serena and Queen Goldengrace appeared in the holding cell with Yaris, Cetus, and their child, blocking the jailers' view. "We've come to save you. But first, you must agree to our terms."

Cetus stepped forward, shielding his family. "What shall we do?"

"The child will bring magic to a new world, but you cannot go with the babe. You and Yaris are immortal deities. The new world has not evolved enough to walk with the Gods yet. To save the child from certain death, we have selected a group of human beings with exceptional healing abilities and knowledge of alchemy. We will teach them magic, and they, in turn, will hone your child's inherited skills. We are sending members of the Black Flame Fae community into this realm to expand our presence around the planet."

With tears brimming her eyes, Yaris held the infant close to her chest. "I cannot give my child away."

"Is there not another solution?" Cetus placed his arm around Yaris's shoulders.

"The child will not see another sunrise if you do not," Queen Goldengrace said. *"You and Yaris will always be in your child's life to intervene as divine guides."*

The clouds roiled again and cleared.

Lavender brushed the tears from her cheeks. "You're speaking of my family, aren't you? That's why I'm here."

"You are here to heal the divide between light and dark magic. Only then will Yaris and Cetus unite."

"I witnessed the exchanged looks between the Goddess of Light and The Lord Darkness the night my grandmother and mother vanished."

"They're in love and can't be together." Cora sniffled. "How tragic."

Brody and Emir kept silent during the emotional exchange.

Serena opened the leather-bound book. "My grimoire holds secrets of the Universe, including spells, potions, and charms. I have written pages on teleportation and time travel."

"Excuse the interruption, but The Lord Darkness isn't evil?" Lavender asked.

"No. He's merely a guardian of those dying and the dead." Serena sipped on her tea. "He does not judge but interferes against evil on your planet when necessary."

"The Princesses of the Dark Night are evil. They thrive on creating chaos." Brody interjected.

"They have learned how to manipulate dark energies present throughout the Universe," Serena said. "Each witch or warlock using magic for ill-gotten gain will never enter the Elysian Fields at death. Their existence is like hitting the rewind button."

Cora tilted her head. "What does that mean?"

Lavender giggled. "We watch plays through a fantastic window carried on waves of light and sound that allows us to move forward and go back and look at it again using a machine."

"Intriguing. I have a great interest in machinery." Emir leaned forward. "Serena, you've been to this world of which Lavender is speaking?"

"Only once, but I may go again." Serena closed the book, pushed away from the chair, and placed her book and crystal on the shelves.

"May I visit this new world?" Emir inquired.

Serena turned to him and smiled. "Not yet. The last thing I want is to create a paradox, which I already risked by bringing Lavender and Brody to our realm. But who knows, maybe someday."

"Explain this paradox." Cora crossed her arms.

Brody poured a mug of ale and leaned back in his chair. "Lavender and I live in another time and place. The Gods may or may not be related to Lavender which could create an element of time in which she and I no longer exist. We live because of magic. If magic ceases to remain, so do we."

Serena clapped her hands. "Excellent, Brody. I couldn't have described it better myself. I witnessed the events on your planet before they happened, so I cannot determine if I caused them or not. Regardless, I desire to rectify the situation and bring peace to both realms."

Lavender frowned. "What if King Valdoor breaches your protection shield before I give birth?"

"That is not going to happen," Serena answered with conviction.

"But it could," argued Brody. "Your shields are strong, but he is the king over your realm, and technically he's king over our world, too. Kyewicket and I discussed laying a trap for him before the protective barrier. If we capture him, Lavender has time to deliver and get our bodies back so we can return home through Queen Goldengrace's looking glass well."

"The premise sounds good, but if you don't capture the king, we're as good as dead." Emir poured a tankard of ale. "He will come with royal warriors."

Lavender rubbed her belly. "In the Doanhart Book of Spells, I memorized a mirroring incantation."

"Hm." Serena's brows rose. "That might work."

Cora looked at Lavender and Serena. "The Mirror Spell. Duplicate the king's warriors but use different colors. If you only replicate the guards, my father will see through it. But if we distort the images and add hues not associated with the kingdom, then creating an optical illusion could work. He hasn't fought in a real battle in eons so that he may parlay with Serena. She is his daughter, after all."

Withdrawing the bejeweled dagger, Cora added, "The blade has magical properties, including astral projection abilities to travel to other realms in the Universe. I have never been out of our realm, but my father has used it before."

Lavender's words rushed out without thought. "Do you think it's possible to travel back in time to the pivotal point in my grandmother's life?"

"Yes, yes." Serena jumped two feet off the ground, waving her hands in the air. "Why didn't I see it?"

"See what?" Lavender inquired.

"We have one chance to save Iris and Peony by stopping the killing of Silver and Aster." Brody added, "That's when Iris gives her soul to the darkness. She sought revenge on the men responsible."

Lavender tapped the side of her face in thought. "If we stop Silver and Aster from going to Hant Hollow, well, until all the family can go together, it gives us a shot. We lived with Hagatha before traveling to America." She continued, "The residual effect of changing those times may not stop Iris from going over to the darkness. She fell in love with Jonathan's father, Thomas. She killed him when he jilted her. It led her to cast Jonathan into the antique mirror for a century." Lavender frowned. Her shoulders slumped. "Without Jonathan's curse, he won't meet and marry Victoria. They have a child."

"There are no easy answers." Serena waved her hands in the air. "It is a big choice, but it's the best alternative to restoring balance. If you and Brody go back in time and save your Aunt Silver and cousin Aster, you mustn't run into yourselves. Changing timelines changes lives."

"You mean that Brody and I could disappear forever." Lavender bit her bottom lip. The consequences could change her feelings for Brody or vice versa. Was she willing to take that risk?

"It is a risk."

"Did I say that aloud?" Lavender inquired.

"I read your thoughts." Serena's eyes softened. "But remember, if you and Brody go back and don't get caught, my dear child, you'll save the day. We'll need to prepare. Create a timeline of events to help you navigate your journey through the looking glass well and ensure you land in the correct time and place."

Brody leaned against the wall with his arms crossed. During their discussion, he had remained quiet, but the scowl on his face spoke to his dark mood.

He dragged his fingers over his five o'clock shadow. "Let me get this straight. Lavender gives birth. The two Gods, Yaris and Cetus, take the child. Then Lavender and I use the looking glass well to time travel to the late nineteenth century, arrive at Hagatha's home in France, and warn Silver and Aster not to go to America alone. We intervene on Iris's behalf to warn her not to fall in love with a mortal she's never met. Lastly, Lavender and I must not run into our past lives because it would cause a worse paradox scenario than we're currently enduring."

Brody shouted, "Piece of cake! What happens to Lavender and me?" He pointed to the crystal. "What does the shew stone say about us? Do we still fall in love?"

Lavender noticed his tense shoulders, the clench of his jaw, opening and closing his fists. She pushed away from the table and went to him. She traced the outline of his cheek. "I would fall in love with you a million times over, Brody."

He turned her wrists over and kissed the soft inner skin. Then he glared at Serena. "Well?"

Serena sighed deeply. "I cannot say. We've never time-traveled to change history. It is forbidden."

"Forbidden," Brody said. "Great." He released his hold on Lavender and stormed out of the house.

Lavender turned to Serena. "Brody will do it for me." She raced out the door and found Brody looking into the forest, pulling fistfuls of his hair in apparent frustration.

She slipped her arms around his waist and placed her cheek on his back. "Brody, we've come too far to stop now. Don't ask me how I know, but it is the way we find Mom and go home."

He turned to Lavender and tucked a strand of hair behind her ear. He searched her eyes, the silence between them lengthening. A lone tear ran down his cheek, and she reached up to stop it. "I've never been able to tell you no. I don't think I will survive if I lose you during this mission. Promise me if something goes wrong, you will find me. Memorize my face and remember this kiss."

He slid his hand through her hair to cradle her head. He leaned in and gave her a gentle, loving kiss, expressing his love with an exquisitely sensual embrace.

The sweet ache of desire, passion, and love swept over Lavender in a heated rush. His arm circled her waist as he pulled her against his length. The incredible feel of his body beside hers was calming, but that wasn't what made her love him more. It was his unselfishness—Brody's willingness to put everything on the line, including his life, to help her.

Chapter 15

St. Lucian's present day

Birch and Hagatha donned protective clothing, helmets with lights, and wading boots used for fly-fishing and followed the monk to the cave under the monastery. The stone steps descended into darkness.

The monk stopped next to a pole and flipped a switch. The interior of the cave lit up. The area reminded Birch of the secret underground tunnels where the Knights Templar met. He had joined them to find their treasure, unsuccessfully.

"We uncovered the cavern during restoration." The monk looked over his shoulder. "There are four connecting floors, and archeologists have dated some of the writings to the Stone Age. We found articles and relics from the Roman Empire too. It is where we found the relic and the scroll that took your friends."

Hagatha's adrenaline kicked in on the lower floor. She extended her hands toward the monk, and he froze with the flick of her wrists.

"There's a potent dagger in this room. The blade can kill a God."

"How do you know?" Birch asked.

"I just do." She closed her eyes and focused on the energy of the metal. She blinked a couple of times to adjust her vision and followed the ray of light behind the tallest of the three stalactites near a blue pool of water. She floated toward the beam of yellow and extended her right hand. "Blade of sight, show me your might," she repeated twice, and nothing happened.

Her ability to exude strength, or perhaps the knowledge she had lived considerably longer than Birch— excited him.

Hagatha's mouth curved into a wickedly sexy smile as she flew back to where he stood. Not a hair's breadth between them created a warmth that was both erotic and soothing.

He brushed a kiss across her cheek, and she smacked him, which lit a fire of passion he could not contain. He circled his arm around her waist and drew her next to him, so close, his mouth hovered over hers, not touching— waiting for her reaction.

Birch wanted her more than he'd ever wanted a woman. "Tell me you want me."

"No, damn it. Where is the dagger?"

"Forget the blade. Look at me and tell me that you want me."

"For crying out loud. I'm trying to find the blade that could save my family. I don't have time for passion." She pushed him away. "Maybe later."

Someone on the upper stairs shouted, "Hello, Father, are you down there?"

"We're down here," Hagatha mimicked the monk's voice. She released the monk from her spell. "Thank you for the tour and for allowing me to view the scroll. But we must return to my home. I have guests arriving."

The poor monk looked puzzled.

Birch grinned sideways. *What a witch.*

He, too, had slipped under Hagatha's spell.

Hagatha held a letter she'd written over a century ago in her bedroom that remained unopened.

Memories of the past flooded her mind.

Could it be true?

She had an uncanny feeling—a sense of déjà vu. A knock rapped at her bedroom door.

"Hagatha? Are you okay?" Birch asked. "Um, Max is getting ready to go to the airport. He wants to see you."

"I'm coming. Just a minute." Hagatha placed the letter in the rosewood vanity box with mother-of-pearl inlay.

Max was distraught over leaving without Lavender. The unopened letter reminded Hagatha that she didn't have to search for Lavender—Lavender would find her. She released a sigh. She'd taken an oath so long ago she had nearly forgotten. She could not reveal her knowledge without jeopardizing Lavender's return. She could not give Max any comfort.

Hagatha merely hoped that all would end well. She had an idea. She took the box and opened the door.

The heated look from Birch gave her pause.

"Are you okay?"

"I'm fine," she replied.

Hagatha pushed by Birch and made her way down the stairs through the foyer, main hall, and kitchen. Birch had followed her, then went out the side door.

Cook touched Max's chin with heart-melting tenderness. "Do not worry. In my heart, I know things will work out as they should."

She coughed, warning them of her presence. Clearly, they had formed attachments.

She offered Max the box. "This is for Lavender. Make sure to declare it in customs. Please keep it safe. I have left a letter inside for her. And do not open it."

"Oh, okay." Max hugged Hagatha. "Will we ever see her again?"

"I am convinced of it." Hagatha air-kissed each cheek.

Birch stuck his head inside the kitchen. "Hey, Max, the car is ready."

Hagatha squeezed Max's hand. "Cook and I shall fly to America as soon as I tie up a few loose ends. Maybe we can make it to the Harvest Festival. I've heard Halloween in Hant Hollow is legendary."

Max's eyes widened. "That's an understatement. I'll look forward to seeing you soon."

Birch took Max's luggage and glanced over his shoulder. "I will return later. Don't run off." He winked.

She felt her cheeks flush as he and Max left.

Cook smiled. "You like the warrior, don't you?"

"He has potential." Hagatha shrugged. "I smell croissants."

"Just out of the oven. You get the tea, and I'll get the plates."

She put on the kettle and retrieved the porcelain tea service. "Cook, do you remember when Iris and her girls lived here?"

"Just like yesterday." He placed the tray of goodies on the table, then stoked the fire before sitting down. "Why do you ask?"

"Oh, nothing, I guess. I had so many wonderful memories when our home was full. What do you say about closing the house and going for an extended stay in America?"

"What about Lavender?"

"Something tells me that Lavender and Brody will find their way to Hant Hollow."

"Then what about Birch? He's drooling after you." Cook slathered butter on the bread and took a bite.

"You think so?"

Cook nodded.

Hagatha poured tea for two and joined Cook at the table. "There is something ruggedly handsome about Birch. A little rough around the edges. I might take him with us."

Cook laughed. "Nothing you can't smooth out."

Hagatha sipped the tea. She didn't want to tell Cook about the contents of the letter. It held significance for Iris and her girls. The letter she wrote when Iris was an infant. Something niggled at the back of her mind.

The broom dropped in front of the kitchen door.

She and Cook exchanged looks.

The hair on her arms rose. "Company is coming."

Chapter 16

The Pleiadean Forest

The sun sunk below the horizon as Cora raced with Kyewicket through the forest. The chill of evening sunk into her bones. Her breath materialized like a misty cloud.

Galloping horses pounded the dirt, edging closer to Cora—the massive beasts bellowing cries released puffs of smoke. The sight of them could scare demons away. The royal army wore mail and armor. Their swords and battle-axes clanking—several warriors shouted from their saddles.

She didn't see her father, the king, and the guards hadn't seen them yet.

Cora stopped and placed her hands on her knees to catch her breath. She looked to the left and right, then glanced over her shoulder. "Kyewicket, you still have time to warn Emir and Brody. You must go to them and alert Serena. Protect Lavender at all costs."

"No, Goddess Cora. You are in danger. I shall not leave you."

Over the last fourteen days, Brody, Emir, Serena, and Cora worked day and night to put safeguards against the crown. Lavender had been on bed rest for several days. Kyewicket had been her constant companion.

"Shush, we'll hide within this hollow tree." Once inside, Cora peeked to see the military approach. The full moon illuminated the army line that stretched beyond the hills.

Her fingers pressed into her temples as she used telepathy to signal her new friends about the impending danger.

Emir was the closest to where they had cast the mirroring spell.

"The royal guard is in the forest. They're heading toward the barrier near the meadow. Alert Brody and Serena. Kyewicket is with me." She paused, then lied, *"I'm sure the guard will not harm us."*

"Do not get caught," Emir replied. *"I will alert everyone and come to your aid."*

The foot soldiers stopped and lit torches.

"The Goddess Cora is here. Search the area," the commander shouted. "You— go to the king's tent. Inform him we are close to the witch's house. I see white chimney smoke."

Cora stilled.

She dared not breathe. She closed her eyes and concentrated on being invisible.

Kyewicket whispered, "The royal guard cannot see the smoke from Serena's. That's a deliberate redirection incantation to lure them away from the house."

"Kyewicket, please be quiet."

From her vantage point, she noticed the commander in charge, Orphic. His red eyes gleamed with hostility as he barked orders. His cruelty was legendary. He dismounted and came near their hiding spot.

Cora held her breath.

Orphic sneered. "I might not see you, but I smell you, witch."

Her fingernails bit into the palms of her hands.

Someone shouted, "King Valdoor is here."

Orphic spat on the ground and mumbled curses.

Her father flew in on his two-wheel flying chariot, surrounded by white lights embellished in gold. Cora didn't know who scared her the most, Orphic or the king.

The chariot came to a stop.

Orphic clicked his heels together and bowed. "Sire, your daughter is here. She is using a cloaking spell."

From her vantage point, her father, King Valdoor, wore battle colors, a regal blue tunic over black sleeves and trousers trimmed in gold with boots up to his knees. He exited the vehicle. He waved the commander away. "I'll find her."

"Cora, come out, dear." Her father's voice sounded as sweet as honey tasted, but she'd been stung by that bee before. A bit sterner, he said, "I will not harm you if you come out. However, your friends will suffer for it if you continue this game of hiding and seek."

He tapped on the hollow log. "Cora, work with me. I know you love your sister, but your allegiance is to me."

The king reached in to grab her by the throat, and Kyewicket went on full assault, clawing, biting, and hissing. Her father threw Kyewicket, who hit the hard ground with a thud.

She cried, "Stop, stop. Don't hurt my cat."

Kyewicket dematerialized.

Behind the mirrored barrier, Brody and Emir readied themselves for battle when Kyewicket appeared.

"Meow," the cat barely cried. "The king has Cora." Kyewicket passed out.

Brody cradled the feline in his arms. Tears formed in his eyes as he cast a healing spell over his furry friend. "Healing energies and blessings this night, cover my friend with pure white light, surround Kyewicket with your love and sight."

Emir placed his hand on Brody's shoulder. "Take him to the house. I will go for Cora. Lavender will need you in case they breach our boundaries."

Brody heaved a deep sigh, torn between fighting or protecting his loved ones. He had to protect Lavender first and foremost. "The royal guard will break through the barrier. You must come to the house when they do, even if they have Cora. It will take all of our abilities to fight them."

Emir bristled at his words. "I cannot leave Cora."

"You'll do her no good if they seize you, too. Be careful, my friend." Brody materialized inside Serena's house. He took the steps two at a time to the second floor and placed Kyewicket on a quilt in front of the fireplace.

Lavender thrashed on the bed.

His throat constricted, witnessing her pain.

Serena used a damp cloth to dab Lavender's forehead. "She's delirious. What happened to Kyewicket?"

Brody relayed the unfolding events. He urgently pleaded, "Can't you ease her pain?"

"No. I would only prolong Lavender's agony." She dipped the cloth into clear water, wrung it out, and then wiped down Lavender's arms. "Yaris is pulling away from Lavender. Her contractions are closer together. Once the baby's head crowns, Lavender and you shall be free of Yaris and Cetus."

Brody swallowed hard. "We don't have much time before the royal guard breaches the barrier. Any idea how long before the baby arrives?"

"Soon."

Lavender moaned, "Don't leave me, Brody." She reached for his hand, and he clasped it.

"I'm here, angel. I'm not going anywhere." He tried to stay calm, but his gut roiled with worry. He could do nothing to help Lavender but sit next to her on the bed.

"That's all I need," she whispered, her breathing labored.

Brody pushed the hair away from her face and kissed the back of her hand. She seemed to ease a little.

"Lavender, I need to check the baby's position. Okay?" Serena draped a white linen cloth over her legs.

Lavender took a deep breath and exhaled. "Whatever you need to do, I'm ready."

"The baby is in position. Can you push for me?"

Brody's head started swimming. "Push, honey."

Serena's hands went under the sheet.

Lavender's face turned ashen. Her lips trembled, and her voice quivered. "Something's happening."

Brody blinked several times. Lavender and Yaris's faces seemed to merge. He looked at his hand, and he had double vision. He shook his head. "Serena?"

Serena glanced up. "The baby's head is crowning. Push, Lavender."

Lavender screamed. Her fingernails bit into Brody's hands.

Wind wildly circled in the room. Raw heat engulfed Brody. Sweat poured off his brows.

He was being pulled apart from the inside out, and by the look on Lavender's face, so was she. The roiling in his gut would not stop.

The wood plank floors shook. Vibrations got louder, reaching a fever pitch. Bright light filled the room, nearly blinding him.

"The baby is coming." A smile lit Serena's face. "Yaris, my friend, you have a ...."

Lavender and Brody flew across the room with a loud whoosh. He smacked into the stone wall hard, knocking him out of breath.

Lavender reached for him, and he wrapped his arms around her.

He searched her face, her eyes. Lavender was back.

Drenched in sweat and trembling, they stood in unison.

Yaris held the baby in her arms. Cetus sat beside her and caressed her face with his hand.

Serena smiled, then looked at Brody and Lavender. "You did a wonderful thing today."

Yaris beamed at the swaddled infant.

Cetus said, "How can we ever thank you?" He kissed the top of Yaris's head.

Lavender moved toward the bed, and her eyes locked on the baby's face. "She has red hair. What will you call her?"

Yaris smiled. "We shall name her—Iris."

The past met her present.

Lavender's eyes rolled back as she hit the floor, and darkness followed.

"Ooh, my head hurts." Lavender opened her eyes while trying to sit up.

Brody scooped her into his arms and carried her to a tufted sitting chair.

She rubbed her temples. "Did I hear you correctly?" Lavender directed her question to Yaris, then looked at Serena.

"Yes, this is Iris, your grandmother."

"No, no, no—this cannot be happening." Lavender closed her eyes. Her hands gripped the armrest. "You brought us here, across the universe. For what? How could you deliberately use me, use us?" she yelled, then clenched her teeth.

With gentleness, Yaris answered, "Serena and I have been best friends most of our lives. I fell in love with Cetus, and Serena helped arrange for us to see each other. We knew my father wanted Cora to marry Cetus, but he loved me. I became pregnant out of wedlock. It meant certain death to Cetus, our baby, and me."

Cetus interjected, "We asked Serena for help. She is Yaris's half-sister."

"Time works differently here. Most beings in the cluster can live forever, but we're not immune to death." Serena straightened her back and lifted her chin. "My mother left me the shew stone. She was a powerful witch—the first of her kind. Yaris and Cetus asked me for help, so I consulted the crystal, and it led me to you, Lavender. Soon, Yaris will time travel to the Iron Age. She will find Hagatha and entrust the child to her care in exchange for magic." She looked at Lavender. "Did your mother tell you about the Celtic healers?"

From memory, Lavender recited the tale of her people. "We descended from the Celtic healers who fought the underworld with the divine powers of the Goddess of Light. Our leader, Dreena, passed down the knowledge and gifts to us. The Doanharts trained with the ancient ones. That's why we possess the sacred scrolls in our library. Wait, one minute. If Iris is a deity, how does Dreena fit in?"

"Dreena is Yaris and Cora's sister."

"Oh my God. That's right. My head is spinning. The men with long black robes, blackcaps, and long beards proclaimed the Celtic healers' magic came from the devil. The Goddess of Light, er well, Yaris, led the women away from wrath to the Pyrenees in France. Who are the men?"

Yaris interjected, "We believe they're minions of my father, King Valdoor, his brother, Odar, or maybe Cetus's family from Orion's Belt. We believe the men in black exist in your present time too."

"Serena didn't want to send for you, but the shew stone revealed that you and Brody are the Gate Keepers." Yaris shifted the sleeping infant to her other arm. "You will free magic not only in your world but the Universe. We manipulated our time and yours, so we must not fail."

"We're the Gate Keepers?" Brody asked.

Lavender raised a brow. "That's why we went to St. Lucian's. The Gate Keepers are supposed to lead me to my mom."

"And, you will find Peony," Serena said. "Soon, Yaris and Cetus will leave our realm to watch over Iris and your family. Yaris will live in Waytherlands. Cetus will reside in Elysian Fields." Serena stepped to the fireplace and checked Kyewicket's vitals. "My cat was a gift for Iris."

The cat purred, "I am fine." Serena placed him back on the quilt.

"Kyewicket belonged to you?" Lavender inquired.

"Yes." Serena nodded. "Look, we don't have much time."

Sprite materialized. "I'm here to take Lavender and Brody to the looking glass well. Queen Goldengrace is on the move."

"Our coup d'état is underway," Serena replied in a shaking voice, then rubbed the back of her neck. "If our plan succeeds, Queen Octavia will come to our aid from the south against King Valdoor. Queen Goldengrace will attack from the west. Emir, Cetus, and I will attack from the north. The river to the east will slow the king's army from retreating."

Brody interjected, "We will fight with you."

"No, you must warn Iris about Silver and Aster. It is her only chance at redemption. Otherwise, she will call on my mother, Urslina."

"Oh man, you're kidding me. Urslina?" Brody paced the floor. "The Queen of the Dark Night is your mother? I've been fighting her soldiers for over a century."

"The crystal shows that your future world is under a dark spell of deception by men in black robes. It does not reveal anything about Urslina. Magic is not the only thing at risk. Your world may lose the ability to make individual choices in life. Darkness is spreading far and wide."

"One thing leads to another." Lavender sighed heavily, stepped over to Serena at the fireplace, and rubbed Kyewicket ears. "We must trust you, Serena. How will we know if we made a difference by changing past events?"

"I'm counting on you. I'm counting on our descendants of magic to intercede and break the spells of deception. You and Brody together create an unstoppable form of magic. Lavender, you, and the rest of your family are born from demigods. You are divine, my dear. And we all tread on a thin veil of magic coalescing with time travel. What we do, we do for the greater good."

"What about the impending battle coming to your door?" Brody crossed his arms over his chest.

"I have watched King Valdoor's uncanny ability to inflect emotional abuse on his daughters for a long time, not to mention his subjects," Serena said. "Fear does strange things to one's soul. My sisters and I will no longer submit to his tyranny. We will not cower; instead, we choose to lift our voices and fight for freedom, even if it means death."

Rumblings from outside shook the house for a second time.

Serena pushed open the window. "Heavens above, Octavia has come through with the air fleet."

"Queen Goldengrace is advancing to the meadow as we speak." Sprite's wings fluttered. "Lavender and Brody must come with me now."

"The babe and I will go with Sprite, too. It is time." Yaris placed the infant on the bed. She caressed Cetus's face with the palm of her hand and then kissed him. "I'll take Iris and Kyewicket to Hagatha through the looking glass well. Cetus, you must stay and fight with Serena. We stick to the plan, then meet at the crossroads where Earth and Waytherlands intersect."

Cetus drew Yaris into his arms. "Please don't take any unnecessary risks. I will not survive without you."

"The crystal doesn't lie." Yaris kissed him lightly on his lips, then turned to Lavender and smiled. "Remember, Lavender, everything that's happened in your life has brought you to this moment in time. You are my blood. You have my power. Failure is not an option."

Lavender straightened her shoulders and lifted her chin. "I will do my best to succeed."

Brody took Lavender's hand. "Remind me again, how do we return to our time after our mission is complete?"

"After Yaris safely delivers Iris to Hagatha, she will guide them to France, and then she will leave the dagger, scrolls, and sculpture in the cave under St. Lucian's castle. The moment you touch any of the three items, you should return to the time whence you left."

Brody frowned. "The operative word is *should*."

Chapter 17

Battle in the Meadow

Cora remained captive in her father's tent. She repeatedly tried to break the chains with magic, but her father had used a binding spell to block her incantations.

The battle in the meadow raged for three long days. Cora agonized, not knowing if anyone she loved had been hurt or, worse, died. She heard bits and pieces from the different soldiers guarding her. The sisters of Pleiades held their own against King Valdoor's royal army.

Night fell, and a new guard brought her a plate of food and a mug of ale. He was young. For each bite he offered, Cora refused to eat. She would not eat or drink anything until she knew if Emir lived.

"Queen Octavia's southward advancing army has outflanked the king. A large battalion is retreating across the eastern river. The fighting is almost over." The young soldier fell to his knees before Cora. "Please have mercy on me, Goddess."

"If you'll undo my chains, I will forgive you."

The lad's lower lip quivered. "I do not have the key."

She screamed, "Father, let me go."

The flap to the tent opened. King Valdoor strode inside, his face covered with blood, his fine clothing dirty and torn. He yanked her from the chair, still bound in chains. The pain was excruciating. "You're coming with me."

"Where are you taking me?" she cried.

"Where your mother will never find you."

Queen Octavia materialized. Her hair was wild and standing on its ends, her crazed eyes pierced the king. "Take your hands off my daughter."

His grip tightened on Cora. "She's my daughter too. You've turned my progeny and subjects against me. You pledged allegiance to me, Octavia."

"You're solely responsible for the subjects following me, and not you. You are not the king I mated. Your greed and lust for power have overshadowed any good you've done in our realm." She pointed her wand toward him. Sparks flew from the tips. "Let Cora go, and you may leave this realm unharmed. You try and take her from me, and I will destroy you."

Emir appeared. His wingspan extended the width of the covered area. With one fluid move, he knocked the king off his feet, sending Cora flying toward her mother. The shackles on her wrists and ankles cut into her skin.

Emir shifted, then readied himself to fight the king. "You do not deserve Cora."

Her father released a harrowing cry as he attacked Emir. They locked into hand-to-hand combat, each grappling for position. They crashed onto her father's desk, then rolled onto the rug covering the ground. Grunts and moans accompanied each strike of their fists and feet.

"You're her father! Look what you've done to her." Emir deflected blows and counter-punches until he had the advantage and subdued the king.

Her father vanished.

The fae prince shouted, "I will come back for you," and flew out of the tent—his glorious wings a shimmering raiment of black, silver, and gold.

Queen Octavia helped Cora to her feet. "Let me see your hands."

"Father placed a spell on my chains."

"Your father's magic is no match for mine." Her wand barely touched the metal, and the shackles fell to the ground. She flicked her fingertips, and Cora's wrists and ankles healed instantly.

"What news of Yaris?" Cora asked, her heart pounding.

"She and the child have left the realm." Queen Octavia blinked away tears.

"Girl or a baby boy? And what of Cetus? Is he—well?" Cora bit her bottom lip nervously.

"Yaris has a girl. And well, Serena took Cetus back to her home to tend his wounds. I don't think they're life-threatening." Octavia tilted her head to the side. "Are you in love with Prince Emir?"

"I know little of love but being near Emir makes me happy. I'm so worried about him, and of course, you, too."

Queen Octavia sighed. "I remember feeling that way about Valdoor a long, long time ago. Would you like to come home with me?"

"I do not fit in at court, Mother." Cora placed her hands on her hips. "I want to stay in the forest."

"With Emir?"

"Yes, if he will have me."

Queen Octavia caressed Cora's cheek. "I've always wanted my daughters to be happy. I understood why Valdoor wanted the Orionnites treaty, but I never agreed to marry my children off to gain it. That is why Serena, Goldengrace, and I worked feverishly to take the throne from him. He may have disappeared, but I doubt it is the last we hear of him. Cetus will leave the realm as soon as he is able. He and Yaris will never return. The Orionnites want him and your sister dead."

Cora's eyes widened. "Where will they go?"

"To another realm, and one day you will visit, and perhaps, my children will carve out better lives for themselves in that place." Queen Octavia reached for the gold chain around her neck and placed it on Cora's. "This amulet will protect you wherever you go."

Cora hugged her mother tightly. "Thank you, Mother."

Yaris wore a dark brown tunic over a linen blouse cinched with a leather belt. She swaddled her infant with nettle fabric, made a sling over her shoulder, and carried Iris close to her chest. She chose comfortable leather boots and a plaid woolen cloak for warmth.

The intense fighting echoed during the day and stopped at night. Her mission was to save magic by crossing into another realm, a place called Earth.

Yaris, Lavender, and Brody would leave with Sprite.

She looked around Serena's one last time, then joined the others on the trail to Queen Goldengrace's secret room. She had never seen the looking glass well. The energies within would take them to another time and place.

She'd walk on a distant planet by nightfall. She wouldn't think about sacrificing Iris for the greater good. She couldn't think about the things she'd miss as the child grew. The crystal never lied, she kept reminding herself.

With every step of the journey, Yaris could feel the baby's heartbeat next to hers, and she smelled the sweetness of her breath. The bond between mother and child, while brief, would have a lasting impact on her for life.

Yaris had fallen in love with Cetus in these woods.

She imprinted the serenading birds, the crisp scented air of evergreens, and the spectacular array of wildflowers in every color, shape, and size.

Large trees offered nature's canopy. Variegated vines, roses, and blackberries grew wildly out of control. The thick, lush underbrush teemed with life.

Sprite's high-pitched staccato belted a lovely song in tune with the feathered creatures of the land.

Lavender and Brody's heads nearly touched, their whispers not decipherable, but the love between them was undeniable.

Yaris was proud of her, so willing to do what was right, regardless of the consequences. And her warlock, Brody, had followed Lavender through time, not knowing if they would ever return home.

True love was a gift and a blessing from The Creator.

Climbing the last hill, Sprite stopped. "Keep moving through the village. Do not make eye contact. Some of the locals were against the war with King Valdoor. Most fae loves a good brawl. Fighting's in our blood. Rumors are circulating about several community members intending on breaking King Odar out from the dungeon."

"And then there's Queen Goldengrace." Sprite hovered near Lavender. "She's sending other magical beings to Earth—an exploration to the New World for our species' survival. A lot of infighting on who's going and who's staying."

"Why would the queen release such information?" Brody asked. "Surely, she knows with so much going on—the whole place is a tinder box of violence."

Quietly, they entered the community near the stables. Faerie horses were lean and strong, and flew fast on the wings of the wind. A white stallion strained his neck in one stall. He shook his head, his nostrils flared, and fire lit in his eyes.

Yaris extended one arm, palm up. The horse slept. They continued along the crushed-stone pathway. Fire pits and torches lit the area.

One table of locals played card games, and another group of fae sang around the fire, drinking mugs of ale between verses.

Yaris felt no animosity here. The night brought with it a chill in the air. She covered the sleeping baby with part of her cloak.

Near the pedestrian bridge, a muscular fae forged a warrior's sword from the blazing pit.

They slid by unnoticed.

The stone path transitioned into a grass walkway. The heady scent of flowers indicated they were close to the castle. Yaris followed the group into an underground tunnel. The dank smell of moist dirt settled on the bluestone walls.

They stopped abruptly at a dead end.

Sprite withdrew her wand and cast a spell. A hidden door appeared, then opened. She waved them in and sealed the entrance behind her.

Yaris, Lavender, and Brody traveled down spiraling stone stairs.

With excitement, Sprite said, "See the pulsating blue light? We're almost there."

On the last step, the baby woke. "I must feed her before we travel." Yaris sat on a white marble bench between two Cypress trees—several dotted within the room's interior with no ceiling.

The babe latched onto her right breast with ferocity. She caressed Iris's soft red hair. She pushed the raw emotion away that strangled her with grief.

How can I give her up?

It's Time to Travel

The room seemed to come alive as Lavender edged toward what looked like an in-ground hot tub surrounded by four Doric columns. Swirls of blues, greens, and white light churned counterclockwise. A large sculpture of Queen Goldengrace rested behind the looking glass well.

Lavender's stomach dipped. She and Brody had arrived in the Pleiades realm unexpectedly via the Goddess sculpture—entering a time well scared her.

"Look under the omphalos stone box." Sprite fluttered excitedly.

Lavender lifted the lid. Several various gems and stones lay on royal blue velvet fabric. "Rubies are stones of passion. They have a grounding effect. Lodestone for protection, tektites are fragments from leftover meteorites used for casting spells."

"Tektites navigate time travel," Sprite said. "Each of you will take one, place it in the stringed pouch, and then tie it to your wrist, including the child. Then, Lavender and Brody, think of the specific place in time that you agreed on at Serena's. Engrain the date, the time of day, and the place. Once you are ready, lock your arms together, then step into the looking glass well."

Yaris looked at Sprite and sighed. "I have the coordinates for our journey." She placed the babe on her shoulder and gently rubbed Iris's back until she belched. Then, Yaris took a cloth from her bag and diapered the infant. She stood and went to Lavender. She kissed each cheek and said, "I will see you again." Yaris hugged Brody. "Take care of our girl."

Brody swiped a tear from his eye. "Something down here is making my eyes water."

"Mine too, sweetie." Lavender smiled and gently touched the baby's head. "I'm glad we spent time together, Yaris. My prayers are with us all."

Yaris wrapped her arms around the infant. Without looking back, she dropped into the spinning matter, then disappeared.

Lavender swallowed hard. "Yaris is so brave. I'm terrified."

"I love you with all of my heart." Brody caressed her face. "I regret nothing if I take my last breath today, but the crystal doesn't lie, as Yaris stated. Let's do this thing."

Lavender nodded and locked arms with Brody. "Thank you, Sprite."

Together they jumped into the looking glass well.

Foam-like matter formed around them like warm silicone or slimy goo. Prisms of colored particles manipulated the geometry of time and space. They landed at Hagatha's chateau near the greenhouse.

Hagatha's Chateau
Summer 1885

"Ugh! How gross was that?' Lavender shivered, then came to her feet in a bed of low-lying foliage and flowers. "Hagatha has always maintained such picturesque grounds. Look at those old trees next to the pond. I forgot how elegant the place looked in the summer."

"That was some nasty-feeling gooey stuff. It went up my nose." Brody sneezed and coughed, then brushed himself off and perused the landscaping. "Oh, yeah. I remember this place." He inspected Lavender. "Well, at least, we appear to be in one piece."

"Gosh, Brody, it's been a hundred and thirty years since I've been inside the glasshouse." She stepped inside and called out, "Anyone in here?" Silence. "Whew. I need a few minutes to gather my thoughts. My brain is fuzzy." Her fingers traced the ledge that held various specimens in pots. Growing along the curved arch was the most spectacular coral-colored bougainvillea.

"Wow, a paradise of color, and the fragrance is sublime," she added. "Hagatha's towering palms and oleanders put mine to shame. Thankfully, the place is far from the main house and encircled by the kitchen's garden walls, so hopefully, no one saw us."

Lavender snapped her fingers and transformed her attire into a plaid traveling dress of the day. "What do you think? I think it's the style of the late 1880s."

"Mighty fine, woman." Brody's grin went wide. His hands traveled over her tight bodice, then slid down the low bustle. "Sets off your figure for sure. I want you so bad it hurts."

"Later, I promise. We need to scope the place out and plan on how to talk with Grams. I wonder if Mom is here."

"Don't go soft on me. We can't cause any ripples in time. Or as few as possible anyway." With a wave of his hand, he donned military garb French-inspired from the war against the Prussians. "Seems like I remember wearing a uniform similar to this one." He turned around and asked, "Well?"

"I am not a fan of red epaulets. And you weren't in the French army."

"No, you're right. How about this?" Brody changed into a tan cut-away jacket with a pair of patterned trousers, a royal blue shirt, matching cuffs, and a white collar.

"Now that's more like it—the spats round the whole outfit. Oh, I sort of miss those days when the public put more effort into appearances. Although, I do not miss corsets."

"Do we wait until dark or inch our way to the main house?" Brody inquired.

Lavender opened the door and stepped outside—her hands went over her mouth.

"Miss Doanhart? Pardon me, Miss Lavender Doanhart."

She slammed the door shut.

"Good grief. It's you, er, well, the *past* you coming this way. I don't remember meeting you in the glasshouse." She glanced over her shoulder. "Hide, back there in the palms. And for God's sake, don't say anything."

Brody frowned but followed her instructions.

Lavender grabbed a gathering basket, then magicked garden gloves and trimmers then stepped over to the roses.

Her heart hammered.

The door opened slowly.

The *past* Brody entered tentatively. "Excuse me, Miss Doanhart. I noticed you on my way to the stables and wondered if I ..." He stopped mid-sentence, staring at her with hunger in his eyes.

Lord, give me strength.

She casually lifted her chin. "Yes?"

He took off his top hat and rubbed the rim. "Again, pardon my intrusion, Miss Doanhart. I thought you were in Paris." His eyes roamed her body, then landed on her lips. He swallowed hard.

"I've returned." She thought it best to say as little as possible.

He took a step toward her, searching her eyes. "You look different."

Drats, she forgot to put her hair up.

Lavender slowly took off her gloves. "In a good way, I trust."

His breathing labored. "Forgive me for my impertinence, but you are most ravishing this afternoon." He reached out and touched her hair. "I've never seen your hair down." His voice dropped an octave, hoarse like a lover's whisper.

Her pulse thundered through her veins. Her heart leaped as he took her hand into his. Warmth pooled in her loins.

Brody was the man she loved, still loved with all her heart. She would spend the next century with him, loving him. But this Brody standing before her was different. It would be years before Lavender ran into the meadow at Hant Hollow and kissed him.

Paradox repeated in her mind.

Lavender took a step back and leaned against the worktable. "Captain Whitmore, compose yourself." Somehow her voice remained steady and calm.

Suddenly, *past* Brody slipped his hand to her nape. His lips next to her ear, he crooned, "Lavender."

Jesus, Mary, & Joseph.

She heard rustling in the back. She had to stop. Any minute, her Brody would storm to rescue her from himself.

Lavender pushed *him* away. "Freeze." The *past* Brody immobilized.

Present Brody stormed toward her. "That lousy bastard."

"Calm down. It is you, after all." She released a sigh. "No harm, no foul."

"Bullshit."

She touched the side of his face, then she went on her tiptoes and kissed him.

His features softened.

"I will give him a memory wipe." She waved her hand in front of the frozen Brody. She turned and said, "Let's hide and see if it works."

They went to the back of the glasshouse and hid in the palms.

Lavender snapped her fingers.

Past Brody stood without moving for a minute, then scratched his head. He looked around and slowly exited the glasshouse, shaking his head.

Lavender relaxed against her Brody. "That was too close for comfort. But it's kind of nice seeing that you were attracted to me way back when."

He cupped her face with his hands. "I fell in love with you way back when. Seeing myself with you, I remember the encounter. Why were you in Paris?"

"I haven't the faintest idea." She whirled her finger, and a blanket appeared next to the fruit wall. "Let's wait until dark. We'll make our way to the main house through the kitchen."

Brody sat on the blanket. "We are going to have to wipe anyone's memory that sees us here, except Iris. I wondered if Serena is living here. She mentioned it briefly."

She joined him on the floor and leaned against his shoulder. "I agree. I dread, yet look forward to, seeing Grams. She was fun in France. What were you doing at Hagatha's anyway?"

He wrapped his arm around her. "Hm. That was a long time ago. I met with Hagatha several times over the years—before us."

"What do you mean you met her?"

"Well, we went to social gatherings together."

With a raised brow, she asked, "And?"

"I never had sex with Hagatha. But she was lovely and well-connected. I enjoyed her company, and she introduced me to Carlton and his father. Carlton and I became fast friends. He was instrumental in my promotion in the military ranks."

"Good. Hagatha is a pill." Lavender yawned.

"Rest, my love. We'll need all our energy to get through the night, and if all goes well, tomorrow we return home."

Brody moved his fingers on his right hand in a circular motion. "Shield us from the view of others, protect us with your light, wake us up at first signs of night."

Lavender nudged into the crook of his neck, and Brody rested his cheek on the top of her head. "I love you."

He whispered, "I love you more."

"I love you most." She giggled.

Chapter 18

Celtic Village

Yaris and baby Iris landed in a cave close to Hagatha's village. She was preoccupied with protecting the child from noticing anything out of the ordinary during the transition of realms. After arriving, she checked Iris for any noticeable changes in her health. Nothing seemed amiss. The baby smiled.

"Lovely child, I'll watch over you. I promise." Her heart sank. "I hope you'll forgive me one day and understand the significance of your sacrifice for new world magic. Hagatha and her coven need you. Black-robed men will arrive soon."

They exited the cave.

The sun rose over the mountain peaks. She watched below as the sea lapped gently against the sandy shoreline. She inhaled and exhaled the briny scent. The water, the wave, and this planet's sun had a soothing effect on her soul.

Earth was not so different from home.

Yaris walked upward, climbing a well-trodden path until the sun was directly overhead.

A hill fort came into view not too far in the distance, surrounded by a maze of ditches and ramps. She and Iris made their way to the village. Before entering, she gazed through the main gate. Yaris changed into more appropriate attire. Then she walked inside without anyone stopping them.

In the pasture, several farmers tended the livestock consisting of cows, sheep, and pigs. The blacksmith was hard at work lifting his sledgehammer, then pounding the metal with echoing pings, creating a rhythmic tune along with the flame's hiss.

She did not see Hagatha with the women curing meat.

Several looked her way and frowned. Yaris couldn't hear what they said. She sensed their distrust or disgust, maybe both—their smudged faces and clothing were covered in soot.

Hunters gathered near the pits. They stared but didn't approach her.

Toward the back of the settlement, she found a large roundhouse made with stone walls. Most dwellings were made of woven sticks, mud, and logs with thatched cone-shaped roofs with fire holes at the top.

On one side of the dwelling, a woman pulled strands of linen off flax's stems to weave into clothing more than likely.

Yaris found Hagatha working in a garden on her hands and knees with two other women.

Hagatha stood, then used her hand to shield the sun from her eyes. "Do you speak Gaelic?" Her dialect merged between old English and Gaul.

Yaris understood her and replicated her speech pattern. "A little. May I sit?"

"Come into my house. I'll fix you a cup of tea. How old is the bairn?" Hagatha swiped her hands on her long apron dress.

"Newly born." Yaris ducked beneath the thatched canopy, following Hagatha through a willow door.

The scent of woodsmoke and meat hit Yaris's nostrils on entering the roundhouse. She was astonished at the neatness. There was a carved oak bed with layers of coverings. Straw and animal skins covered the clay floors. Some skins hung from the ceiling. There was a stone fire pit in the center with large pots hanging on a dual crane device.

Painted motifs of stars decorated the walls.

A long, rough-hewn table with wooden chairs was on the other side of the room. Shelves held various clay jars of special spices and herbs if the scents were any indication.

"From where you hail?" Hagatha asked as she prepared a concoction of root tea with some sort of brew. She handed Yaris a hand-made ceramic cup.

"Thank you." She took a seat in one of the chairs, rocking Iris in her arms.

"It'll put hair on your chest, but it warms the belly." Hagatha laughed. "May I take the child? She can rest on my bed."

Yaris nodded.

Hagatha held Iris in her arms. "What a beauty." She laid the infant down and returned to the table. "You might as well spit it out. I see there's something on your mind." Hagatha picked up her cup and sipped.

Yaris relayed the story that brought her to Hagatha. She summarized, hitting the high points on what the future held for the Celtic healers.

"Argh, you're a teller, I see." Hagatha slapped her knee.

With a flick of Yaris's wrist, the room filled with floating candles. "I'm telling you the truth." She snapped her fingers, and the Doanhart Book of Spells appeared on an ornate podium. She waved her hand, and the shew stone appeared. "I'm the Goddess of Light."

Hagatha's eyes widened. She fell to the ground prostrate before the Goddess.

"Rise, Hagatha. I do not mean to frighten you, but time is of the essence. I understand you're confused. Allow me to show you. Look into the crystal. See the past and glimpse the future." Wispy mist circled within the glass, then several memories of what transpired over the last fourteen days materialized. The image emerged of a local woman hanging from a tree.

Hagatha blinked several times as she watched the scenes unfold. She placed her hands on the table, palms down. "Holy Mother of God." Her face turned ashen. "You're a witch."

"No. I'm a Goddess." Yaris placed her hand over Hagatha's. "We must gather the other healers and leave. A group of men dressed in long black robes will arrive soon. They want to stamp out magic before it begins on this planet. They will charge the healers with witchcraft."

"The men are here." Hagatha's voice quivered. "They're with our chieftain. Who are they?" She glanced to the door, then back to Yaris. "Are we in danger?"

"Yes. I believe it's my father and members of his royal guard. He knows we seek to spread magic to your world. They will use religion to kill many healers over hundreds of years."

"Your father. He is a God too?"

"He's a vengeful God. Healers are more receptive to the possibility of magic. My daughter and I possess pure white magic. Our abilities are good. However, those men and men like them will accuse healers of sleeping with the devil. But do not believe them. That is a deception implanted by my father. Some men are weak-minded, and strong women threatened their power. They will seek to destroy you all." She narrowed her eyes at Hagatha. "I will save you if you raise my daughter."

Hagatha didn't speak for several minutes. "I-I can't have children. Why can't you keep her?" She glanced over her shoulder at Iris sleeping on the bed. "How will I care for a Goddess? What happens when I die?"

"If my father finds me with Iris, he will kill us on the spot. He doesn't know you. My sisters and I witnessed you raising my heirs through the shew stone. If you agree with my terms, you'll receive partial immortality, and so will your coven. You will live for thousands of years. However, you're not immune from accidents, malicious intent, or death. The Book of Spells will teach you as Iris grows, and her natural abilities will enhance your own. I will watch over you."

"How? Stay with us?"

"I cannot. It's the bargain I made to save my child and the one I love. You will be Iris's mother in every sense. You will prosper with her. And when she comes of age, Iris will conceive three daughters, and those daughters will bear three daughters. They will be your family, your tribe, your coven. You must also provide a haven for the other magical beings coming to the planet."

"What is a planet?" Hagatha asked. "Do they relate to the stars in heaven?"

"We don't have time for questions and answers. I know you just met me and have no reason to trust me, but you will prosper and possess much power if you do as I request. We must flee before my father finds us. And, Hagatha, the crystal I give you this day never lies."

"I will bring the healers here at once." Hagatha stood.

"I'll wait."

Yaris gathered her thoughts and began weaving a spell in her mind. The magic would transport them to the Pyrenees the place where she would create a home for her child and a village for the healers. Yaris knew her father would sense her presence once she uttered the powerful incantation. She must be quick.

She went to the bed where her infant slept. Oh, how she loved the child.

Yaris took a deep breath and exhaled. She resolved herself to the path set for her and her descendants.

The door opened.

Hagatha ushered in a group of terrified, shivering women into the roundhouse. "These are our healers, Tabitha, Hidee, the twins, Naola and Etoil. Then there's Claudia and Thel."

Claudia asked, "Don't we get to tell our kin?"

"Do you want to live or tell your kin and die?" Yaris stood with her hands planted on her hips.

"We don't know this woman," Thel said.

"Hush," Hagatha replied. "I have seen the truth. Do you trust me?"

One after the other nodded.

Yaris gave Hagatha the nettle fabric and placed the infant within the sling. "Gather in a circle around the fire. Grip the person next to you by the inner forearm."

The women complied.

The sound of a carnyx reverberated as the voices of an angry mob approached outside.

"They're coming to kill us." Hidee blinked rapidly.

Naola shook her head. "Oh, Lord. The war horn's blowing."

"Urslina isn't here," cried Tabitha. "We must save her."

"Urslina brought the black-robed men to your village," Yaris snapped.

"No," Thel said, "Urslina is one of us."

"You may stay or leave. If that's your choice, release yourself from the group, or prepare yourself to travel." She narrowed her eyes at Thel, but none of the healers left the circle.

Yaris raised her arms. "I call on the Earth, our roots. I call on the Air, our life force. I call on Water for our intuition. I call on Fire for transformation." A gusty wind swirled around them. The fire flames shot through the hole in the roof.

The healers' grip tightened; their clothing ripped during the transition. The physical and the supernatural worlds merged.

Blue light energy fields shot forth from Yaris's body and surrounded the coven with a protective shield as King Valdoor burst through the door.

"Witches!" The king's eyes locked onto Yaris's. "Satan is here."

"Beware of wolves in sheep's clothing," Yaris shouted, then their coven vanished from the king's sight, and they reappeared within the forest of the Pyrenees.

The women fell out onto the ground, wailing and weeping.

Tabitha placed her hand over her heart. "What have we done?"

"He called her Satan." Thel pointed at Yaris.

"What is a witch?" Hidee asked.

Hagatha uncovered the nettle fabric. "There, there, wee one." Baby Iris babbled with a grin.

Yaris came to her feet.

She opened her hand, and a golden staff appeared. She slammed it on the ground, and each woman in the newly formed coven came to attention. "I am the Goddess of Light." She started with Hagatha then pointed to each one. "A new dawn. A new heart. The Doanhart Coven shall never part."

"In exchange for magic, I give this land to you, each of you will pledge alliance to light, pure magic. Never surrender that light, or I shall banish you from this group. You swear an oath to protect Iris and guide her with all righteousness. And never forget, those men in the town will hunt you from now until the end of eternity. Together we stand, divided we fall."

Yaris held out one hand, palm down. Hagatha placed her hand on top, then each woman, one by one, did the same. Each one pledged fealty to the light.

Yaris withdrew and turned. She raised her hands and watched Hagatha's home come into being, and by the next sunrise, Yaris had completed the healer's village.

She put each member to work.

Hidee, the hunter.

Thel, weaver of thread.

Naola and Etoil, the farmers.

Claudia, the smithy.

Tabitha, the brewer

Hagatha, leader and teacher of magic.

Yaris lived with the healers and Iris for a time. She left before Iris entered the age of reasoning. Yaris said her goodbyes, then made her way to the cave of St. Lucian's. There she buried the Dagger of Destiny, the Prophetic Scroll, and the Goddess Sculpture.

Yaris closed her eyes and conjured Waytherlands, a place where the supernatural and physical planes meet. A perfect world for all magical beings free from plots, authoritarian leaders, and evil of any kind. It was fashioned like the Pleiades without the formality of court.

In Waytherlands, each being, regardless of birth or circumstance, was equal in station. Any being that dared try to enter her haven with nefarious deeds in mind would evaporate into the ether.

Waytherlands opened the door to the imagination. Majestic waterfalls, pristine beaches, and turquoise seas. Lakes, mountains, and plains. A virtual paradise with ease of mobility with no heavy rain, no winter storms, or harsh winds. She liked a steady drizzle of rain, the kind that lulled her to sleep.

She wanted each to be free to create their own home and habitat and stay compatible with everyone who sought refuge within its borders.

Yaris created a Library of Magic in the metropolis center, which held copies of manuscripts, scrolls, and books she had memorized during her Pleiadean training. She left room for area growth with varying shops to keep busy, but work was not a prerequisite to entering her realm. Her world included crystals and several looking glass wells to intervene in the lives of those she loved.

Lastly, she carved out a particular section in the world for her own devisement—a place where she hoped to build a life with Cetus when he wasn't helping magical beings cross over to Elysian Fields.

Yaris waited for Cetus and waited for him. He never entered Waytherlands. Eons later, she understood why.

Chapter 19

Cora burst through Serena's door in a panic. "Is Emir here?"

Serena tended to Cetus as he lay on a makeshift bed near the fireplace. "No. I thought he went to save you."

"He fought the king for me, and when Father fled, Emir went after him. Queen Goldengrace, Mother, and I searched for him to no avail. Please, Serena, ask the shew stone." Wringing her hands, she said, "I have a sinking feeling something is dreadfully wrong."

Serena finished bandaging Cetus's hand. "Try and drink the Camellia sinensis. It will help with the inflammation." She stood and squeezed Cora's hand. "Inhale and exhale slowly before you pass out. Let's go into the kitchen. I'll ask for help." She took the crystal from the shelf, removed the velvet sleeve, and placed it on the table.

"We lost a lot of good folks today." Serena released a heavy sigh. "The forest weeps for the beings." She closed her eyes, her hands flat on the table. After what seemed like an eternity, Serena stared into the glass. Wisps of mist circled. Her eyes widened. "Stay calm, Cora."

"How can I stay calm? What do you see?"

"Emir is on the other side of the river. Let me grab my medicinal herbs, and we'll go to him."

"What's happened to him?" Cora's throat constricted. "Tell me, or I'll go mad."

"He's nailed to a tree," Serena paused and added, "His wings are charred."

Cora's nostrils flared. "I will kill the king for this. I swear by all that's holy." The rage within her boiled, and only her father's blood would silence it.

"Release the rage. It doesn't do him or you any good. We must fly to Emir."

"I'm coming with you." Cetus tried to stand but fell back onto the bed.

In two strides, Serena was at his side. "We will find Emir. The wound near your heart can kill you, Cetus. Promise to stay put."

"King Valdoor will pay for the bloodshed today, I swear it." His breathing labored. His jaw clenched.

"I vow it," Cora added. She and Serena left the house and took to the sky.

They flew low over the east river, searching for any sign of Emir. They descended into a grove of sequoias—waning sunlight filtered through the lofty branches.

Cora spotted Emir in one of the giant trees.

His head lolled forward. His once glorious wings burned—nails went through his wrists. The king had beaten him beyond recognition.

Her heart lurched.

Was Emir alive?

Serena and Cora hovered in front of him.

She whispered, "Emir, it's Cora. Oh, Emir, I'm so sorry."

He didn't speak.

"We must remove the nails." Cora glanced at Serena.

"Give me a minute. I'm thinking. He could bleed out if we don't do this right." Serena chanted, "Mighty sequoia trees, come to our aid, give Emir the strength he badly needs."

Wind swept through the grove. The nearby branches moved with fluidity.

Orbs of light surrounded them as The Black Flame Fae materialized. They joined in with Serena's spell.

Emir slowly raised his head. His eyes locked with Cora's.

"I'm here, my love. We're going to save you," Cora said. "Please fight, Emir. Don't leave me."

The fae attached themselves to the massive tree one by one—it seemed to pulse and glow. Cora surmised each one gave Emir a part of their life force.

Two faeries, Dune and Stone, stayed close to Emir, one on each side.

Serena turned to Dune and Stone. "When we remove the nails, support Emir."

They nodded in agreement.

Serena formed a ball of blue-violet energy. She turned to Cora. "You remove the nail swiftly from his right wrist."

Cora pressed her lips together as powerful, healing energies went into her fingertips. She ripped the metal from Emir's right wrist, then his left one.

His screams echoed in the forest.

Serena quickly applied the light to his wounds while Dune and Stone supported Emir. Emir passed out.

"Dune, Stone, take him to the river. The water will cleanse his wings. From there, we will go to my house."

The sun descended behind the mountain. It was not dark, though. The Black Flame Faeries lit the sky with what seemed like a thousand twinkling stars.

Queen Goldengrace swooped in, releasing glittering magic dust turning the river gold. She entered the water and took Emir from Dune and Stone, then lifted her chin—looking to the sky. "Heal my son with your light, heal his injuries with your might, heal my son, O Creator of light, help Emir to fight." The valley echoed as the faeries joined her.

Cora watched Emir transform from bloodied, beaten, and burned into the most majestic being in her world. His mother released him, and then Emir strode out of the water.

The Black Flame Fae cheered with thanksgiving.

Emir's beautiful wings jutted upward, fully restored.

His body glistened in the moonlight. His eyes searched for Cora, and she went to him. Cora would love him for the rest of her life.

Hagatha's Chateau, 1885

"Wake up, Brody." Lavender nudged him. "You snore like an elephant in heat."

"Huh, what?" He woke swinging his fists.

She ducked. "You nearly hit me."

"Sorry, love. Too many years of battle. You never know when someone is on the attack. Did I hurt you?"

The inky sky was visible from the glasshouse. Brilliant stars twinkled with no clouds in sight.

"No, I'm fine. I'm familiar with your sleeping habits." She pointed to Hagatha's house. "I forgot how gas lamps cast such a buttery glow. Anyhoo, Hagatha has outdoor post lights. We should teleport into the kitchen just in case someone mistakes us for burglars."

Brody came to his feet and stretched. "Okay, we teleport into the kitchen, then what?"

"We'll listen to make sure Hagatha isn't throwing a soiree. If not, we'll start with Iris's room, the library, then the solarium. To the best of my memory, she was a creature of habit. Same daily routines. I wonder what time it is?"

"Not a clue, but I'm starving." Brody's stomach growled.

"I am too. We can eat later. Oh, Brody, I miss Rockvale. I miss the Red Rose, and I miss Hant Hollow. Max, Jasmine, and Aunt Isidore are probably worried sick."

"We can't get emotional, sweetheart. We need to think clearly." His hand slid over the back of her head, and he kissed her forehead.

"True. Grab my hands."

He took her hands. "On the count of three."

She nodded. "One. Two."

"Three," Brody said.

They materialized in the kitchen. Someone stood at the basin, peering out the window. The walnut plank floor creaked. Someone turned.

Serena gasped. "Oh, thank God. I was wondering when you guys would show up. I thought I had the time period miscalculated." She hugged Lavender and took a step back.

"Serena?"

She nodded.

"Tell us everything. What happened after we left? Did we win? How are Cora and Emir? Any news of Yaris and Cetus?"

"I'll go into detail after everyone goes to bed. But for now, you and Brody follow me. Iris is reading in the library. Hagatha is entertaining in the dining room, which should give us some cushion if Iris pitches a fit."

"What do I say? How do I start?" Lavender asked.

"Just start with; we come to you from the future." Brody chuckled, and she elbowed him in the gut. "Ouchy. Can't a guy have a little fun?"

"No." Lavender and Serena answered in unison.

Serena lit a lantern. "This way."

"Into the pantry?" Lavender inquired.

"Secret passage." They followed her. Serena opened a small door hidden on the back wall.

Growing up at Hagatha's, Lavender and Jasmine had searched every nook and cranny, or so she thought. She was clueless about the passageway. It was roughly ten feet high by five feet wide, surrounded by stone walls.

A rat scurried in front of Lavender, and she bit the back of her hand not to scream.

They went along a narrow path. Lavender reached for Brody's hand.

"Don't be afraid," he assured her. "I'm right behind you,"

"It's silly, but I feel like I'm in an episode of *Dark Shadows*."

Serena chimed in, "We're almost there. Watch out for the low beam. Don't bump your heads." She pulled on a sconce, and they entered through another secret door to the library.

In the late nineteenth century, the room had richly carved rosewood bookshelves. Red velvet drapes hung next to the open window overlooking the property. The scent of varnish and leather filled Lavender's nostrils.

The open ceiling with exposed timber made the room seem bigger. Oriental rugs covered parquet floors—dark wood wainscoting with chair rails covered the walls. An ornate floral screen was placed in front of the summer hearth. Several cut-glass gas lamps with blue crystal prisms lit the room.

Curled into a leather chair, Iris was so engrossed in reading that she didn't hear them.

Lavender stepped forward and coughed to get her attention.

Iris straightened, then frowned. "I thought you were in Paris." She glanced at Brody. "Why are you back?"

Serena said, "Iris, we must speak with you with the utmost urgency." She prattled on about Iris's origins and the catastrophe which loomed ahead.

"I believe you've had too much sherry, Serena." Iris placed her book on a marble-top rosewood side table.

Lavender went to her grandmother and knelt before her. She took Iris's hands and searched her eyes. "We're serious, Grams. If you send Silver and Aster to America alone, they will die. Men from the local town will kill them. You'll call on Urslina, which makes you go over to the dark side of magic. Eventually, it tears our family apart. I'm not in Paris because Brody and I come from the twenty-first century. We have traveled far and endured much to save you. A battle between light and dark magic erupts, and The Shadows take you and Mom into the abyss. We search for you and stumble onto a sculpture that takes us back in time. Please, please wait until we can all go to America together."

"I've been reading *Alice's Adventures in Wonderland*." Iris took a deep breath. "I'm not sure I believe what you're saying, but I see you do."

"Lavender speaks the truth. She and Brody cannot stay here long. We've conspired to arrive here at this interval in your life," Serena said. "We risk what is called a grandfather paradox. For example, if I travel back in time and kill Peony in her infancy, Lavender will cease to exist."

Serena paced the room. "By changing your decision regarding Silver and Aster's travel arrangement, we change future events for the better, we hope. We can't say for sure we're doing the right thing, but this decision changes your life's trajectory in a bad way. Your decision now may be your only chance for redemption in the future."

Iris stood. "You're telling me that I am the daughter of the Goddess of Light and The Lord Darkness?"

"Yes, Grams."

"Poppycock." Iris turned to Brody. "So, you are from the future too? It seems odd that you were here earlier today. Is this some kind of ruse?"

"It's not a ruse. You saw the past me," Brody replied. "We almost ran into him outside. Look, Iris, we've gone through so much to get here. You open your veins the night of the battle that destroys the Doanhart Coven. Your father, The Lord Darkness, takes you with him to the underworld. We believe Peony is in purgatory, neither alive nor dead."

Iris clenched and unclenched her fists. "Maybe we shouldn't go to America at all."

Lavender began to panic. Her life was in America. She fell in love with Brody in Hant Hollow. She turned to Serena for help.

"Iris, the Doanhart Coven accomplishes many things in America. Good and bad. Only you can make this decision. I cannot sway you either way. But I will add, there is great evil in this world. I believe your grandfather, King Valdoor, searches for the Goddess of Light, and The Lord Darkness. He's intent on killing them. From what we have gathered to date, he rules the Black-Robed men, and Urslina has aligned with him to overthrow the Mage Alliance you help create."

Iris frowned. "There is something else you're not telling me. What is it?"

"Grams, after Silver and Aster die, you become a different person. Unseen forces of good and evil battle for your soul. If you change this one decision, it may save you and my mother." Lavender sighed. "We love Hant Hollow. We build a good life there. We love

America with all her warts. It is the one place on Earth that gives the whole planet hope. We are a part of that hope."

Someone knocked on the library door.

"We must go." Lavender kissed Iris's cheek. "We can't get caught here. I know whatever you decide, it will be for the best."

Brody took Lavender's hand. "You have a wonderful family, Iris. I love your grand-daughter very much."

"We will travel to a portal which sends us to present day," Serena said. "I pray we see you there, Iris. Thank you for listening without judgment."

Tears rolled down Iris's cheeks. "I love my family. I will do what I must to protect them."

Lavender smiled. "I know. That's why we're here."

She, Brody, and Serena left through the secret passage.

Lavender wanted to look back at Iris but kept moving forward.

Only time would tell if they made the right decision.

Chapter 20

Going Home

Lavender and Brody munched on homemade bread, cheese, and apples while riding in Serena's carriage. Memories of summer's past came back to Lavender suddenly. Those free-spirit days of doing whatever she felt like without conforming to rules or ideologies. She used to stay up all night at balls and small get-togethers, drinking until dawn, and even sometimes stripping off her clothes for a dip in a fountain or running naked in the woods. She always connected deeply with the Earth and its creatures.

She'd been a hopeless flirt. Not necessarily superficial, she appreciated any healthy and somewhat muscular male regardless, if they were wizards, werewolves, or vampires, and occasionally, a delightful human.

All that changed when she fell in love with Brody. From the first time she kissed him, the stars aligned. She was at home with Brody, and even though they disagreed from time to time, their chemistry together just clicked.

When the Doanhart Coven split, Lavender changed. Too much had happened in her life.

But traveling along the rough and rocky terrain, the wildness inside of her very soul begged to come out. She supposed that girl still existed and maybe needed a little dusting off.

By the time they reached the Abellio trail, the sun had peeked over the mountain with pastel pink, orange, and golden hues merging with the blue-gray skies. The rugged, untamed Pyrenees made travel treacherous in the nineteenth century, but the sublime landscapes still inspired her.

Lavender said, "I hope we can find the entrance to the cave. I don't think monks find it until the restoration."

"Not to worry. We don't have to travel to the castle," Serena replied. "I found another entry point just around the next bend."

Brody stored the leftover food under the black cushioned seat. "I'll tell you. I'm somewhat apprehensive, not knowing if we made a positive difference on our mission."

"We'll know soon enough."

Charles, the Stealth driving the carriage, came to a stop. He jumped down and opened the passenger door. "I will accompany you to the cave."

"No need." Serena held Charles's hand, stepping out onto the ground. "Thank you, my dear." She waited for Lavender and Brody to exit, then said, "We need to change clothes." Snapping her fingers, Serena appeared in hiking attire and combat boots. "Hopefully, we'll arrive in the same season. If not, we can change when we get there. Remember that the timeline may reveal differences, so brace yourselves."

Lavender changed into similar attire.

Brody opted for combat fatigues. "I'm hoping for the best but preparing for the worst."

Lavender didn't reply. She was too nervous.

"Well, onward we go. I can't stand the suspense." Serena followed a cattle path snaking down a sloping hillside.

Lavender and Brody traveled close behind her. She nearly slipped on a loose rock, but Brody grabbed her arm.

The farther they went into the mountains, the lusher the flora. Sun dappled through the trees as it rose into the midday sky. The wilderness held a heavy scent of evergreen, wood, and wet rock. The opening of the cave came into view.

Lavender's stomach dipped.

Time travel was scary. She prayed they didn't wind up in the Paleolithic era.

Serena stopped and magicked headgear with flashlights. "It's very dark once the light of the entrance fades. With any luck, we'll arrive at the spot Yaris left the divine relics in about thirty minutes. Stay close together."

"Why can't we just teleport to the spot?" Brody asked.

"Too many twists and turns, not to mention gigantic stalactites that could impale us."

"We're close. I hear the buzzing in my ears, the same sound when we first traveled. Do I hear rushing water?" asked Lavender.

"A powerful stream runs through the cave," Serena said. "I've heard there's even a waterfall, but I didn't see it when I searched a few days ago. Oh, and don't talk unless you need to. We don't want falling rocks to crush us."

Lavender and Brody replied in unison, "Agreed."

The flashlights offered some visibility. Navigating the cave required acrobatic balance, and Lavender nearly busted her behind several times. Then, something quite spectacular happened. Several multi-colored lights started pinging off the limestone walls.

Could it be the Black Flame Fae?

Faeries resided in the area. Lavender and Brody had witnessed them driving to St. Lucian's.

Her heart raced. She turned to Brody and used telepathy. *Do you see what I see?*

Yes. I see them.

The fae appeared as orbs of light and created a road to the relics.

In a low voice, Serena said, "We're here."

Sprite materialized in front of Lavender. "We have gifts for your travel." She took out a gold pouch and handed Lavender, Brody, and Serena bracelets with black tourmaline, white quartz, amethyst, and jasper.

Lavender glanced at Brody with tears in her eyes. "Your bracelet. They've made your bracelet." She turned to Sprite. "You're so kind. How can we ever thank you for helping us? I trust all is well in the Pleiades?"

"All's well, milady." Sprite bowed.

"Good." Lavender tilted her head to the side. "Will we ever see you again?"

"I am traveling with you. So you may count on it." Sprite giggled.

"You're most gracious." Brody kissed Sprite's cheek.

Serena extended her hands out, palms up. "It's now or never."

Lavender wrapped her arms around Brody's neck. "Let's go home."

"I'm all in, love." He circled Lavender's waist. "Let's rock."

St. Lucian's Present Day

Brody jerked awake in pain, sitting in a metal chair with his wrists tied securely behind his back. Barbwire bit into his bloodied chest. He tasted copper. He couldn't see out of his right eye and could barely see out of his left.

One room. No windows. One keyless light. But it was clear, that King Valdoor leaned against a concrete wall with his arms crossed over his chest.

"Brody Whitmore, Hand to the Regent. You are one tough bastard." The smirk on the king's face relayed he enjoyed the torture he inflicted. "Tell me what you remember."

What do I remember?

He, Lavender, and Serena entered the cave. The Black Flame Fae had been there. Brody glanced to his left.

Oh my god.

Sprite's lifeless body was enclosed in glass. *Is she still alive?*

He tried to speak, but his swollen lips made it painful.

"Where's Lavender?" Brody croaked; his throat dry. He feared for Lavender's safety which made him seethe with anger.

The king leaned in, placing his hands on either side of the armrest. He searched Brody's face. "You don't remember materializing in St. Lucian's cave?"

"What year is it?"

"You're back on Earth the day after you visited Adam Bissett." King Valdoor threw his head back and laughed. "A lot of things have happened to the world since you left. You cost me my kingdom." Brody could see the blood rage in the king's eyes. "You and Lavender cost me, my family, and my queen."

"You did that by yourself."

King Valdoor backhanded him.

Brody's head snapped to the left. He spat blood onto the dirty linoleum floor. He stretched his neck until it popped, then he glared at the king. "I'll kill you if you touched one hair on Lavender's head."

"Get in line," the king shouted. "You're going to help me. Or I will destroy everything you hold dear, including Lavender."

"For crying out loud, Lavender is your great-great-granddaughter."

"I have no family. They are all traitors. I'm no longer a king. Address me as Valdoor."

At least Queen Octavia won, Brody surmised. He wondered what other changes had happened in the new timeline.

Did Silver and Aster live?

Did they save Iris?

His chest tightened. He had to escape and find Lavender.

"Good luck with that, Whitmore. I still read minds. And, FYI, I came to this realm with all my magical abilities. Silver and Aster live, but Iris still killed Thomas Rogers. She cursed his son, Jonathan, and the night of the Hant Hollow ball, Iris called on The Lord Darkness, but I appeared instead disguised as Cetus. Iris works for me now, as does Orphic, Claudia, and Etoil. You will find Yaris and Cetus for me if you ever want to see Lavender again."

Brody gritted his teeth. "Where is she?"

"Hm. She? Do you mean, Lavender? She's with the Doanharts. And the fae," the king pointed to the cage. "Sprite isn't dead. But a word to the wise, do not try to escape, or I will squash the fae under my boot." Valdoor left the room, then locked the door.

Brody closed his eyes and used his mental skillset to find any audio or visual recording devices. Once he homed in on the locations, he mimicked the equipment so those watching him would only see him tied to the chair.

Then he opened his eyes. It took him about thirty minutes to find the right spell in his wheelhouse to release himself from the constraints. He went to the small fae imprisoned in glass. "Sprite, can you hear me? It's Brody."

Her wings fluttered a bit, then drooped again.

"Please, Sprite, fight. I can get us out of here if you help me."

Sprite slowly raised her head. She used her hands to push herself into a sitting position. "The king's stolen my magic." A lone tear escaped down her cheek.

"Look at me, Sprite."

She raised her gaze to meet his eyes.

"Valdoor cannot steal your magic. He's not fae. He must've used a self-loathing spell. Do you remember what he said?"

Her wings fluttered but did not lift her from the glass floor. "I didn't understand the king's words. Something like, I take your magic from your soul and placed it in a hidey-hole."

"Bullshit scare tactic. Valdoor took nothing from you. Do you hear me?"

The corners of her lips upturned into a smile. "Really?"

"Really." Brody searched for the bracelet Sprite had given him, but it was gone. "I'm going to summon you, Sprite, to my command. I will release my hold over you once we get out of this jam, okay?"

She nodded.

"I call on Sprite, the powerful fae, to come in haste to my aid. By the beating of your wings brings freedom when you sing."

Sprite rose to her feet, and her wings fluttered a little, then a lot. The glass disappeared, and she touched Brody's face. She sang, "I shall heal your wounds, mighty warrior." Pixie dust rained on Brody, restoring his health, and renewing his strength. "We don't have much time. His spies have learned you've tricked them."

"Into my pocket, my friend." She flew into his shirt pocket. He snapped his fingers, teleported them beyond the prison walls, and reappeared outside St. Lucian's castle.

From the castle tower, King Valdoor and Orphic watched Brody and Sprite escape into the mountains.

Orphic turned to the king. "Tell me again. Why are you allowing them to go?"

"You never see the big picture, my friend. Brody is Hand to the Regent, Carlton McGrath. He's entrenched with the Mage Alliance. Sprite works closely with The Black Flame Fae. They are leading me to magical beings that I will use to build my growing army. I'll need to recruit seasoned warriors. Placing spies within their inner circle is key to my success within this realm. I learned from my mistakes and will take whatever time is needed to do so." He pointed, then said, "They're going to help me do it."

Hagatha's Chateau Present Day

Lavender opened her eyes. She lay in her canopy bed with the intricately curving pole design, gold scrollwork on the footboard, and a mile-high mattress with goose-down pillows. She would've liked nothing better than to stay between the crisp cool sheets and sleep for a decade, but instead, she panicked.

How did she get here? Where was Brody?

She threw the covers off and jumped out of bed. She glanced to the side table and spotted her cell phone. She tapped the screen. "Call Brody."

"I don't see Brody in your contacts. Who would you like to call?"

She swallowed hard. *No Brody?*

Lavender wore a nightgown, and with a whirl of her forefinger, she changed into jeans and a slouchy sweater with black ballet slippers. She raced out of her room and down the staircase. She heard people talking in the library.

She braced herself and entered the room with Hagatha, Serena, Cora, Emir, and... "Mom?" Lavender cried. "Is it really you?"

With tears in Peony's eyes, she hugged Lavender tightly. "Yes, it's me. How do you feel?"

"I have a killer headache." If her mother was alive, then what other changes had occurred? She turned to Serena. "Where's Brody?"

"You may want to sit down, dear." Hagatha motioned to the sofa.

"I'll pour you some brandy." Peony released her.

Lavender's heart pounded. Her pulse raced. "What happened to Brody? Somebody tell me something, and for God's sake, I don't need brandy."

Serena said, "We have Birch searching for Brody."

"Where? And, by the way, what year is it?" Lavender cried.

The French Pyrenees

Birch searched for Brody in the mountains with Irick and Adel. The dark green trees, thick shrubs, and bushes made the path difficult to follow. He sensed someone or something close. The wind blew in a storm. Lighting shot across the sky, and thunder rolled.

If Birch and his team didn't find Brody soon, they'd have to call off the search until later. He raised his hand to stop Irick and Adel.

Time seemed to stop.

Birch held his breath. One. Two. Three. Four.

He lifted his weapon of choice for hunting in the woods, a Remington pump-action rifle. It may not kill an immortal, but it would slow one down. He zoned in on a sound so light that it was undetectable to most humans, but Birch wasn't mortal. He was a warrior wizard.

A rustling in the leaves tipped the balance in his favor.

Suddenly, an orb of light flew fast in his direction. Birch didn't have a chance to move, much less warn his team.

In a second, the fae materialized. It was evident from her bruises someone had hurt her. "Quick, we must hurry. Brody's dying."

Was she a friend or foe?

She shouted, "I'm on your side. Please, come."

Birch nodded and then motioned to Irick and Adel. "Follow the fae."

Between the approaching storm and the forest, Birch nearly lost the flickering fae wings while he raced through the woods— branches and twigs scraped against his flesh. He winced with pain but kept moving forward—the muscles in his legs burned from the climb up the mountain.

Birch spotted Brody. His heart hammered in his chest. Brody was not only his boss but also a trusted friend. "Good God, what happened to him?"

"Valdoor captured us." The fae hovered. "We escaped, then Brody fell into a trap. The stake went through his right leg, and he went down. He's lost so much blood. I could not heal him."

Birch went on bended knee. "Hey, buddy, it's Birch. We're going to get you help, my man." He took Brody's wrist and felt a faint pulse. "Calling Doctor Conway. Brody needs you. Come straightaway. Don't delay."

Irick and Adel knelt on the other side of Brody.

Doctor Conway materialized in a tuxedo, holding a martini in his right hand. He drained the glass, and it vanished. He shouted, "Move." He opened his hands and formed a glowing golden ball. He hovered it over Brody.

Brody blinked a few times.

"Commander, I'm going to remove the stick from your leg. Then with the help of Sprite, we'll teleport to my hospital in Paris," Doctor Conway said. "I cannot operate under these rough conditions. Do you hear me?"

Brody nodded but did not reply.

Doctor Conway turned to Sprite. "Will you assist me until we arrive, my dear?"

"Yes, doctor."

"Birch, you and the others, go to Hagatha's. Lavender is there. Bring her to my hospital within the Pantheon. Go to the entrance, and you'll see the sign of the Mage Alliance, only visible to members, then use the Witches Honor Code to enter."

The ground underneath them shook as Doctor Conway removed the pointed stake.

Brody's piercing screams echoed over the rumbling thunder.

In a flash of light, Brody, the doctor, and Sprite disappeared.

Chapter 21

Lavender paced near the fireplace, waiting for an explanation. "What has happened?"

Birch burst through the door. His face was ashen. "We must leave at once. Brody is hurt. Doctor Conway took him and Sprite to Maelstrom Medical in Paris."

"What happened to him?"

"Valdoor nearly killed him."

Lavender gasped. "No time to ask questions. We must teleport."

"I'll give Bea a call to ready the house on 16th Arrondissement," Hagatha said.

Lavender paced until she thought she'd go mad. *Brody, live. Fight, my love.*

Would he hear her pleas?

Birch went into detail about how he found Brody. But no one knew the specifics of what Valdoor did to Brody or Sprite. She pulled her cell out and called Jasmine. The phone rang several times before she answered.

"We just heard, Lavender. I wish I were with you. Carlton's notified the Mage Alliance in France. They're putting together a swat team for St. Lucian's and Paris." Jasmine continued, "Carlton seems to think Valdoor has vacated the premises. There's an active threat to you and Serena. Birch is not to leave your side."

Lavender brushed a tear from her cheek. "He hasn't. Birch is with me. I won't survive if anything happens to Brody. I won't live without him."

"Don't talk nonsense. Doctor Conway will heal him. He has an excellent staff. Oh, hold. Max wants to talk with you."

Max cried with broken breaths. "Oh, Lavender. I should've stayed at Hagatha's. I'm so sorry."

"It's not your fault. Max. Mom's alive."

"There have been quite a few changes since I returned to Rockvale, but we'll talk soon. Here's Jasmine."

"Lavender, please call me once you have any news. I contacted several witches, and we're weaving spells to protect and heal, Brody. I love you."

She sniffled. "I love you too. But, Jasmine, it's my fault. If I hadn't pursued Adam Bissett, none of this would've happened."

"You and Brody changed many things for the better," Jasmine replied. "Silver and Aster live. Peony survived. The Doanharts are the only ones that know what really happened before you time traveled. Lavender..."

"Yes?"

"Iris still killed Thomas and cursed Jonathan in the mirror, but Dreena and Raine freed him. Jonathan and Victoria are happily married, and they have a little girl. Valdoor took Iris during the Battle of Hant Hollow," Jasmine added.

Lavender hyperventilated. "We gave her a second chance. How could she screw that up? Have you heard from The Goddess of Light or The Lord Darkness?"

"Yaris and Cetus live here, in Hant Hollow. They're no longer in control of the Mage Alliance."

Lavender closed her eyes and tried to calm herself. "They live in Hant Hollow?"

"Yes, and Cora and Emir live here too."

"Holy Heavens. It's too much. Don't tell me anything else. My only concern is Brody. Everything else will have to wait. I'll call you when I have news of his condition once we arrive in Paris." She ended the call.

Hagatha came into the room. "It's time to teleport."

"Lavender, remember, changing the past changes the future," Serena warned.

She narrowed her eyes at Serena. "You summoned me. I swear, if Brody dies, you will pay."

Two weeks later, the 16th Arrondissement house

Brody watched Lavender sleep in a chaise before swinging his legs off the bed. His injured leg still hurt like a mother, but he didn't vent it to anyone. The last thing he wanted was more sympathy. It was bad enough to get pitying looks at the hospital, but he was grateful for the kindness shown.

Hagatha owned a four-bedroom in an exclusive Paris neighborhood. She'd renovated since he last visited over a hundred years ago. Walk-in closets as big as his old apartment. The bedroom suite where he'd been recuperating had a large bathroom fitted for an invalid. Him.

Brody didn't use the cane as suggested by Doctor Conway as he walked to the window and pushed it open. He gazed at the immaculate, sunken garden.

Doc said he had a good chance the limp would eventually go away, but that wasn't what bothered him. Instead, something evil grew inside him, gnawing his guts.

Brody didn't tell Lavender. He'd caused the dark circles under her eyes. She sensed the shift in their relationship after returning to the present. The closeness between them evaporated with each passing day.

A purple orb bounced toward the window.

He turned to make sure Lavender still slept.

Sprite materialized.

Brody pointed to Lavender. "Whisper. She's not sleeping well."

"Something is wrong with me. Something bad. Valdoor spelled me."

His eyes widened. "Valdoor did something to me too."

She landed on the windowsill, then placed her hands on her knee. "What do you remember?"

"Not much. I gotta get away from Lavender and the Doanharts before I hurt them. I've had dreams of choking Lavender to death, and I liked it." His fingers went through his hair.

"I've had nefarious thoughts as well," Spite interjected. "The Black Flame Fae council has summoned me. They want me to testify about what happened. I don't remember. I'm scared, Brody."

"We must speak with Serena in private. Valdoor is her father."

Serena stepped out into the sunken garden and lit a cigarette.

"Now's our chance," Sprite said. "Can you lower to the garden without causing yourself additional pain?"

He sighed. "Only one way to find out. I'll meet you down there." He levitated over the ledge and floated to the ground.

Serena blew out smoke. "You and Sprite ganging up on me?" She stubbed out the butt into a stone trash receptacle. "It's good to know you can still fly, Brody. What's on your mind?"

It took all his willpower not to strangle her.

He spoke through gritted teeth. "What did your father do to Sprite and me? You know, I see it in your eyes."

Sprite hovered near Serena. "She knows something."

"I'm not working with my father. And Iris killed my mother— one piece of history that didn't change. If you're under Valdoor's spell, I need to test you, but not under Hagatha's roof. It's dangerous. Did Doctor Conway scan for any implanted devices?"

"What kind of devices?" He glanced around to make sure no one heard him. "I was out for three days. I don't know what he did or didn't do. The only person I trust is Sprite. She also feels evil inside her."

"Ah, we're getting somewhere. Evil's growing inside you." She tapped the side of her face with her forefinger. "Hm. The king is slippery, and I hear he's building an army." Serena opened her hands, palms out. Without touching Brody, she scanned the front and back of him, then Sprite. "I do not detect tracking devices. But, if Valdoor cursed you, we should conduct a magical screening at my place. It's not far."

He pressed his lips together and nodded.

"I have a furnished flat in butte Montmartre. Are you familiar with the artist district?"

"I know it well. It's where the French cancan was born and the Moulin Rouge. Give me your address. I'll meet you there at midnight. You're not to tell Lavender until I figure out what is wrong with me." Brody crossed his arms over his chest and frowned. "Understood?"

"I will not lie to Lavender, but I'll not offer any information unless she asks me."

Sprite fluttered her wings. "I don't like hiding things from Lavender, but I feel it is for the best."

Serena magicked two cards with her address and gave one to each of them. "See you at midnight."

Brody levitated to the third floor and entered the bedroom. He leaned down and kissed Lavender's forehead.

"You're awake. How do you feel?" She looked at him with so much love it shattered his heart. She would never forgive him for dodging out without telling her why.

But if he told her, it'd take dynamite to pry her away from him. "I'm fine but feeling a little guilty." Not a lie. "You need to rest, Lavender, in your bed, not mine. I can't sleep knowing you might be uncomfortable."

She tilted her head to the side. "You're not telling me something. Do I need to call the doctor?"

He sighed heavily and rolled his eyes. "No. I don't need Doctor Conway. I will sleep better knowing you're in your room, sleeping. Okay?"

She glanced at the clock over the fireplace mantel. "Okay. Only promise you'll call if you need me."

"I promise."

"Brody, I know something is going on with you. Please talk to me."

He chewed on the inside of his cheek. His stomach dipped. "I gave you space, remember?"

Lavender pushed away from the chair. She cupped his face with her hands and kissed him softly. "I love you, Brody Whitmore."

"I know."

She took her blanket and walked to the door, then stopped. "You didn't tell me."

Brody smiled. "I love you with all my heart."

After she left the room, he went to the door and locked it. He had no phone or clothes, so he whirled his finger. He wore a black leather jacket, the same color sweater, and jeans paired with black combat boots.

It was time to see if his magic was intact. So he teleported to the address on the card and knocked on the door—praying Serena wasn't sending him into a trap.

Serena opened the door. "Come in, Brody. Sprite is here. We have no time to lose." She walked into the living area. "My room is a safe place." She waved her hand, and the furniture disappeared. "I always make sure the five-pointed star is upright toward the Pleiades. So our magic is pure and uncorrupted by evil."

Sprite fluttered close to Brody. "What are you going to do to us?"

Serena snapped her fingers, the electric lights extinguished, and the room filled with floating candles. "I intend to bridge my consciousness with yours, then replay what spell Valdoor used during your captivity. It's physically painless, but the buried horrors may cause emotional stress. I will channel my divine powers to counter the king's."

Brody took a step closer to Serena. "We merge our magic."

"No." Serena frowned. "I believe Valdoor's spell is deep within your memory bank. We should purge before we merge. But you make a good point. Once you and Sprite are clean, combining our power will make our magic much more potent than Valdoor's."

"Is this dangerous for you?" Brody asked.

"Any dealings with my father are potentially deadly, but what choice do we have?" Serena stepped inside the circle.

"I will use an interplanetary and dimensional block to keep Valdoor from entering our mind space. Once you both enter, I'll close the loop. I will call on you to close your eyes and open your mind to let me in. If by some chance, Valdoor used a spell resistor, then I begin the purification process. It is imperative to stay within the circle until I release you. Do you both agree?"

Brody said, "I agree."

"I agree," Sprite said.

"You may enter my sanctum." Serena opened her hands, palms up. She watched as Brody stepped in, and then Sprite followed. "Brody Whitmore, and Sprite, the Black Flame Fae, do you surrender to my control so I may enter within your mind's space?"

"I, Brody Whitmore, surrender control to Serena of the Pleiades."

"I, Sprite, the Black Flame Fae, surrender my mind's control to Serena of the Pleiades."

With a jolt, Serena appeared within Valdoor's interrogation room. Sprite had a far superior intellect and battled the king with a contest of wills in the beginning. She hovered in front of him, countering with a litany of curses, her wings beating wildly.

Serena did not dare move and kept her breathing shallow for fear of discovery.

Suddenly, King Valdoor minimized his size in scale to Sprite.

Serena couldn't understand his spell, but Sprite flinched with each word, closing her eyes. In between his tirades, the king smacked the fae repeatedly until she lay unconscious on the floor. Then, Serena caught one fact; Sprite was in love with Queen Goldengrace.

The king returned to his full stature, picked Sprite up by her wings, and covered her with a glass dome cloche.

Serena turned to Brody. Blindfolded, gagged, and chained to a metal chair secured to the floor—barbwire bit into his chest. Anytime Brody tried to maneuver his constraints, it drew more blood and pain.

Valdoor repeatedly hit Brody in the face as he chanted in his native language. Serena listened carefully, trying to interpret his words. Eventually, the revelation came to her. *Brody Whitmore, Hand of the Regent, you agree to spy for me, and I set Lavender free. However, I need places, dates, and times of any meetings with time-sensitive information regarding plans to capture me.* With every strike to Brody, the king repeated his mantra until he broke Brody mentally, spiritually, and physically. Finally, Valdoor left the room with smugness and a smirk.

The spell placed within Brody and Sprite had a resistor clause.

Serena broke in and manipulated the king's words, relinquishing his control over their minds. Then, just as she released Brody and Sprite, the king's face materialized within her mind space.

"I see you, Serena. Help me regain my throne, and you will sit by my side as we conquer this planet."

"No! You've done nothing but hurt me. You've done nothing to save your family. You are selfish and mean-spirited. I will not open the door to evil and allow it to come in." She extended her arms, and created ancient hand gestures, then repeated, *"I bind you, Valdoor, from hurting my family and friends, I bind you from hurting me. I bind you, Valdoor, from spreading evil in this realm."*

Valdoor raised his foot and attempted to step between the sacred circle's boundaries, and Serena closed it with haste.

A burst of blue-green light surrounded the trio within the circle. "Awake, Brody and Sprite." Serena clapped her hands three times. "Quickly, we must merge our powers and create a protector spell. With any luck, it'll buy us time for our journey to Hant Hollow so that we may join the Doanhart Coven. Then and only then will we be safe." She wiggled her fingers and lit sage incense to burn in the room.

One by one, Serena, Brody, and Sprite clasped each other's arms and merged their magical powers. Wind swirled as intricate golden vines grew around them, creating interchangeable runes imprinting on their biceps and down their forearms, allowing their conscious and subconscious minds to interconnect.

"It is done," Serena sighed.

The floating candles disappeared simultaneously as she turned on the electric lights.

"We return to Hagatha's before dawn." Serena glanced at the antique clock on the wall. "Then arrange travel immediately to Hant Hollow. Once the coven accepts us, Valdoor cannot use us. Together, we'll initiate a plan to send the king back to the Pleiades, where Queen Octavia awaits to execute him."

"The evil is gone. I don't feel it anymore." Brody hugged Serena, then reached for Sprite, who landed within the palm of his hand.

"Oh, thank you, Serena." Sprite added, "I no longer possess a heavy heart."

"Grab hands," Serena said. "We'll teleport to Hagatha's as one."

Chapter 22

Lavender woke with a start.

Something's wrong.

She jumped out of bed, ran to Brody's room, and flung his door open. He was gone.

"No. Don't leave me, Brody," she screamed.

She pressed her eyes closed and sent him a telepathic message. *I love you. I will help you if you just talk to me.*

Peony materialized in the room and engulfed Lavender in a loving embrace. "It's okay, darling. I'm here."

"No. Mom. I must find him." She jerked away from Peony. "I did all this for you. Answer me, did you ever turn to the dark side? Did you join Iris? Do you have any idea what Brody risked saving you?" Tears streamed down Lavender's face.

"Iris tempted me. I won't lie. I love my mother. Approval from our parents, even when they do wrong, is a strong emotion." Peony frowned.

"I tried walking away from Dale Rogers. But, I was so ingrained with sexual deviance I couldn't stop. Eventually, I killed him, but Iris had already left with Valdoor. That's when I prayed to our Creator. I offered myself as a sacrifice to save you. The Creator healed me and removed the darkness from my soul. But, I will never get back the time I lost with you. And, I will spend the rest of my life begging your forgiveness."

Peony stepped toward Lavender. "I learned you and Brody are the Gate Keepers. Your trip to the Pleiadean realm created a power shift in the Mage Alliance."

"King Valdoor, am I right? Is he here, in Paris?"

"We're not sure. Maybe." Peony reached out a hand, and Lavender took it.

"Mom, you never have to beg for my love or forgiveness. I have always believed you had goodness within your soul. I convinced Brody, and that's why he helped me."

Peony wiped tears away from her cheeks. "Thank you, daughter. Thank you for not giving up on me."

"Let's go downstairs. I need caffeine. Does Hagatha have an espresso machine?"

Peony nodded. "I think so."

They held hands as they walked down the staircase.

In the foyer, Brody, Serena, and Sprite instantly appeared surrounded by a blue-green orb. They released hands, and the aura vanished.

Brody searched Lavender's eyes. The tightness in his face alerted her to danger.

"Where have you been?" She resisted the urge to punch him and instead circled her arms around his neck.

"We need to leave, now." He pulled her arms away. "Everyone in the house related to the Doanharts must evacuate immediately."

Birch, Hagatha, and Cook entered the foyer from the kitchen.

Birch extended his hands, palms up. "What's up?"

"Valdoor is coming.," Serena said, "No time to pack. Who's in the house?"

"This is it except for the Stealth staff and Bea." Hagatha frowned. "Why is Valdoor coming?"

A loud explosion erupted, startling Lavender.

The front door blew open—fragments turned into projectiles and flew across the room, but Brody swiftly cast a power shield to deflect them.

King Valdoor stood in the opening.

"Ready to fight, Father?" Electrical currents shot from Serena's fingertips.

Brody, Lavender, Peony, and Sprite released overlapping streams of light toward the exiled king.

Cook, Birch, and Hagatha readied themselves for battle.

The Princesses of the Night flew into the room, dressed in black military armor.

The witches from the dark side went on the attack. They countered with streams of black, sulfurous smoke, fire, and brimstone.

Lavender recognized Etoil.

"Lookie, lookie, who's got Cookie?" Etoil laughed.

Lavender glanced over her shoulder.

Hagatha held a knife to Cook's throat.

Brody seemed to grow two feet. The thunderous scowl on his face relayed emotions words could not express.

"I'll hold the stream with Brody and Sprite." Peony shouted, "That's not Hagatha. That's Mom. Kill her, Lavender."

Lavender used a translocation spell, appeared behind Hagatha's impostor, and initiated a foot sweep to knock the witch off balance, sending the knife spiraling to the floor.

Cook pinned the poser to the ground as Iris materialized under him.

"Why Grams?" Lavender implored. "We gave you a second chance, and you threw it away."

Iris's eyes bulged. Her mouth twisted grotesquely, and drool dripped from the corners. She was spellbound.

The witch before Lavender was not the gentle grandmother she left in the past.

Iris vanished in thin air.

The windows and doors in the house shook.

"I will seek revenge on those that destroyed my kingdom," Valdoor shouted. "Come with me, Princesses of the Night. We live to fight another day." He turned to Serena. "You will pay for defying me."

Etoil shielded the king with her body.

Serena's steely gaze locked with the king's. She used rapid finger and hand gestures, molding and casting brilliant blue rays of energy, chanting in the ancient Pleiadean language. She snapped Etoil's neck, then shouted, "I am not afraid of you."

Valdoor and his minions dematerialized.

Brody rushed to Lavender. "We can't stay here. Valdoor is building an army."

"He spelled Brody and Sprite," Serena said. "I used my powers to release them, and the three of us are one, magically speaking." She took a step back. "I glimpsed Valdoor's intentions to destroy the family. The Doanharts must invite us to join their coven."

Brody cupped Lavender's face. "I know I'm a wizard, and the Witches of Hant Hollow is like a secret club, but Valdoor has Iris. The Doanharts need us, and we need you."

"Of course, we accept you with open arms." Lavender kissed him. Then she turned to Cook. "Where is Hagatha?"

Cook sprinted into the kitchen, and the rest of them followed. He went into the walk-in pantry.

Hagatha sat in a chair, her hands bound and a pillowcase covered her head.

Cook removed it and untied her hands. "Are you okay?"

"No. Iris tricked me." Hagatha rubbed her wrists. "What happened out there?" She left the pantry, opened the liquor cabinet, and poured a shot of whiskey.

Lavender gave her a quick recap. "We must leave. No packing. We take the next flight out of Paris to Nashville."

Hagatha called Andre and Bea. They materialized in the kitchen. "Will you get rid of the mess the king made in the foyer, then close the house?"

"Yes, Miss Hagatha."

Hagatha addressed Andre. "Once you lock down the house and the chateau, then you and Bea travel to Hant Hollow. It looks as though I'm building onto the property." Hagatha squeezed Lavender's hand. "You're a brave witch, but I'm staying awhile longer. I want Valdoor to think that I've fled the city too. I'll stay at a friend's B&B. It offers me cover to investigate his operations. We need to know their numbers and the extent of their power."

Birch stepped next to Hagatha. "I will stay to help Hagatha."

"I'll stay too," Cook added.

"Valdoor is dangerous." Lavender frowned. "He blames me for what happened to Yaris and Cetus. He'll use his hatred of me against you."

"I've lived a long life. I cannot abide the look in Iris's eyes. She's spelled, or worse, cursed. I'm not making excuses for her, but she deserves another chance if she is being controlled."

"I'm not sure Iris deserves any special treatment," Brody added with a thunderous scowl.

Either way, she is oblivious of her connections with us or the Doanharts. Once I find out who's helping them, then we'll meet you in Hant Hollow, I promise."

"You are always welcome, Hagatha. My sisters will agree," Peony said. "Hant Hollow is a refuge for all magical creatures. We have a direct door to Waytherlands. Yaris and Cetus have placed advanced security measures on those entering our sacred place."

"Does anyone have a problem with Sprite traveling with us?" Brody asked.

"No. Sprite is family." Lavender grabbed Brody's hand. "We'll discuss a plan of action once everyone arrives in Rockvale."

Twenty-four hours later

It was dark when the plane began its descent into Nashville. The clear sky allowed an incredible view of the city, along with a string of red lights from cars snaking across the interstates and highways. The jet's force hit with a jolt, coming to a stop as the pilot geared down and lowered the tires.

Lavender's natural time clock was so out of whack.

Exiting the plane, there was a bevy of passenger chatter, loudspeaker announcements of arrivals and departures, and the roar of engines on the tarmac.

Tennessee was Lavender's favorite place in the world. Her book of life today started again today.

Max, Jasmine, and Carlton met Brody, Peony, Sprite, and her in a café within the airport.

"I've missed you guys so much." Lavender hugged each one. "I can't wait to spend time with you and share what happened after we time traveled. But I'm exhausted. I didn't sleep on the flight." She pointed to Brody. "He, on the other hand, slept like a baby."

"Hey, I can't help if I fall asleep faster than you," Brody replied. He dropped his arm around her shoulders. "Oh, this is Sprite."

Sprite had altered her fae size, to around five feet, for the trip to America. She peeked out from behind Brody's shoulders. "Hello. Thank you for a haven against Valdoor. Are there any Black Flame Faeries in Hant Hollow?"

Max sidled next to Sprite and placed the faerie's hand in the crook of his arm. "I should say so. Emir and Cora live on the property. He is fabulous!" He glanced over his shoulder. "Let's go to Rockvale, eh?" He patted Sprite's hand. "We're going to be such good friends."

"Oh, Maxie, I have missed you." Lavender laughed. "No luggage, so let's ride."

He winked at her.

"How about Sprite and Peony ride with Max, and Lavender and Brody ride with Carlton and me?" Jasmine turned to Lavender. "Will you be staying at the mansion?"

"The ride arrangement works for me." She shook her head. "But no, Brody and I will reside at the Red Rose. Of course, Sprite is welcome to stay with us."

Sprite turned her head. "Oh, that's okay. I want to see Emir. I think I'll stay with the Doanharts if they'll have me."

"Absolutely," Peony interjected.

Two hours later, Lavender unlocked the front door of the Red Rose. It seemed like a lifetime ago since she'd left. Entering the first floor of her elegant bookstore, she sighed relief. The recessed lighting set to dim indicated the shop was closed. She inhaled the lemony scent of freshly polished furniture.

She was home.

Emily ran down the stairs. "I can't believe you're back. Good grief, we thought someone kidnapped you. Did you find what you were looking for?" She looked at Lavender and Brody.

"Yes, we found everything and then some." Lavender sighed. "This is Brody, by the way. He's moving in."

Brody chuckled.

"Oh, I know all about Brody from Max." Emily blushed.

"What did Max say about me?" he inquired.

"All good." She turned to Lavender. "I kept the Red Rose tip top. Your rooms are clean, and the fridge is full. Max called earlier, so I went ahead and packed my bags. Oh, the store is doing great."

"Thank you, Emily." Lavender squeezed her hand. "Feel free to take a few days off with pay."

"You don't have to do that."

With a raised brow, Lavender said, "I insist."

"Okie-Dokie." Emily looked at Brody. "Nice to meet you." She left from the side door.

Lavender turned to Brody and rubbed her hands together. "Goodie, I have you all to myself." Then, with razor-sharp clarity, she realized it was not luck that had brought them together but destiny. Her gut-deep need for him created feelings so raw and uncontrollable it was hard to breathe.

Brody backed Lavender against the entry wall as his hands roamed her curves. "I am holding you to that promise."

She tilted her head back as he pressed featherlight kisses along her neck. "What promise?"

"We settle down and tie the knot," he said with labored breath. "I'm in love with you."

"I was so worried when you disappeared. What happened?"

"Not now. Later. I don't want to waste another minute talking about Valdoor or your grandmother. I want you, woman." He scooped her into his arms and strode up the staircase. "Which floor?"

"Top one." She giggled. "Am I too heavy?"

"Like toting a Marlin." He chuckled. They bypassed Max's art gallery and went up one more floor, then entered the vast suite with a state-of-the-art kitchen, fourteen-foot ceilings, a cozy living room furnished with Doanhart antiques, and her comfortable canopy bed.

"Wow." He twirled her around.

She wiggled her feet. "Aw, Emily left fresh flowers and lit the fireplaces. Let's leave the lights off. I love a room lit by crackling flames."

"Very romantic." He looked up. "Cool skylight. It's a great room."

She nudged her nose into his neck. "Your room. My room. Our room."

"Quoting Dr. Seuss?" He threw his head back and laughed.

"No, silly. I'm going to take a shower." She pointed to the main bathroom. "Come with me?"

"Thought you'd never ask."

He put her down inside the lavatory. She turned on the water until steam filled the room. She flipped on the silent vent fan, then stepped into the shower.

"Are you getting in?" Water pelleted against her skin.

"Yeah, just enjoying the view." He slid in behind her and kissed the nape of her neck. His fingers skimmed her arms. "Mm. You're satiny smooth, skin like silk."

Lavender turned and kissed him on the mouth.

"I'm going to wash your hair," he said.

"Sounds lovely." She sat on the built-in bench.

He poured a generous amount of shampoo into his hands and worked the lather in her hair. He used his fingers to comb out her locks during rinsing. He bent over and kissed the nape of her neck—giving her pleasant goosebumps. She lifted her face ever so slightly, and Brody leaned down, kissing her again before gently washing her body.

She returned the favor.

Her fingers slowly slid down his muscular chest, gently grazing each scar he had earned in battles over the centuries. Next, she moved down his flanks—taking time, allowing the hot water to loosen his tired muscles.

After toweling off, she said, "Honey, I have a wine cooler in the kitchen. Grab a bottle, your choice, and meet me in bed."

He walked through the suite of rooms, naked.

Dang, he had a fine body.

He made every day worth living.

Lavender slipped on a satin robe without using the sash. She pulled down the covers, then sat on the bed with one foot tucked under her and the other dangling, not touching the floor.

Brody brought in an ice bucket with Nebbiolo in one hand and held two flutes in the other one. "Goddess Divine." He handed her a glass and clinked the crystal.

"Great choice." She sipped. "Did you know this wine has more melatonin than all the reds?"

"Really?" He raised a brow.

"You knew, didn't you?"

He nodded and joined her in bed.

She nearly burst out laughing when he gulped the wine, then placed his glass on the side table. She put her glass on the matching side table and allowed her hand to rest on his thigh.

"I could stay in here with you forever." He slipped his hand through her hair to cradle her head.

"Me too. Make love to me like it's the first time, no— the last time."

His grin went wide and warmed her in all the right places. "What do you want, love?"

"I want it all."

Brody was magnificent in every way. He loved her enough to travel to otherworldly realms and back again. He never judged her. He was a constant force of stability. His love surpassed all others.

Never will anyone or anything come between us again.

Chapter 23

Paris

Hagatha, Birch, and Cook exited the house on 16th Arrondissement through the staff door. Under a cloud of darkness, with fog so thick that Hagatha could barely see her hand, she made her way through the back streets of Paris's art district with her comrades. The frigid temps had most tourists and residents indoors.

Her friend, Jean-Micel Soyer, ran The Paragon. The exclusive Bed and Breakfast for magical creatures was rumored to have belonged to one of King Henry VIII's mistresses.

It was past midnight when she checked into one of his apartments overlooking Pont Neuf. Jean-Micel's staff were discreet and competent. The double bedroom connected to the king suite with a shared common room. The silk and linen fabrics, wallpaper, and art pieces were inspired by the Neo Regency era from the nineteenth century.

"I shall reside in the suite. Cook, you and Birch will share the other room." Hagatha sat on the sofa next to the window. Jean-Micel had left a bottle of champagne on ice on the coffee table.

Cook opened the bottle and poured each a glass. "Where do we start?"

She leaned back and sipped. "The Blind Shuffle, it's a mage-only club and is close to the Moulin Rouge. It stays open all night, and it's not accessible to mortals." She glanced at her watch. "I say, let's change into more appropriate attire and hit it. We split up inside and see what shakes loose."

"I suggest changing appearance. Hagatha, you're well-known in magical circles." Birch closed the drapes. "You place a target on all of us."

She stood and snapped her fingers. "Does this meet your approval?" Hagatha wore a bobbed haircut, a black bandeau maxi dress with a matching low-slung sequined belt, and sandals. She draped a gray faux fur over her arm.

Birch swallowed hard. "Yeah, that'll do." Then, with a wave of his hand, he wore a black turtleneck, black trousers, and a black leather trench coat.

She smiled, then turned to Cook. "Well, I'm waiting."

Cook frowned as if in deep thought. "How about this?" He extended his hands out, palms up. He wore a floral print shirt paired with a complimenting maroon velvet slim-fitting jacket, dark wool trousers, and Oxford shoes.

"Nice," Hagatha said. "We look for those on the dark side." She made a triangle with her fingers and then chanted, "Open our eyes to members of Valdoor's army while shielding our real identities." A burst of wind entered the room and dissipated. "Use telepathy if in a bind. I will find you. We'll teleport to the entrance."

The club materialized into view, past the Moulin Rouge. Hagatha walked up the steps, and the bouncer looked at the three of them. "Witches Special tonight," said the large man with a bald head and rippling muscles with runes tats.

Hagatha lifted her chin without responding and entered the posh establishment with deep red, gold, and black Baroque interiors—dripping crystal chandeliers and Rococo artwork dispersed through the club along with furniture covered with richly woven textiles.

The pulsating music boomed. The multi-colored lights changed in sync with the DJ's jams. High-energy magical creatures filled the crowded dance floor.

Hagatha nodded to Cook and Birch. They went their separate ways.

She weaved through the crowd and noticed a familiar face. One of the original Doan-hart witches sat in the back corner of the room. Tabitha was alone, but it didn't mean she wasn't with someone. Hagatha went to her booth and shouted over the chatter and music, "May I join you?"

Tabitha's back straightened. She nodded and waved her hand, indicating her approval.

Hagatha slid in next to her. "Do you come here often?" Lame question, but she needed to start a conversation.

A waiter brought Hagatha a shot of whiskey. "Compliments from the gentleman at the bar."

Hagatha looked at Birch and smiled.

Thank you.

He nodded. *You're welcome.*

Tabitha chuckled, and Hagatha's shoulders relaxed.

"I see through your disguise, my friend. What are you doing out this late? You ole witch. And who's the hot wizard?"

"A friend." Hagatha placed her forearms on the table and leaned forward. "I need your help."

"But of course, you do." Tabitha leaned against the back of the sofa. "How may I assist you?" Her long black fingernails tapped with the beat of the music.

"Valdoor." It was all Hagatha needed to say to receive a response.

Tabitha looked to her left and right, then leaned close to Hagatha. "Why do you ask?"

"Two questions, first."

"Okay."

"Are you aligned with Valdoor?" Hagatha inquired. "Or do you stand with the alliance?"

"It's funny you should ask me those questions. I met him tonight. Valdoor sat in the same place where you sit now. He offered me riches and power beyond my comprehension. He also hit on me. Can you imagine?" With a raised brow, she added, "I already possess both, and I don't need a king to get laid. And to answer the second question, I stand with the alliance that you and I helped to create."

"I'm glad to hear it. Do you know any details about Valdoor's army?"

Tabitha waved her hand. "The room is full of his warriors. Be careful. They want to change the old order and issue a new one. I'd estimate, in Paris alone; he has at least one thousand in his ranks." She sipped on a fruity cocktail. "The young magical creatures no longer see the benefit of our protection or honor our traditions. They no longer want to work to enhance their craft. They want it handed to them on a silver platter."

"Does Valdoor know your position?" Hagatha asked.

"Do I look like a fool? No." She opened her hand, and the Pleiadean crest hovered over her palm for a second, then vanished. "His soldiers wear tattoos of this image on their left inner wrist. Several of his militia members are looking at us. I suggest you mingle."

Hagatha cupped Tabitha's face and kissed her soundly on the mouth. "I will always love you." Then, she pushed away from the table and walked away without looking back.

She found Cook on the dance floor. The young wizard he danced with seemed enamored with Cook's good looks. However, Hagatha noticed the crest on his wrist.

She tapped Cook on the shoulder, lowered her lashes demurely, then looked in his eyes. "Dance with me, monsieur."

"Go away, he's mine," sneered the militia member.

Hagatha hissed and extended her claws which had grown longer and sharper.

The young male narrowed his eyes and retreated.

She wrapped her arms around Cook. *The place is crawling with Valdoor's army. Where is Birch?*

He went into the restroom with a witch.

The hair on her neck rose. *We're going in. Follow my lead.*

Hagatha wrapped her legs around Cook's waist inside the unisex bathroom and began kissing him.

His hands gripped her buttocks.

She looked through the opulent gilded mirrors and noticed the last stall was occupied.

They bumped against walls and doors.

Several guests primping at the mirrors stared at them and left, cursing under their breaths for them to get a room.

She banged on the last door, and no one answered. She dropped to her feet. She made sure no one else was in any part of the rooms, then locked the main restroom entrance.

"Watch the door, Cook, and do not let anyone magick themselves inside."

She materialized inside the last stall where Birch stood over a half-dressed female. Her neck was broken.

He looked at Hagatha. "She's one of Valdoor's minions. When I didn't respond to her invitation to join the revolution, she became suspicious and tried to leave. I had to stop her."

"Looks like you succeeded. But unfortunately, we'll have to take the dead witch with us." She stepped out into the dressing area and adjusted her belt. "Cook, we have a problem."

In one swoop of magic, the trio stood in an alley that backed up to a closed restaurant. "Put her in the dumpster. Then we travel to Hant Hollow in the morning. The army has grown exponentially. The Mage Alliance is aware of their growing numbers." Hagatha placed her hands on her hips. "We must make the Doanhart Coven impenetrable by calling on all the Goddesses of the Pleiades to stand with us."

Birch took the lifeless witch, placed a five-point star pointing to heaven on her forehead, and gently laid her within last night's garbage. "In this war, we take no prisoners, *mon cheri*." He jumped onto the road and dusted off his pants.

Cook added, "I agree."

They materialized inside their suite of rooms.

Minutes later, Hagatha stood under the showerhead while hot water rained on her skin. Sometimes, she felt every year of her age. It seemed like she was continually battling someone or something. She was bone tired.

Afterward, Hagatha conjured a nightgown and laid out a traveling outfit: a long gray cardigan, white T-shirt, and a paisley pashmina for her trip to America. Finally, she slipped between the warm flannel sheets. She tucked the pillow under her head and closed her eyes.

Her mind raced with thoughts of an impending war.

A soft knock at the door made her sit upright. "Come in."

Birch opened the door. His arms braced against the jamb. "May I?"

The ruggedly handsome warrior made the air back up in her lungs. "Yes. Is Cook asleep?"

He nodded and entered the bedroom, closing the door behind him. "I've received an interesting call from Irick." He pointed to the edge of the bed. "May I sit?"

"Sure. What did he say?"

He eased down onto the mattress. His eyes locked with hers.

"Our sources with the Mage Alliance have seen a mass exodus of magical creatures in the last twenty-four hours." His hand inched forward next to hers. "One of our informants stated Valdoor created an interdimensional doorway. To where? We don't have the answer. But the king has left this plane of existence."

"He's gone? To where? The Pleiades? Does Queen Octavia know?"

"Hold up." He grabbed her hand and squeezed. "We do not know where he is. However, I assure you the Mage Alliance has alerted all concerned parties."

"Any other details? It could be relevant to Valdoor's intentions?"

He rubbed the soft skin between her thumb and index finger. "Only that Adel went with them, undercover. To my knowledge, most of Valdoor's militia has fled with him."

He inched closer to Hagatha. His hand slid ever so lightly up her arm. "You and I both know the king is up to something."

She swallowed hard and looked into his dreamy eyes. "It buys us time to prepare for his eventual return."

A fire ignited in her soul. She was drawn to Birch and threw back the bed covers. Sexual tension hung thick between them. She leaned forward and brushed her lips against his.

Birch reached up and caressed her cheek. Then, he leaned in and pressed kisses along her neck.

His skilled hands made her stomach flip. His desire matched hers as he took her into his arms, and boy did Birch know how to kiss—teasing and nipping her top then bottom lip: a languorous kiss.

"I want you more than I've ever wanted anyone in my life. But I know you are way out of my league." He lay next to her. One arm propped his body as the other hand cradled her head.

"Shush. Don't ruin the moment with words. I don't want them. I only want you."

She took her time opening the buttons of his shirt, tracing her nails across his glorious chest. Oh, the things she wanted to do to him. "Take me." She pulled the gown over her head.

He pressed kisses in and around the sensual parts of her body. Her resolve weakened as he gave her what she needed.

"More," she cried. Her fingernails clawed his back.

She read his mind. He wanted more than sex. Birch was in love with her.

"I cannot love you back. I've suffered enough heartache from men of magic. So don't love me."

"You can't tell me what to do."

He intended to make her his in every way, with every fiber of his being.

Her cheeks flushed with heat. Her body quivered under his expert manipulations. Her fingers tunneled through his hair.

Mine. He screamed in her head. *You are mine.*

A rush of endorphins flooded her body. She pulled him toward her.

"Tell me what I want to hear even if you don't mean it." He wiped his mouth with the back of his hand.

Her hands ran lightly over his biceps. Then, with a labored breath, she rasped, "I love you."

"Was that so hard to say?" His grin widened.

"You have no idea how hard it is for me to love someone," she whispered. "To risk, another heartache is more than I can bear."

They searched each other's eyes.

"Give me what you can, and I will take the rest."

Hagatha arched her back and took what Birch offered. A tantric relationship might not last a lifetime but would give them the closeness each desired.

Tangy and sweet, Hagatha would not discard this lover. No, she would keep Birch around, at least, for a little while.

Chapter 24

The Doanhart Coven

The last several months seemed as if she'd lived three lifetimes. Lavender guessed she had, in a way. She and Brody first time traveled before the Rockvale Harvest Festival and returned close to Winter Solstice.

Lavender rode with Brody to Hant Hollow. She set the passenger seat into a reclining position and watched the white, fluffy clouds turn into images of animals, faces, and angels.

"Did you get any sleep last night?" Brody quickly glanced at her, then gripped the steering wheel.

"I haven't slept well in so long I wouldn't know how it feels. I am excited to see everyone again. A cup of Jasmine's special tea will perk me up."

"Holy Heavens. Hant Hollow has certainly changed a lot since we left."

Lavender came to an upright position.

Black railed fences lined the perimeter of the property. Several new upscale homes appeared as they entered Hant Hollow. "Look, modern-day farmhouses. I love the wide front porches and tin roofs. It's like stepping back in time with a twenty-first-century twist."

He pulled up to a security gate and pressed the button.

Peony's face appeared on the small screen. "Oh, hey, I'll buzz you in. The passcode is 1917 for future reference."

"Thanks." Brody shrugged.

The gate opened, and they drove through the entrance.

"Wonder what else we've missed." Lavender twirled her fingers in his silky, shoulder-length hair.

"We'll know soon enough. Man, they turned the place into a neighborhood."

She giggled. "Yeah, full of witches and magical creatures, I bet."

"The post lights remind me of the early twentieth century."

"I'm glad they incorporated the woods into the lots," She added.

"Walking trails." Brody shook his head. "They have walking trails."

"Brody?"

"Yeah?"

"Let's get married and build out here. We can keep the Red Rose."

His smile warmed her heart. "I'm in. Today, tomorrow, and for the rest of our lives." He parked next to the newly painted white barn.

Tennessee Walking Horses grazed on hay in the front corral.

"We'll tell everyone when it's the right time." She winked. "Before we leave today."

He leaned over and kissed her forehead. "I've waited for you for over a hundred years. I don't think I'm going anywhere."

They exited the car and walked up the sidewalk and steps.

She knocked, but no one answered. Finally, she pushed the door open.

A wave of nostalgia hit her in the chest.

The Doanhart Mansion had been completely renovated. Her gaze went to the shiplap entryway and dark wood floors mixed with their heirloom antiques. Soft whites and grays seemed to be the new theme of the interiors. The result created a down-home kind of feel.

Laughter and loud chatter filtered throughout the house.

"Laven-door," squealed Finis. He ran toward her, and she picked him up and whirled.

"I have missed you." She kissed his chubby cheeks. "Did you miss me?"

"Mama cried." Finis frowned. "She was very worried. Don't go away again."

"Not on your life."

Finis wiggled out of her arms and ran upstairs, chasing Kyewicket.

The drawing room had been converted into a large living area with a sixty-inch smart television mounted over the mantel.

Carlton, Birch, and Draum watched a football game.

"Ref, you suck." Birch turned. "Brody, my main man is in the house."

Carlton hit the mute button on the remote.

Draum said, "Hey, I'm watching that." He glanced over his shoulder. "No offense, Lavender."

"None was taken, Uncle."

Carlton hugged her and then fist-pumped Brody. "How the hell are you? We thought we'd see y'all sooner."

"Brody and I needed time to ourselves."

"Gotcha. Stressed out, I'm sure. The gals are in the kitchen with Max and Cook." He punched Brody in the arm. "Grab a beer out of the fridge and come back. The game is in the fourth quarter. I'm betting on Tennessee."

Lavender and Brody walked through the hallway toward the kitchen.

She had to fight to keep from crying, albeit happy tears, not sad ones.

The kitchen was transformed with washed-out woods, white walls, natural wood ceiling, beams, and state-of-the-art appliances.

She and Brody stood in the doorjamb. "All the sadness in the place is gone." She leaned against his shoulders.

Max and Cook chopped vegetables on the island, each wearing a His & His apron.

Hagatha washed dishes at the sink.

Jasmine stirred a pot on the stove.

Peony walked out of the pantry. "You're here!"

She smiled as the group swarmed her and Brody with well wishes, hugs, and kisses.

"Enough already. I missed you all too." Lavender laughed. "The place looks great. I love the new style, so open and airy."

Max said, "Thank you."

Jasmine hip-bumped him. "You didn't do it all by yourself."

Isidore came in the back door with bottles of wine, followed by Cora and Emir.

"So, tell me, who's here, and who lives in the new houses?"

Jasmine tucked her hand in the crook of Lavender's arm. "Let's sit and chat. Brody, beers in the fridge."

He chuckled. "Yeah, that's what I hear."

Lavender blew him a kiss.

He grabbed a brew and left the kitchen to join the guys.

At the table, Isidore joined her and Jasmine with a bottle of wine and goblets. Serena wiped her hand on a dish towel and sat at the bar.

"Let's see," Jasmine said. "Peony, Silver, and Aster live in this house with Mom and Dad. Hagatha and Cook whipped up a new wing on the back and share it with Max and Birch." Jasmine sipped wine. "Um, Cora, Emir, and Sprite live in the first house on the right. Yaris and Cetus built the cottage across from them. They also live in Waytherlands. Serena built a cabin in the woods, close to the river, and we still live in Carlton's family home but visit here often. The Doanhart estate owns two thousand acres now. Dad and Mom started a real estate company in town."

"It's like a dream," Lavender said. "Our family is back except for Grams. Any word from her?"

Peony turned down the burner, checked the oven, then took a seat next to Lavender. "We've heard nothing about Mom since the attack at Hagatha's."

"Oh, I don't have the strength to talk about my mother." Isidore took a gulp of wine. "Today is a reunion and our ceremony to reunite our coven. We'll eat dinner, then head to the top floor."

Lavender's stomach dipped. "I don't know if I can go up there. So many bad memories."

"You do not have to worry about the top floor." Serena placed her hands on her knees. "The entire house was renovated, including Iris's room of terror."

Cora and Emir sat on the sofa in the bay window, next to the kitchen table.

"We made sure no one has access to this property without an invitation." Cora held Emir's hand. "The only door into other realms is accessed behind the outdoor kitchen area and the Doanhart library."

"No more looking glass wells?" Lavender asked.

"We have evolved." Serena took a swig of beer.

"Are there other magical creatures here or in town?" she inquired.

Sprite flew into the room. She went from pint-size to adult-size in a flash of light. "Many Black Flame Fae live on the property."

"Oh, several things happened for the better because of you and Brody. Oh, Cora and Emir opened a cozy restaurant near the park, and the fae staffs it," Hagatha added. "The town loves it, I hear."

"Let's not forget, Peony and Isidore opened a bohemian-style clothing shop across from the Red Rose. Silver and Aster are working at the boutique now and will join us for the ceremony later." Max took the chopped veggies and added them to the pot.

"Really? I love bohemian styles," Lavender interjected.

"We know," Peony, Isidore, and Jasmine said in unison.

Cook stepped forward. "The bread is ready in ten minutes. Then it's dinnertime. I put the extra leaf on the dining room table. Tell the boys."

Over dinner, Lavender relaxed and enjoyed the old familiarities of her youth. They reminisced over the fun times and waxed over the sad times. At times, they laughed so hard, that she cried. It was a good feeling to be among her family and friends.

The Doanharts weren't merely magical "witches." They were born of Pleiadean royal blood, born of Goddesses.

Lavender straightened her back as the conversations waned and raised her glass of wine. She tapped on the crystal with a silver spoon. "May I have your attention?"

Brody draped his arm around her shoulders.

Everyone looked at them.

Jasmine shouted, "Enough already with the suspense."

"Brody and I are getting married."

Whistles and shouts of joy erupted from the table.

Max left the room and returned with two bottles of French champagne. He glanced at Hagatha and smiled. "From my dear friends, Stephan and Mel, we shall toast to Lavender, finally saying I do."

The entire table roared with laughter.

Brody leaned over and kissed Lavender's cheek. "She's worth the wait."

"Aw." Jasmine sighed. "That's so sweet."

"Kiss her." Finis clapped his hands. The rest of them joined his chant.

Brody pushed away from the table and reached for Lavender's hand.

She stood, and he dipped her back and kissed her with gusto with her eager family members clapping and shouting woohoos.

After cleaning the dinner table and leaving the dishes in the sink, the Doanharts made their way to the top floor using the main staircase.

On the second-floor landing, Lavender pointed to the portraits of witches, centuries-old, as they came to life, giggling and nodding their approval of her choice in a mate.

On the third floor, Lavender hesitated.

"I am right beside you," Brody whispered. "I will never leave you again."

The rest of the family had entered the room and changed into white garments, including Silver and Aster. Lavender hugged them. "We must catch up soon."

Peony handed the ceremonial robes to her and Brody.

The mood turned somber.

On the floor, the five-star emblem pointed to the heavens. The wind blew into the room in a swirl. Yaris and Cetus materialized next to Lavender and Brody.

"My dear girl, how can we ever thank you for the sacrifices you and Brody made to help us? We will forever be in your debt."

Lavender circled her arms around Yaris's neck and cried. "I'm so glad you and Cetus made it, and you're together?" She took a step back.

Cetus shook Brody's hand. "Yes, we are married."

"What about the Goddess of Light?"

"Remember my sister Dreena?" Yaris asked.

Lavender nodded. "Of course."

"She and Raine Moonfall oversee those duties assigned by the Mage Alliance. The Goddess of Light and The Lord Darkness is something the council votes on now. And, it is not a life sentence anymore, thanks to you." Yaris kissed Lavender's cheek and joined the others around the star.

Serena stepped forward and snapped her fingers—the room filled with floating candles and sage incense. "This is a sacred circle. Each one standing here tonight will commit to the Doanhart Coven. Hold the hand of the person next to you, and we will seal the coven with a prayer."

She raised her arms toward the heavens. "Thank you, Creator God, for bringing my family together. We praise your holy name."

One by one, each person in the circle repeated Serena's offering.

Next, Yaris opened her hands, and a ball of fire hovered. "I will love my coven unconditionally. Our coven lives in harmony with each other and nature."

They followed protocol. Each one in the circle repeated the second rule.

Cora's hands went into prayer mode. "I will respect each member's supernatural powers and share my energy of light."

Hagatha created an orb of protection. "I will call on our coven if I feel threatened by charm, spell, or curse initiated by anyone outside our protected circle."

One by one, each member, including Max, committed themselves to each other and the coven.

Serena, Yaris, Cora, Hagatha, Silver, Aster, Isidore, Peony, Lavender, and Jasmine took a white feather and gave one to Cetus, Emir, Birch, Draum, Brody, Carlton, Cook, and Max.

The women danced in and out, weaving around the men and singing, "Following the coven rules is a must. Fill our coven with friendship, love, and trust. Remember, good or bad, what goes out comes back to thee in threes. Celebrate our coven with heart, soul, and me. That is our fervent prayer and utmost goal."

They held hands.

Lavender shouted, "Here's to The Witches of Hant Hollow!"

The coven shouted, "The Witches of Hant Hollow!"

Epilogue

Rockvale Christmas Tree Lighting

Lavender and Brody had spent several days decorating the Red Rose Hotel for the holidays. Snow flurries in the air enhanced the feeling of the seasonal spirit.

She watched and waved at the passers-by. People laughed and talked, moving along the flagstone sidewalks lit by the new LED streetlamps. There was no better way to usher in the holidays than Rockvale's Christmas Tree Lighting Ceremony.

She held Brody's hand as they exited her doorway. They walked by the church, and she waved to Pastor Green. Christmas bells chimed a lovely tune from the tower.

They continued by the grocery store, bank, and The Fox Hunt Lodge.

She peeked inside the windows of her mother's and aunt's clothing store, Peace Out. "I can't wait to try on clothes one day soon."

"Think they'll give you a discount?"

"They better." She winked.

Carolers sang at every corner decked out in Dickens style.

She and Brody strolled around the historic Georgian-inspired town hall. Twinkling white lights and decorations filtered throughout the park. Local food vendors had set up booths. The Ladies Auxiliary Club hosted areas for children's activities, including visiting Santa at a custom gingerbread house decorated with real frosting and enormous lollipops.

Silver, Aster, and Sprite dressed as elves. Sprite even sported her real wings. They handed out peppermint to the kiddies.

"Let's stop by Cora and Emir's booth and grab a hot cocoa," Lavender said.

Brody patted his coat pocket. "I have my whiskey flask."

She giggled. "Of course, you do."

Musicians played from the white gazebo bandstand near the park center while folks sat in lawn chairs watching their performance.

She waved at Max. His and Victoria's tent offered winter art for sale. Cook and Jonathan handled the cash register.

Lavender was thrilled Max had found love.

Others enjoyed ice skating on the frozen pond. Burned barrels offered residents and tourists a spot of warmth as they checked out the celebration venue.

Lavender and Brody joined Jasmine, Carlton, and Finis with Isidore and Peony near the Christmas tree.

"Laven-door, I saw Santa," Finis exclaimed with glee.

"And did you tell him you were a good boy?"

"Uh-huh. Auntie Silver gave me papermint."

Brody chuckled, then discreetly handed the whiskey flask to Carlton.

Carlton nodded. "Mighty obliged, sir."

Draum stepped onto the stage and tapped the microphone. "Testing. Testing. Can you all hear me?"

Crowds of people replied, "Yes."

Hagatha and Birch stepped next to Lavender.

"This little town is so charming. It reminds me of home," Hagatha said.

"We love Rockvale." Lavender smiled, then sipped hot cocoa.

"Welcome to Rockvale's Annual Christmas Tree Lighting Ceremony. I trust you all have sampled our local businesses and shops. If not, please do before you leave. One side note. Please make sure you watch the children near the open flames." Isidore joined him on stage. "This is my lovely wife, Isidore. She will initiate the lighting of the tree."

The audience cheered.

"The Doanhart family has long roots in the area." Isidore looked at her family and grinned. "Our family walked through the woods of Hant Hollow recently. The gorgeous evergreen, before you, seemed to beckon us to its location, so we decided to donate it to the town. My grandson, Finis, will now do the honor of turning on the lights."

More cheers filtered through the park.

Finis bounded up the stairs with the help of Draum. The little boy shined from the inside out.

Isidore offered Finis the large switch. "It's ready for you."

Finis turned toward the crowd. His chest lifted, and shouted, "Merry Christmas."

"Merry Christmas," many shouted in response.

Then he flipped the switch.

The tree lit to perfection.

Oohh's and ahh's erupted from the crowd.

Lavender looked around at her family. So much had changed since she and Brody time traveled. She'd never take love for granted again—ever.

There were family and friends she'd probably never see again. The division between light and dark magic still existed. She supposed it always would. The drama created by Valdoor and Iris would create ripple effects later in life, but for now, she chose not to live in fear.

Lavender intended to love more, forgive often, and laugh at every opportunity.

Brody must've sensed her musings. He leaned down and cupped her face. "My heart is bursting with happiness."

"Mine too, Brody, mine too."

The End

Enjoy this book? You can make a difference.

Reviews are my best and most powerful resource to attract new readers. But, unfortunately, I do not have the muscle of a traditional New York publishing house, nor do I have the marketing funds to place full-page print ads, subways, or broadcast ads. Well, not yet.

Honest reviews help so much. Please consider taking five minutes to post a review. Or go to:

https://books2read.com/TheWitchesofHantHollow2

Thank you very much!

D.F. Jones

Character Key

Spoiler Alert

Word of warning before heading into significant spoiler territory with The Witches of Hant Hollow character reference. It is in the reader's best interest to leave the deep dive until you read the books if you do not want to know what happens.

First Witches

    Urslina, Queen of Dark Magic, Serena's mother

    Hagatha, Iris's Guardian and earthly mother, leader of the Doanhart Coven.

    Hidee: the hunter.

    Thel: the weaver of thread.

    Naola and Etoil: the farmers.

    Claudia: the smithy.

    Tabitha: the brewer

The Doanhart Coven

    Hagatha: the matriarch

    Iris: mother of Silver, Peony, and Isidore

    Silver: first daughter of Iris

    Peony: second daughter of Iris

    Isidore: third daughter of Iris

    Aster: daughter of Silver

    Lavender: daughter of Peony

    Jasmine: daughter of Isidore

Wizards and Warlocks

    Draum Locke: wizard of the light, Jasmine's father, married to Isidore

    Carlton, Regent of the Mage Alliance, lives in Jonesboro, married to Jasmine

    Carlton "Finis" McGrath III, the young son of Jasmine and Carlton

    Brody Whitmore: Hand to the Regent

    Defenders: an elite force of mage warriors

    Christian Birch: mage warrior

    Irick and Adel: brothers and mage warriors

    Cook: a wizard that lives with Hagatha

    Dr. Conway: magician, wizard, and doctor to all those supernatural, practices at Maelstrom Medical Hospital

    Jean-Micel Soyer: owner of The Paragon, Hagatha's friend

Mouijah Stones: sacred relics

    Waytherlands: supernatural world and a haven for magical beings

    North American Mage Alliance changes to Mage Alliance

Stealths: magical domestic staff

   Mordecai: Hant Hollow Mansion

   Andre: Hagatha's Chateau

   Charles: Hagatha's driver

   Bea: Hagatha's Paris house on 16th Arrondissement

Mortals Book 1

   Jonathan Rogers: mortal that falls in love with a witch.

   Mae Morgan: mortal that needs Jonathan's help

   Anthony Morgan: Mae's father and bank president

   Tom Jordan, Billy Sprat, and Horace Smith: town bullies

   Sheriff Watson: Rockvale

   Dale Rogers: Jonathan's uncle and Anthony's business partner.

   Max Dupres: Nashville art dealer and Victoria's best friend

   Will Lamb: Jonathan's best friend, attorney

   Louise Lamb: Will's sister

   Doc Smith and his wife, Lizzie: Rockvale physician

   Mr. Hubern and his wife, Margaret: the General Store owners

   Earl the Pearl: barkeep at The Fox Hunt

   Pastor Daniel Dyer: Rockvale Church

   James Rogers: Jonathan's grandfather

   Thomas: Jonathan's father

   Earlene: Jonathan's mother

   Alan Higgins: the owner of the picture show

   Briar Morgan: Anthony's estranged wife and Mae's mother

Mortals Book 2

    Emily Ellen: mortal, college intern that works for Lavender

    Professor Browning: Silver Meadow University, rare book collector

    Pastor Green: Rockvale Church

    Adam Bisset: curator of antiquities

    Stephan & Mel: owners of the Wine Bar, Crush

Otherworldly Realms

    Seven Sisters of Pleiades

    Nona: sister one

    Ravvyn: sister two

    Dreena: sister three, Lady of Light, and eventually Goddess of Light

    Thagna: sister four

    Moria: sister five

    Raella: sister six

    Cora: sister seven

    Yaris: sister eight, falls in love with Cetus, Goddess of Light

Seven Wizards of Orion

    Linus: wizard one

    Cornelius: wizard two

    Vudale: wizard three

    Cane: wizard four

    Saylor: wizard five

    Fedois: wizard six

    Cetus: wizard seven, falls in love with Yaris, The Lord Darkness

King Valdoor: Ruler of the Pleiades

Queen Octavia: Ruler of the Pleiades

Orphic: Pleiadean Commander, ruthless

Odar: King of the Fire Throne and Ruler of the Black Flame Fae

Queen Goldengrace: daughter of Urslina, married King Winterwood, after his death, married Odar to save her people, ruler of the Black Flame Fae

King Winterwood: rightful ruler of the Black Flame Fae, married to Queen Goldengrace, father to Emir, killed by Odar

Emir: former prince of the Black Flame Fae, an emissary for Odar

Serena: Powerful witch of the Pleiades, illegitimate daughter of Valdoor, mother Urslina, Queen Goldengrace's sister

Urslina: Dark witch, mother of Serena and Goldengrace, killed by Iris Doanhart

The Black Flame Fae

Crystal: fae spy, works for Odar, King of the Fire Throne

Dune and Stone: fae that helps Emir

Sprite: tiny fae loyal to Queen Goldengrace

Book 1 side notes:

Victoria Frost, unbeknownst to her, is a goddess and possesses power from the Guardian of Water and Sky, and Dreena, Goddess, the third sister of the Pleiadean Realm, and Lady of Light

Raine Moonfall, the lineage from the Guardian of the Water & Sky, and Victoria's biological father

Terry and Sarah Frost, Victoria's adoptive parents that died in the Nashville Flood

About D.F. Jones

USA Today Bestselling Author D. F. Jones began her career as a broadcast consultant at the ABC Affiliate in Nashville, which led her to open an advertising agency. Over the years, she's created many campaigns for clients, but she fell in love with writing fiction.

D. F. Jones is married to the love of her life. They have two gorgeous sons whom she loves and adores. She's a fan of the Tennessee Titans, MT Blue Raiders (Alumni) and enjoys working in her flower gardens.

Whether it's angels or demons, time travel adventures, witches and wizards, her books are action-packed with supernatural and romantic elements.

Go to DFJonesAuthor.com to register for updates, and follow me on social media.

Also By